Praise for *Five Rivers Met on a Wooded Plain*

'**Wonderful** . . . I was hooked from the first page. Barney has the real novelist's ability to inhabit different characters, and to make the texture of life tangible and compelling. Everything he writes about love, loss, grief, desolation, and moments of hope and illumination rings absolutely true. It's the real stuff.'
Michael Frayn

'**Powerful** . . . this young writer is capable of convincing compassion.'
The Times

'Looks well beyond the literary intelligentsia's world, describing with great humanity five ordinary lives, and coming close, as it does so, to being a "state of the nation" novel – albeit one with none of the bombast the term usually implies . . . **deeply affecting . . . a tolerant and insightful debut**.'
Guardian

'Barney Norris's first novel has the **deep emotional power** and accuracy of his admired plays, and more: a sweeping study of how, in everyone's lives, memory and imagination may intersect with chance.'
David Hare

'Norris writes beautifully, unearthing **extraordinary** depths in the everyday . . . a **memorable** writer, mature beyond his years.'
Sunday Times

'**Extraordinarily involving and perceptive** . . . a picture of a society evoked through its injured members. A most **remarkable** book.'
Bernard O'Donoghue

'Outstanding . . . a **moving**, strangely uplifting novel that grapples with the coarse substance of everyday existence and poetically celebrates its passage. **Superb**.'
Mail on Sunday

'A novel of **overwhelming** cumulative power, each of its five voices naked in their honesty: ordinary lives made extraordinary by the humanity and artistry of an **amazing young novelist**.'
Nicholas Hytner

'**Compelling** . . . Norris never loses sight of the love there is to be found in the world as long as one is willing to seek it out and fight to keep it.'
Evening Standard

'**Brilliant and multi-layered** . . . the author has an uncanny ability to capture even the tiniest nuances of each character.'
The Herald

'Norris has a gift for tapping in to ordinary lives and finding the extraordinary in them . . . **emotional, compelling and thought-provoking**.'
Daily Mail

'**Riveting**.'
Radio Times

Turning for Home

Barney Norris

Doubleday

LONDON • TORONTO • SYDNEY • AUCKLAND • JOHANNESBURG

TRANSWORLD PUBLISHERS
61–63 Uxbridge Road, London W5 5SA
www.penguin.co.uk

Transworld is part of the Penguin Random House group of companies
whose addresses can be found at global.penguinrandomhouse.com

First published in Great Britain in 2018 by Doubleday
an imprint of Transworld Publishers

This book is a work of fiction and, except in the case of historical fact,
any resemblance to actual persons, living or dead, is purely coincidental.

Every effort has been made to obtain the necessary permissions with
reference to copyright material, both illustrative and quoted. We apologize
for any omissions in this respect and will be pleased to make the
appropriate acknowledgements in any future edition.

A CIP catalogue record for this book
is available from the British Library.

ISBNs 9780857523747 (hb)
9780857523754 (tpb)

Typeset in 11/15pt Giovanni by Falcon Oast Graphic Art Ltd.
Printed and bound by Clays Ltd, Bungay, Suffolk.

Penguin Random House is committed to a sustainable
future for our business, our readers and our planet. This book
is made from Forest Stewardship Council® certified paper.

1 3 5 7 9 10 8 6 4 2

For Charlie

i.m. Albert Norris

Wither is fled the visionary gleam?
Where is it now, the glory and the dream?

William Wordsworth, 'Intimations of Immortality
from Recollections of Early Childhood'

Robert

IN THE FIRST young years of the new century, a team of researchers affiliated with Boston College attempted to collate an oral history of the Troubles, recording the recollections of combatants on both sides. They persuaded their subjects to speak by telling them that their lives offered lessons to future generations, and that a record should be made of how and why things had happened in Northern Ireland as the people involved saw it, while their stories could still be captured. The subjects were given assurances that nothing they said would be made public while they were living, a necessary step for securing cooperation that perhaps, with hindsight, was asking for trouble.

The project was initiated by a small group of Irish journalists and historians, men I had known in the course of my work in Belfast. I admired what they were doing – it still strikes me as an important undertaking. After all, the bloody century I spent most of my life in has to offer some lessons to the years that will come after me; otherwise it will all just have been murder piled on murder, loss without meaning, and more bloodshed will surely come as a result of the failure to learn from those lives which were lost before. There is no task more important than asking people to rewind a moment, look closer, take stock. The world has been changing so fast all the way through my own life, and there have been earthquakes wherever I look all around me. People have a responsibility, I think, to learn to manage the aftershocks, as the endless churning of the world continues to accelerate, and generate new worlds, and overtake everyone. So I think the importance, even the necessity of a project like this one is self-evident.

But things didn't work out as planned. Instead of explaining the motivations that had driven them into their war, as the project's architects expected, the men they spoke to started confessing to things they had done in the past. They unfurled details of killings and the chain of responsibility behind them. Perhaps old men were settling scores, pointing out those they believed had betrayed them in the long ago, in the knowledge their testimony would become public with their deaths, and might then hurt someone they hated. Or perhaps there was a guilt weighing on them all, and the lure of the confessional took over whenever the Dictaphone started to record. Or maybe they simply believed they had nothing to hide any more, under the blanket of secrecy promised to them by the interviewer sent from Boston College. Whatever the reasoning, more was given up than could ever have been expected. Murder on murder was traced back to its source among those black and flashing spools of ribbon where the stories were spilled out like soldiers disembowelled.

After a while the Police Service of Northern Ireland got to hear of what was being said and, as a result of that, the project briefly became an international preoccupation.

Last week, lawyers acting on behalf of the British government issued a series of subpoenas to Boston College, seeking access to the recordings in order to assist Her Majesty's Government in the investigation of historic crimes in Northern Ireland. I read the news of this latest earthquake cocooned in the comfort of my armchair, the story printed in the pages of the papers everyone else who lived in my village bought, not the briefing papers that had once been rushed to me by car and by night, letting me into their secret world long before anyone else I went to church with heard about their contents. I wondered whether anyone would call me about what was going on, whether I was going to be needed. Although no call came in the first week after the story broke, I kept hoping. No one wants to be forgotten, not in their own lifetime.

Then came the news, in yesterday's papers, that Gerry Adams had been taken in for questioning on the strength of some of the interviews given to the researchers, and the Boston Tapes were briefly on everyone's lips.

They called them the Boston Tapes in the papers, not discs, not sound files. I thought that was strange at first; it made me wonder how the interviews had been recorded. I suppose it's just the phrase still echoing onwards, even though we've surely all left cassettes behind by now. There is something about a tape that means the image holds interest long after it has been rendered technologically obsolete. The idea of a ribbon of speech, a voice speaking one truth on one side and then saying something else completely different on the other, two stories that might have contained anything at all, separated only by the breadth of the tongue they were told by.

That is magical. And I think perhaps it's very human as well.

Isn't the life of any person made up of the telling of two tales, after all? People live in the space between the realities of their lives and the hopes they have for them. People spin myths from the quotidian roots of their experience, in order to create a small cocoon of space in which they can live between the dream they could never hope to grasp and the indifferent ordinariness of everything around them, in which they can tell themselves things might be about to get exciting, no matter how cramped the quarters seem, how dark the dawn, how low the ceiling. That is the duality in everything. The whole world makes more sense if you remember that everyone has two lives, their real lives and their dreams, both stories only a tape's breadth apart from each other, impossibly divided, indivisibly close.

And still there's more to it than that. There's more that's seductive in the image than only that; it wasn't just about dreaming. It seemed to me once I thought about it that these tapes laced through with murders and remembering were a vision of the speeches and silences that defined every life, the all-too-human need to make a statement, to cage oneself into a set of words. They were about wanting to tell the truth. Wanting the days of your life, and the acts of your life, to be known to have happened, and to have had some weight, to have left some kind of meaning behind them, imprinted at least in language, if nothing else. They were about laying out the mess of the self for others to unravel, trying to participate in the argument of the world after you'd left it, and longing to live for ever, to be clearer, to be seen and to see things as you thought they really were.

But I'm getting ahead of myself. At the start of the day, all this still waited like a bomb in the back of my mind, and talk of the Boston Tapes lay hours off in the future.

from Interview 18

[All interviewees' names redacted to maintain anonymity]

I joined up after Bloody Sunday. A lot of us did. The Brits had killed a kid, for God's sake, they'd shot this kid through a wall. They said they were returning fire from some IRA men up in this block of flats, and that's where the boy was sleeping in his bed, and that's when they shot him. He died in his bed. You hear that from a lot of occupying forces, you know – we were only returning fire from fellas who were hiding in among civilians. If you believe all you read, that's what the Palestinians spend all day doing, hiding among civilians. I don't know about it. For our lot, human shields, that'd be a disaster, wouldn't it? We need people on our side. Anyway, there was this guy doing the rounds in the wake of it all, that week after Bloody Sunday, went from house to house asking whether now might be a time to think of joining up. I thought I should. I thought we all should.

Kate

Perhaps we had been running through a wood without end. Perhaps our teeth had fallen out. Perhaps the whole world had been reduced to the colours it was painted in, and there was nothing solid to anything around us any more, only brushstrokes, only torrents of feeling, soul after soul adrift in an ocean of blues and greens. Perhaps it doesn't matter what the dream was. Days would be easier to get through if none of them meant anything, after all, if all life was only the ruffling of the surface of a lake. Perhaps in our sleep we glimpse that ease, that peace, and bite down on silence to taste it swilling round us.

I didn't draw the curtains when I went to bed last night. Now, the light of morning paws catlike at my face and the eggshell blue of the room grows bright around me, beckoning. As if the house is opening its eyes. My hair's in my eyes; my mouth is dry. I lie foetal in the middle of the bed, try to remember what I was dreaming, but the story has already vanished. All that remains is a vague unhappiness clinging to me, the feeling of someone having just left a room. Like the water on your shoulders when you've stepped out of the sea, light burning it away leaving only salt behind.

I have the feeling that in the dream I was one of many

people standing in a line, but even as I try to bring the image to mind, it clouds over, falling away from me, the memory of the dream drifting back into the fog and shadow waiting always at the cliff-edge and the limit of my thinking.

I pick up my phone, see it's still only seven-fifteen. Earlier than I'd wanted to wake up, but I won't be able to sleep again now, not in the grip of this beautiful morning. I'd only hoped to sleep longer because I wanted to try and treat today as a kind of holiday, and sleeping in is what people on holidays are supposed to do. It's always the same simple dream for me these days. I only want to be like other people. Surely that isn't too much to ask?

It was the vibration from a text that woke me. Sam, as I knew it would be the moment I saw my phone light up. I went to sleep almost certain I'd get this very text from him by morning. *Hey. I'm really sorry, but I'm afraid I'm not going to be able to make it today. Something's come up and I have to be in Bristol. X.* I don't reply. I put the phone back on the table and lie very still on my side, staring at the wall, staring at nothing, and wishing I didn't care so much.

Some people put their phones on silent when they go to bed, so that nothing wakes them. I've thought about doing the same. But I get nervous when I don't know where my phone is. I can't help myself. I'd feel too much anxiety turning my phone off at night, I think. I wouldn't be able to sleep for fear of what I wouldn't hear about until it was over, all the things that might pass me by.

When I was in the hospital, lying in bed and thinking my life was over and there wasn't any point to me any more, only the occasional visitor to make me still feel part of the world, I didn't feel able to use my phone a lot of the time. It was my link to everything that wasn't that place, that room, that feeling, and I found I couldn't bear the thought of all those things it stood for – all I believed I had lost. It didn't seem to hook me into the world where my friends were still living, their songs playing on without me. It only showed me how far from them all I had drifted. I would look at my phone and see only the echoes of the life I'd lost, the places I could never revisit, the dreams I'd cherished that would never come true now, after what happened to me. So I left my phone alone, and the texts and emails of friends checking how I was doing went unanswered. After a month or so, most of them stopped trying. How many times can you tell someone you're thinking of them, if all you hear back in return is silence? What no one knew, though, was that all the time I wasn't replying to the messages people sent, I was reading them and rereading them like poems I was trying to learn by heart. I would stare with mad longing into the water of the world that seemed to glimmer at arm's length from where I lay, fascinated by what was happening to everyone else, in love with the life of the person I had been, the person I had once thought I was going to become. I would read all the messages again and again, and the real world came to seem like a story I could follow, tuning in every day to find out what happened next as lives bled out little by little all around me. My friends seemed moth-like and beautiful as they tried to reach me, beating their wings against the screen of my phone. That's why these days I feel like I can't be without it. From the confines of the hospital, it came to seem like it contained the whole world.

*

It's quieter here at Grandad's house, and darker at night, and I slept well even though I was swaddled in a strange bed, not somewhere I felt I was really safe. I need a shower to wake me up, but in fact, lying still and thinking about it, I have to admit I don't feel bad at all.

Sleep has come and gone in the last couple of years. I've battled with it. For a long time I hated sleeping on my own, it was the one thing I wanted to avoid more than anything else. But that loneliness isn't as bad this morning either. Perhaps I'm getting better. It has occurred to me over the last few weeks that there's been a small change in the way I'm feeling. Things don't seem quite as frightening as they did in the dog days of last year. I can look at the way the trees have started flowering now the clocks have gone forward, and find it beautiful. I can stand and look at the green leaves budding at the fingertips of a tree, and lose myself for a moment in the sight, feel a quietness growing in the heart of me. It gives me hope. Perhaps as time passes it's all going to flow back into my body, the life I thought had left me like blood pouring out from a wound. My desires can be everyone else's, and I can try to be normal again. That was the test I set myself by coming here today – I decided to come back here and try to get through the day of the party, knowing my mum would probably turn up at some point, knowing I might have to talk to her, and see if I was strong enough, and see if it might just be possible to start slotting back into the life all around me.

Grandad has thrown these birthday parties all my life and longer. It was Grandma's idea in the first place, so the story goes. She turned Grandad into a host, then kept him at it when he might have given up, if left to his own devices. Family was always important to her; I remember she used to seem like she lived for us and through us all, and she always loved to mark the little rhythms of the year, the birthdays and the holidays. They were the waves she swam over as she made her way out into the open water of her life. Her life always seemed to organise itself around preparing for the next celebration, the next wave rising to meet her.

She never made anything like as much fuss about her own birthday. Only Christmas really rivalled Grandad's party for the work she put in. These celebrations were Grandma Hattie's days.

It's the house that makes it all possible. You need a bit of space to really give anything the attention it deserves. That's why all the best ideas happen when people are out walking – things flower when they're given room. Like a body of water, a day will expand to fill the space it's given, so moving into this big, rambling old house with its sprawling garden meant Grandma could fashion the occasions she dreamed of: a Christmas tree towering up through the stairwell in the hall, chestnuts and bonfires in autumn, the happy crowd of guests raising a toast to Grandad on the sunlit lawn each spring.

Grandad invites his whole family and all of his friends to the parties. When I was younger, that meant entertaining over two hundred people. He and Grandma used to hire caterers to feed all the mouths, and clear the plates, and stop the whole construction from collapsing. The stock of guests was topped up over the years, as couples from that first guest list had their children and watched them grow, and as new people came into my grandparents' lives from other parties, other meetings, other days. But the list has mostly been shrinking again for the whole span of my life, because, of course, Grandad's friends started to die, and once he was retired he didn't meet as many new people. On top of that, once the parties were established as a family tradition, people started to feel like they could miss one every once in a while, if it was difficult for them to come. Everyone knows there will always be another gathering next year, after all. So these days there are always some faces missing.

This time, Grandma will be missing too. I can't imagine what that's going to feel like, not to see her here, not to hear her laughter. This will be the first year Grandad will have to live the day of the party without her. I've tried to imagine it, but I don't really know how he's going to get through. That is the other reason I've come here today. I need to be here to support him.

The congregation is so diminished that Grandad doesn't even hire caterers any more. This year Aunt Laura will do all the cooking, and people will eat from paper plates, which makes it easier to clean up. I don't really know how Aunt Laura will manage so much work, but she did it all with Grandma the last seven or eight years since the caterers stopped coming, and perhaps she wants to carry on on her own because she feels no one can replace her sister at her side, not just yet. Grandad told me last night that Aunt Laura started preparing everything a week ago, to give herself time to get everything ready for the day. He talked about her like she was something from a myth, said she would battle the day with no weapon but the sweat of her brow, regal, defiant, as terrifying as any general. She would make a cold lunch for everyone, because that made timing things easier than hot food. And no matter what troubles beset her, she would surely come through. In the years ahead, I suppose it will only get easier for her to carry on doing things like that, as the tribe my grandad sprang from continues to thin, and fewer and fewer people make it to the party.

All the same, it's still a significant occasion, this day. Once the sky's turned ripe with the fresh fullness of the sun in May, and the morning's in full swing, the lawn will fill with bodies, pressed a little closer together than they might have chosen if the party wasn't happening so early in the spring and the weather was warmer, and the air will hum with years-old conversations, picked up again for the duration of an afternoon.

Today is the first time I've come here in three years. Because I was in hospital, some of that time, and because I was trying to keep a distance between me and Mum. And, now I think about all of it, I'm afraid. I'm dreading the day, even though I slept better than I expected.

I lie on the bed and carry on staring at the wall, thinking of all the things that might happen this afternoon. I'm scared of how different everything might seem, how much everyone's lives might have moved on after three years. I don't know whether I'll feel much connection to any of those people, my relations, any more. I don't know what they might all have been told about me since I last saw them, what they might be thinking about me behind my back, and what they might think of the way I look. I wish with all my heart that I could go back in time and spend today at the party I went to four years ago. Or go back to any of the other years that are gone. Things seemed possible then. Things used to seem easy.

I say a last goodbye to the thought of going to sleep again now my mind's whirring, and try to steel myself for sitting upright and beginning. I let the grogginess slide away, and I feel as ready as I'm ever going to. In the bathroom I turn on the shower. It's always strange to undress in someone else's house, even a house that's familiar to you, even your grandparents'. I stand naked in front of the mirror and force myself to look at my reflection, then run my hand down the side of my body, over my breast, my stomach, my hip.

Every morning while I wait for the water to run hot, I stand like this and watch my body in the mirror. I remember a time not so many years ago, after my twentieth birthday, when it seemed to me that the person I was had somehow set, become fixed, become inevitable. A childhood of possibility had passed, and I decided I was comfortable with the idea that this was my face, and this was my body, and this was the life I was going to live. I felt happy enough with the skin I was in, back then. I live in hope of feeling like that again some day. When I was younger, before the accident, I never knew how precious it was to be at peace with yourself, and let yourself be loved. For a while, till the accident changed everything, I felt that way. I stopped playing the game of imagining other lives laid over my own, the teenage game of dreaming your life. Now I look at myself and I know that stability was just an illusion. Now the sight of my body in the mirror makes me feel sick. I never really stopped pretending to be other people, I don't think. I just got better at it, so I hardly noticed what was happening any more as I slipped out of one skin and into another, minute by minute, whoever I talked to, whatever I was thinking.

No matter how hard I look at my reflection, at the other self I only ever meet when the two of us stand either side of this mirror, I can never believe a stranger would be able to tell even a single one of my secrets or stories from looking at me. It's strange that the body can hold so much, and still seem so unreadable.

Some people never recover from learning that there is no world on the other side of the mirror, I don't think. No Narnia, no Wonderland, and none of the world of your dreams coming true just by wishing, by walking through a mirror or falling down a rabbit hole. Some people never get over the fact that all those longings we carry within us have to be willed into being if we ever want to really see them come true. I don't know whether I've properly got over that myself.

I get into the shower and flinch as the water hits my back. It's much hotter than the shower at home. It makes me smile. People say money can't buy happiness. But it pays for better boilers; it wakes you up faster in the mornings.

Downstairs, I find Grandad in the breakfast room, staring out of the window with the light washing pale over his face, the remains of a boiled egg on a plate in front of him, the smell of burnt toast and butter like a memory in the room. He turns and smiles when he hears me come in.

'Good morning. How did you sleep?'

I smile back at him. 'Really well, thanks. You?'

'Oh, I slept all right.'

'Are you looking forward to today?'

Grandad laughs to himself, as if the idea of today being something to look forward to seems unimaginable to him. 'I suppose so.'

'Oh my God – happy birthday! Sorry! I should have started with that.'

'Thank you.'

A strain of the dream I had last night comes back to me suddenly. A cliff pocked with caves where a town on the clifftop hid away all their children, who survived there, and grew up believing they were birds, not men and women, and learned to sing and fly through the heartstopping air like the crows that nested in the dark places of the cliffs hung all around them. And I remembered a dream the night before that of broken men sat cowed, slobbering and naked inside gauze cages, kept apart from visitors by ropes and string under low ceilings, no light anywhere, forgotten and unwashed.

'I might have some cereal,' I say.

'Help yourself. There's lots in the pantry.'

'OK.' I go through to the pantry on the other side of the kitchen, and open the door, and breathe in the memory-rich aroma of the dark, cool room. I've always loved it in here: the smell of shortbread and marmalade, tins and caddies stacked high over my head like a cave of wonders, shelves closing round me like an embrace. It's dark and womblike and anything I reach out and touch is a treasure: delicious, brightly packaged, wrapped up like secrets. When I was very small, the walls of food seemed to stretch on up above my head for ever. I look at the shelves now, a little more thinly stocked without Grandma to keep an eye on them, the larder of a cook with a little less imagination.

Last night Grandad cooked for us. A lentil stew and treacle pudding. 'The sort of thing you used to have when you came to stay in the holidays, Kate. I hope that's all right.'

'That'll be lovely. Thank you, Grandad.'

When dinner was served, I could see it was all from tins. There would be no more of the rich smell of Grandma's favourite recipes drifting through these rooms; he didn't know how to make them. On the shelves I see stacks of corned beef and jars of pickled vegetables instead, waiting to be ladled out on to one plate after another. Something else is missing now as well. It's as if there's no magic to the shelves any more, no splendour lingering. Is that because Grandad doesn't keep the larder as well stocked as it used to be, or is it me seeing things differently?

When I was a little girl I used to try and see how long I could hold my breath underwater. One time, swimming in an outdoor pool, I lay like a crocodile against the concrete belly of the deep end, daylight dappling gently on my shoulders, tiger-striped, and kept myself down there till my head began to hurt, till the very last moment I could bear to keep waiting. When I felt my lungs start to burn I pushed back up towards the light, but found to my horror that there was a lilo looming above me. Instead of getting to the surface and gulping at the air, my hands met the cloying plastic of the sun lounger, and I thought for a moment of pure panic that I was going to drown beneath it, disappear completely and for ever.

That's what it's felt like to battle through any given day for a long time, all my life passing and all of it filled with the same desperation. The memory of clawing at that heavy plastic as my blood started to sing in my veins, my blood screaming out that my lungs were bursting, comes to me time and again these days.

I look around for cereal. All I can see is All-Bran, so I take the packet back into the kitchen and pour out a bowlful, measuring as carefully as I can without the proper equipment. I've been trying to go vegan for the last few weeks, but of course there's no soya milk or almond milk or anything else like that here; those are the discoveries of another generation. I wonder how I'm even going to be able to stay vegetarian today, if Grandad has any say in the food. He believes a meal hasn't really happened if it doesn't contain meat. I did think of mentioning it to him before I arrived, but decided against it, because he would have worried, and prepared something specially, and I didn't want the attention; it's easier to get on with my own problems without anyone watching how I deal with them.

Grandad looks up when I walk back into the breakfast room, and seems surprised at first, then smiles. 'Find what you wanted?'

My stomach tightens, and I don't know how to answer, but he doesn't know he's asked the wrong question. His hands lie flat on the table, either side of his plate and placed very deliberately, as if he's been examining them. 'Yes, thanks.'

He nods, and looks away from me. I want to get him talking, because the silences at this table used to stretch out like cats in the sun when I was younger, if it was just Grandad and me, and everyone else had gone out. The memory of how frightened of Grandad I used to be, his fierce and distant frowning, lost in some newspaper or briefing note, still disturbs me. Besides, he won't want to sit in silence either, probably. I'm here to cheer him up a bit, to distract him from thinking of Grandma.

'You seem a bit preoccupied, if you don't mind me saying.'

'Oh, well.' He looks back out to the garden, and I don't think he's going to say any more. I wonder whether he really wants me here right now, or whether he had in fact been enjoying this breath of time alone before the business and busyness of the day began. I sit down opposite him, feeling awkward. Then he turns to look at me again. 'I heard you in the hall and for a moment I didn't quite know who was going to come in.'

'What do you mean?' I search his face, worried that something is wrong. It's always my instinct now to reach at once for the worst thing that could possibly be happening. I wonder whether he's had a stroke. His face hasn't dropped. Has his mind somehow slipped? What's happening?

'I suppose I thought it might be your grandma. Isn't that silly?' He smiles at me, and rolls his eyes, and it's the same face he used to pull to make me laugh when I was six years old, and I can't help smiling, even though what he said worries me. I see with sudden clarity how alone he is now, rattling round this house, listening for an echo of Grandma, drowning in the silence she left behind. It's cruel that people have so much taken from them as they near the end. Not that Grandad is even very old, that's the worst of it – he might even have to get through another twenty years with no one to share the day with.

His smile fades again, and he looks down at his hands where they lie very still on the table. Is he afraid of becoming upset, is that why he doesn't want to look at me? I know that's when I have to look away from other people. Or perhaps he laid his hands out like that to stop them shaking, and is looking now to see whether they're giving him away.

'I'm sorry. You must think I'm going mad in my old age.'

'Of course I don't.' I think he's looking very old though, much older than I remember from last time I saw him, and that's a strange thing, because he seemed so strong to me once, so proud and frightening.

But that's what happens, in the end: people get older; their time ticks down. Grandad had a heart scare five years back, when Grandma was still alive. We all thought then that it would be him who went first, and not the other way round. In truth, it was a relatively mild heart attack. He never lost consciousness as far as anyone knew, and they kept him in hospital for two weeks, and gave him angiograms and ECGs, and talked to him about lifestyle and taking things slow, but then he was allowed home and life went on much as it had done before, with a little extra medication.

They looked for genetic reasons, and it emerged there was one waiting inside him. He was diagnosed with hypertrophic cardiomyopathy, a thickening of the walls of the heart that meant the muscles had to beat harder, which could create strains and risks over time. At first there was talk of giving him a pacemaker to safeguard against another collapse, but in the end they decided they didn't need to, not yet.

As the problem was an inherited condition, Mum and I had to get checked out for it too, and I was asked to lie on hospital beds with the ultrascanner pressed painfully into my ribs while a nurse looked things over. I felt ill knowing as I lay there on my side that if I only turned over to face the other way, I would be able to see a film of my own heart beating, the engine that drove me, the muscle that would one day relax for the last time and bring me to a conclusion. I could watch the thing very gradually running out of beats. I hope I'll never have to see a picture of it. It would be terrifying. I think watching your own heart beat would be like meeting your doppelgänger. I think it might kill you. Make the world end.

Neither Mum nor I were diagnosed with the condition. But we were told it could develop later in life; we were not safe from it, we might suddenly hear its voice calling us years from now, and so we would need to get ourselves checked every five years or so. The time's approaching, I suppose, when I'll need to get another check-up.

Does everyone wish in the same way I do that we could hold on to more of our lives as they happen to us? I think it's a weakness in me, but maybe it's the whole world's instinct. I'd rather not feel as if I'm always losing the day around me. I want desperately to be able to think of life as a kind of travelling: a landscape we cross like explorers over sand dunes, seeming bright to us at first but then vanishing into the distant dark behind us. It would make everything so much easier if I could be happy with that, think of time as an adventure. It's just that the idea is terrifying to me, and it scares me to think that everything I've lived through has gone for ever.

Grandad pushes his chair back from the table. 'I might get some more tea. Do you want a tea, a cup of coffee?'

'Coffee would be lovely, if that's all right?'

'Of course.' He gets up and leaves the room, and I plough

into my All-Bran. It's the worst cereal in the world, the roughage you might feed to horses, but it's all that's going and I will get through it, no matter what. I chew on my cereal and count the number of times I chew, trying to do things properly, and stare at the wall, and once again see things I left behind miles in the past.

A long time ago they used to pin my paintings to the fridge in the kitchen next door. All gone now, of course. Grandma used to tell a story about my painting and drawing. She said when I was very small I used to love drawing, but I never drew anything in particular. Just different colours and different lines. Then when I was about a year old Grandma took me to some kind of check-up for first-time mothers, and Mum was busy. She went back to work very soon after I was born because she said she was going crazy in the house all day, then complained about having done so and missed out on my childhood for the next twenty years. The health visitor asked whether I was being encouraged to draw things. Grandma told her that I loved drawing, so the health visitor asked whether I could draw a house. Grandma said she didn't know. The health visitor said I should be able to draw a house by now, and asked me to have a go. So I took the crayon I was offered, and drew a box with other little boxes inside it that might have been windows, and might have been a door. And that was the end of making up shapes for myself.

'Here we are. Proper coffee.' Grandad comes back into the room with a cafetière and a mug for me and another mug of tea for himself on a tray.

'Thanks so much.'

I watch as the steam of the coffee rises up through the light coming in through the window. Grandma used to wait for three minutes exactly before she poured her coffee out of this very cafetière. That way it was easier to press down the plunger. I remember her standing in the kitchen, watching the second hand ticking round, *Woman's Hour* faint in the background and the smell of the brewing coffee rich in the room.

It's a perfect morning. It's turning into the most beautiful spring. The garden is filled with expectation. There's something about the light on the grass that seems unreal, the whole view of the lawn from the window softened so it takes on the quality of a painting, inflected like a canvas to say something more than the sum of its parts. The view through the window is as vivid as a feeling. It reminds me of the way brick buildings seem to be suffused with a new colour at the end of the day, a life of their own, and almost glow. There are colours in the world which happen for only a few moments in a day, a year even. Dawn breaking over Stonehenge on a midsummer morning, light aligning with Purbeck stone for a secret, dancing moment. Once they vanish, you can't bring those moments back into being. The only way to drink them in is to watch the world more closely than anyone else, and gather up secrets, and learn how to look.

Spring is the most exciting season. The daffodils shine in the sun. You can stare at one, and it will seem to become more beautiful every moment you watch, until you can hardly bear to look at it.

'What are you thinking about?' Grandad asks me.

'Oh, sorry. I was just thinking it's a nice morning.'

'Yes.'

'Perfect for a party.'

He smiles, and his smile seems painted on, poorly acted. Have we ever really talked before, one person to another, not grandparent to child? I feel nervous of him now.

'You know you'll probably have to see your mother today, don't you?'

'Yes.' I wonder what I'm supposed to say. The thought of her makes me tense, my skin pricking, like I'm being hunted. It upsets me to think I'm a cause of tension for people like my grandad, who don't need to be affected by the gulf that's opened between me and my mum. I suppose I've let him down by refusing to see her all this time. I wish it could have been different. Thinking of talking to her again today makes me feel sick now, makes me want to hide away. I'm not ready. But if I wait till I'm ready whole decades might pass, we might never meet again, and that would be another reason for hating myself.

'Will you be all right, do you think?'

'I don't know. I hope so. I'm sure I will.'

'Just come to me if it feels too much.'

'Thank you.'

'I haven't done anything, don't thank me yet. I just don't want you to dread the moment when everyone starts arriving.'

'I'll be fine. I know I'm going to have to see her eventually. Today is probably as good a day as any.'

By which I mean, of course, that there will never be a good day. I'll always feel like a failure as a daughter. I'll always feel afraid of her.

*

And the thought of Joe rises and breaks through the surface of the day, and I didn't even make it through breakfast before I felt myself caught in the undertow, a shrill lament of memory like a curlew calling over a lake, and found myself thinking of him.

'Why not just tell her how she makes you feel?'

We were lying on his bed, wasting an afternoon, staring at the ceiling, our legs intertwined and the light of a rainy day coming in through the windows. I remember him taking my hand.

'I could never do that.'

'Why not? I don't understand. How can you solve it if you don't talk to her?'

'You can't solve it, that's naïve. It's something I just have to live with, and the only way to survive is by not talking about it and making it worse. You're assuming that life is fundamentally all right, that it's possible for everything to work like a clock. But what if the whole thing's actually broken or random and everything that doesn't go wrong is some kind of miracle? Why is that less likely than things magically working out?'

The first time I ever really felt close to someone else, as if another person was a part of me, was Joe. That was when I realised how much Mum and I had never got on. We were still speaking at that point, things hadn't gone completely wrong just yet. But time with Joe showed me how lonely I'd felt all the time the centre of the world had been my parents. That was why I set about turning him into my family, and drifted away from the people who had brought me into the world. The whole of the world, in the years we spent together, was Joe.

I have to try not to dwell on him now, because I need too much of myself today to get lost in the memory of him. I have the meeting with Mum to think about – the terrors of the present, not the past. The past is played out and I can't rewrite it. All I can find the words for is now.

All my life, there's been some deficit, some absence in the space where feeling should have welled up between Mum and me. I think it's the flaw at the heart of me. I don't love enough; somehow I never learned how to love when I was young and living at home. I've always felt like a part of me must be missing. People tell me I'm exaggerating when I try to describe that, say it's my insecurity speaking, but all the same, when I was growing up, I believed I was broken. My heart didn't quite work. Sometimes I think all the darkness I've ever experienced welled up out of that emptiness, and fed on it, and used it to grow and live.

Not now, I can't be thinking about this now, I have to live in the day around me.

'Your shower's very good, isn't it?'

This is the stuff life is made of, I think. Small thoughts strung together so people who love each other too much to say so have something to share. Love among the rubble of an ordinary life, sprouting up weedlike through the difficulty of ever really saying what you mean.

'Oh, do you think so? I'm so glad,' he says.

'I can't get mine anywhere near as hot.'

'You probably need a new boiler.'

'Yeah, but if I said that, the landlord would probably stick his fingers in his ears.'

Grandad laughs, and I smile, because I've made him happy, in a way.

'You know you could always come and stay here, if you ever got tired of things like that. The troubles that come with a rented flat. It's a big house; you know there are plenty of rooms.'

'Thank you. That's really kind.'

'I know you have your work, and your life, you have a whole network of things to keep you where you are, as everybody does. But you can always come and stay here if you want to.'

'Thank you.' I drink down to the bottom of my coffee, leaving the last mouthful so I don't have to swallow a thimble of grains. I'm afraid to look back up from the bottom of my cup. Shy of this sincerity, this kindness from him. I wish I was brave enough to look at him, and tell him how much I appreciate his generosity, but I don't know how, I can't quite manage it. I feel like I must be blushing, colour spreading across my chest. Then the moment of seriousness passes, and Grandad sighs, and gets up from the table.

'I'd better get ready, hadn't I? Aunt Laura will be here soon. She'll murder me if I'm still in my pyjamas.'

'I might go for a little walk before everyone turns up,' I say. 'Would you mind?'

'No, of course not. Go ahead.'

'I'll wash this up first.'

He shakes his head. 'There's no need. Just put it in the dishwasher.'

I laugh. 'I always forget you have a dishwasher. Houses like this don't feel like they should, you know?'

He laughs. 'Oh, we're very modern here.'

The clock begins striking in the hall beyond us. There's always something ghostly in that sound. The sound of a clock striking the hour in another room always seems like a door back into memory, into lost worlds, forgotten possibilities. I know the clock calling out belonged to my great-grandfather once; he carried it with him when he travelled from Wales to London, and he carried it again when he travelled from London down to Wiltshire, where he lived, where Grandad was born. The sound of it striking has sounded in the ears of my family for a century, or even longer. How many minutes has it counted out? Has the millionth hour chimed out and passed without anyone noticing? It might well have done. Milestones like that must be reached and passed all the time, and no one notices them.

'I'll see you in a bit then,' I say, stirring myself.

'All right. See you later.'

He turns to leave, and I think maybe I should tell him that Sam isn't coming. I don't want to admit it to anyone, really, but it's Grandad's party and he said I could bring someone when I asked. He effectively invited him. I should tell him so he doesn't feel kept in the dark.

'Oh, Grandad, I meant to say. My friend who was going to come can't come.'

He turns back and looks at me, and I have the eerie feeling that he understands all of it. He somehow heard everything I didn't say.

'All right. I'm sorry about that.'

'Sorry about the late notice.'

'Don't worry at all.'

*

I load the dishwasher, then put on my shoes and step outside, closing my eyes for a moment to drink in the heat of the sun as it falls snow soft on my face. I feel bad leaving Grandad on his own. A few minutes ago, I was worried about talking to him; I thought I shouldn't bother him, like when I was younger and he was in his study with the door shut. But he didn't growl at me, and now I can see a kind of vulnerability he carries with him like a cloak. It's so strange to find I don't know who he is at all, not really. It makes me feel uneasy to think I used to be small enough for him to hold, and even then he seemed old to me. A moment ago, it feels like, I was starting secondary school; now I'm twenty-five, and all the plans I made have collapsed like old houses, like sandcastles at high tide. How can I be flying so fast through everything? There was optimism in me once; there was a great open future like snow no one had walked in. How could it all have fallen apart so suddenly?

Mum was the start of it all. The root of what happened, the trouble that brimmed in my life and cut me off from everything – from love, from people, from mirrors, from hope.

I suspect Mum never really wanted children. She might have once liked the idea of having a child in the abstract, but she ended up feeling let down by the reality, the tiredness, the work. When I left home to go to university, Mum said as we were carrying my stuff out of the house that she felt she was getting her life back. That was the sound of the lid closing finally on our relationship, I think.

I cross the mounting yard, happy at the sound of the gravel crunching underfoot as I approach the quiet freedom of the road beyond the walls of the yard, a road that leads out to the wide world and home and anywhere you can imagine. I set off out of the front gates up the hill into the village. In a place like this, walking past the pub and hearing the bells of the church, you can almost believe the world is beautiful. Of course, at the back of my mind I know that places like this are only possible if other people have nothing, but the old lanes here still make my heart lift. That's one of the struggles I always have with socialism – it's such a shame, but it seems, in the end, like you can't be fair about things and still believe in nice houses. It seems like a flaw in the plan.

I feel awake enough now to talk to Sam. I know I have to speak to him, or he'll be there at the edge of my mind all day, casting a shadow over all the celebrations. I want to feel angrier with him for letting me down, but I can't, because it's so entirely predictable. If what you expected goes and happens, can you really claim to be disappointed? I call, and hear the Vodafone woman's familiar tones instructing me to leave a message.

'Hi, it's me. I got your text. I'm sorry you're busy. I'm sad you won't be here today. I'll be busy now so I can't speak, but maybe we can speak tonight. OK. Bye.'

I should have demanded more of an explanation, but I've always preferred to hide myself away when anything hurt. I've never liked asking for anyone's attention, asking for anyone to care. It always felt like weakness, like failing. Mum used to make me feel like asking for any help at all was only putting a burden on her.

It used to feel like Mum didn't want me there, as far back as I can remember. Like I was a trouble that couldn't be cleaned up or mended. First she got tired of doing things for me, and would tell me I was old enough now to open my own curtains in the morning. Then she would decide I was opening the curtains wrong, and rush into the bedroom to do them again, as if she was putting out a fire.

'You have to get it neat,' she'd say, tugging at the curtains so they hung straight, framing the window. 'It's ugly if you just leave them half-open; you have to get it neat.'

'Why?'

'Because that's how it's supposed to look. You can see that, can't you?' She would gesture exasperatedly at the window, arranged now just as she wanted. 'Can't you see that's how it ought to look? Really, Kate, it's easy.'

Whatever happened, whatever I was doing, I was always doing it wrong. And there were other ways she let me know how much trouble I was. I remember the locks on the kitchen cupboards that stopped me eating except when I was given my three meals and my snack after school. I suppose it was a way of controlling the household spending. It was a way of exercising control, too.

I've walked as far as the church, so I go into the churchyard and start wandering in between the graves, watching the light as it comes through the trees and reading the names on the stones. I decide to call Lizzy, and dial, and remember too late that it's still quite early on a Saturday morning and she might be asleep.

'Hello?'

'Hey. I didn't wake you, did I?'

'Little bit.'

'Shit, sorry.'

'It's OK. I should get up anyway.'

'It's a beautiful morning.'

'Yeah? Oh, yeah.' I imagine her sat up in bed, reaching across to the window in her bedroom to lift back the curtain and take in the sky.

'How are you?'

'Er . . . I don't really know yet.'

'Sorry, I shouldn't have called so early.'

'Are you all right?'

'Yeah.'

'You sound a bit grumpy.'

'Sorry. Funny morning. I'm just a bit pissed off with Sam.' I feel ashamed to have called her now, to have ruined her lie-in with my problems. She doesn't need to hear about this, doesn't need to hear from me.

'What's happened?'

'Nothing really. I'm at my grandad's eightieth and Sam was going to come down, and I knew he wouldn't, and he texted this morning to say he couldn't, and now he isn't picking up. It's just boring, you know? He could have just said when I asked.' It's sad, anyway, now I say it aloud. Nothing much has happened at all; there's no reason to have called her, except that I felt alone. But perhaps she knows that. Perhaps Lizzy always knows that's what makes me pick up the phone and call her.

'Yeah.'

'I don't know what I'm doing really.'

'Do you feel like you don't want to be with him?'

'Not really. I don't know. I do want to be with him. The trouble is I feel like I never actually am with him. You know? He's always so fucking far away.'

'Yeah.'

'I'm sorry. I know what you think.' Lizzy doesn't have much time for Sam. The whole situation's too difficult for her, really. She's Joe's sister, after all. I wish I had another friend I felt close enough to talk to, wish I hadn't rung her like this.

'You just have to try and have the conversation with him, don't you?'

I've arrived at my grandma's grave. I stand over the flourish of grass and the stone at the head of it, and look at the dates. It's terrible to imagine Grandma's body in that ground beneath me, under the mud weighing down like years, like memory. I turn and walk away as quickly as I can. 'I'd better go now. Got to help setting up.'

'Are you having a party?'

'Yeah, big one.'

'Will she be there? Your mum?'

'Yeah.'

'And you'll see her?'

'Yeah.'

'Is that why you're freaked out?'

'Why do you say that?'

'Because you called me. And I can hear it in your voice.'

'I'm sorry. I guess that is why I'm calling, yeah. I feel like a bit of a wreck. I hoped Sam would be here. Now I'm on my own.' It's pathetic of me, really, not to be able to face things by myself. Why can't I do this by myself? Why do I wish Lizzy could be here, holding my hand?

'You're not. I'll be thinking of you.'

'Thank you.'

'I'm always here for you, mate, remember that.'

I stop for a moment when I reach the road. My throat feels tight. It's weird, but it always throws me when someone shows me kindness. I never think I deserve it. Even when I need someone's sympathy, it still makes me feel sick to ask them for some understanding, because I'm sure one day, when I want reassurance, I'll call someone and they'll tell me I'm not worth their time, they've seen through the act, they don't want to know me any more.

It can be very unhealthy, depending on your mood, to come back to the scenes of your childhood. All around you, wherever you look, there are layers on layers of memories, glimpses of who you were when you came here before, and who you can never quite be again. And I think you always find you were someone else back then. More optimistic, more naïve.

I used to wish Dad could have calmed Mum down, and held us together when we started to fall apart, but he was never the one who made the decisions. Mum was always more driven than he was, and he was too happy to let things lie.

Because Mum was the busy one, she only cooked dinner for the three of us one or two nights a week, and it was always a time to steer clear of her. She would make me peel carrots or potatoes if I came into the kitchen, and then I'd have to concentrate on getting that right, on not causing Mum any trouble, or she'd lose her temper and shout at me for things I didn't even know I'd done.

'You have to get those bits out with the end of the peeler! Can't you see them? Why would you want to eat them? They're disgusting. You have to get them out like this.' She would snatch the potato and the peeler from my hands, and finish the job for me, sighing and harried. By the time dinner reached the table, and I sat down with Mum and Dad to eat, the air in the kitchen was usually thick with the threat of her censure.

'Well, I'll be up far too late getting through the work I have to do tonight,' Mum would say.

'I'm sorry,' Dad would reply. 'You should have let me cook.'

'Why would that make any difference? The work would still be there, wouldn't it? That wouldn't make any difference.'

'Sorry, darling. I just meant it would have been possible for you to get started on it earlier.'

'Can't you let me have some pleasure in my life? Am I not allowed to enjoy cooking for my family?'

Mum loved the martyrdom of bearing so much on her shoulders. She savoured the tiredness, the endless midnights, she let them breathe like wine and then drank them down. She loved to make everyone else feel she worked harder than they did. And she's never seemed to get a handle on her temper in the whole of her life. She never found ways to stop herself snapping at the first sign of stress.

'You must understand, Kate,' Dad would explain, on the nights when he had to come into my room and comfort me, 'your mum does a very high-pressured job to pay for all these things we have. We're very lucky your mum is so wonderful, and works so hard for us. But she has to bottle up all the stress while she's at work, or she wouldn't be able to do her job. So you have to remember that when she comes home she's very tired, she's very stressed, she's had a long day and she needs some peace around her.' I learned from Mum the idea that life was a punishment for something everyone had done to her, life was a burden to be borne.

Dad's work drove him less fiercely. He was good at it, and he cared about it, but it didn't consume him, and he found ways to switch off and take holidays. He qualified as a teacher, and stayed in the same school all his career, and worked his way up over time – he's head of Geography there now, but that's not really the story of his life. His real life happened in his evenings, his weekends, his time away from work, when he liked to be with me and Mum and read books and listen to his CDs, when he liked to go out walking. My parents have always been defined by very different things. Perhaps they were first attracted to one another because they showed each other such different visions of what life could be like. That can be attractive when you're at the beginning of everything. Since they got married, though, one vision has always been in the ascendant. Dad's happy in Mum's shadow, so he's never quite been able to disagree with whatever she chooses to do, or mend his family where it seemed to be breaking.

When I was a child I spent a lot of time in this place, visiting Grandma and Grandad; we'd stay for weekend after weekend in the summer, and come for Christmas and half-term. But those visits tailed off as I got older. That means the ghost of the distant past is all I see today – walks in borrowed wellies, lemonades on the bench outside the pub, snowmen on the green wearing hats Grandad didn't know he'd donated.

There are no more recent memories to build on, to soften the sense of loss. And how could there be? I've been more or less out of the world for the last few years. I haven't been living, only floating through time, pinned in my body, with not much real experience of anything but my anxiety and the hollow sadness at the heart of me to show for the years that are lost.

On good days it can become beautiful, all this reminiscence. As I walk through the landscapes where my sunny childhood days played out, I sometimes feel like I'm living them again. I'm trying hard today to hold on to that sensation, because when I let my mood get dark, it makes me feel the past as an undertow instead, and as I look around me, memories of the times I ran down this road as a child seem to reproach me, gurning out like old graffiti that hasn't quite been washed off a wall. Like the memory of a crime on an anonymous street corner, where bunches of flowers mourn and die. I walk back in the direction of the house.

Lizzy's been my friend since university. She's from London, and she used to spend the weekends at home rather than staying in halls. She'd invite people over to eat dinner there, real food with vegetables in it that hadn't been cooked in a microwave, so I spent a lot of time at Lizzy's house while I was a student. That was where I first met Joe, her brother, one hungover Sunday morning. That was where I first kissed him, one drunk Saturday night.

Joe was a little older than me, about to graduate from Bristol while I was in my first year and getting to grips with London. He would come home sometimes when he wanted a night out with his friends from school, driving across the country with the radio roaring for company along the roads. He read English like I did. I think we both knew we liked each other the first time we met. We had too much in common for nothing to happen between us. That age when anyone with a little chemistry between them ends up falling into bed with each other.

I used to love visiting their home. I liked their parents, because other people's parents always seem less complicated than your own. It's like experiencing the idea of home as it might look in a brochure, never having to look at what's swept under the carpet, never having to do any of the chores. I hadn't realised before then that my own home was unhappy, but I had to confront that fact after my first evening at Lizzy and Joe's. It made me feel at sea to be in the middle of so much laughter.

'I wish they'd stop making *Bake Off*.'

'Why?'

'I've got a better idea anyway. *Bake Off*'s rubbish.'

'It isn't!'

'It's definitely rubbish. Wanna hear my idea?'

'Go on.'

'*Who Wants To Be A Milliner?* It's *Bake Off* for hats.'

The friendship I had with that family taught me the world could be a little more beautiful than I had suspected. They made me think things could turn out all right. You could fall in with a group of people who seemed to fit around you, and make you feel the world was welcoming, and look forward to a whole lifetime of knowing them all.

Then trouble rose up and claimed us. This was the second

lesson I learned from Lizzy and Joe and their family, and this one was harder. Sometimes things don't turn out all right at all. Sometimes, no matter what you might have wanted or planned, trouble comes for you, and there's nothing you or anyone else can do about it. And all of the hopes you might have cherished need revising in an instant.

The magnolia tree at the top of my grandad's road is blooming. I didn't notice the flowers on it before. I suppose I was looking at my phone. The blooms shine like bright shocks of flame, and I have to stop and stare at them, drink them in. The good weather's coming; there's blossom on the trees again. Surely everything can be better now we've all come through the winter?

A car pulls up next to me, its engine still running, and I look through the window to see Aunt Laura smiling out at me, resplendent in a floral print dress that would have been loud in July.

'Hello, dear,' Laura says.

'Hello! How are you?'

'I'm all right. What about you, have you come through all the trouble?'

I should have stopped being surprised by now at the insensitivity people are capable of, but it still amazes me. With Laura, it's usually only an attempt to be kind, and the words coming out wrong, when it might have been better if they hadn't come out at all. Aunt Laura comes from a very different generation, when the world didn't know what to say to someone like me. Perhaps she believes being blunt about weaknesses is the best way to deal with them. Perhaps that's all part of grasping the nettle and keeping a stiff upper lip and so on, and I'm just a snowflake if I let myself think otherwise.

'Yes, sort of. I hope so.'

'Are your parents here yet?'

'Not yet.'

'You've come over from Bristol, have you?'

'Yes.'

'Last night?'

'Yeah.'

'Well, I'm glad you're here, there's plenty to do.'

'Looking forward to it,' I lie. Of course there's always loads to do, and I always find myself enlisted whenever I come to these birthdays. I've let myself forget that, since the last time I was here.

'See you in there in a minute, then. How is your grandad?'

'I think he's feeling . . . thoughtful.'

Laura stares through the windscreen at the house a few yards ahead of us, and nods to herself. When she's serious, she looks just like Grandma. 'Yes. All right. Well, I'll see you in a minute.' Then she drives the stone's throw down to the drive, and turns in through the gates.

I watch her go, and don't start walking till the car's out of sight. This might well prove to be a very long day. I find Aunt Laura exhausting sometimes. She always makes me look after the bar at these parties: she's decided for some reason that it's my thing; she thinks I love doing it and talks to me about it like it's a treat, a nice job where I get to chat to everyone and be the centre of attention. I hate looking after the bar.

I didn't really want to spend today in charge of anything at all, I wanted to be quiet and stay out of sight, but of course I won't have any say, I'll have to go along with the flow of things, however much I'm dreading it. I'm really not sure I can face it all when I think about the day looming like a mountain up ahead. But there's nothing to be done now, I've committed myself. And perhaps I'm wrong, perhaps I'll end up enjoying whatever the day holds. Stranger things happen at sea.

I look up at the house as I walk back towards it and try to imagine what it would feel like to have really lived in this place, spent a childhood here like Mum did, rather than only visiting and playing here through the summers. It's strange to think Mum's mind must be shaped so differently from mine. For me, this house has only ever been a getaway. It's always stayed magical and unusual; there's a sense of holiday about it, because those were the times when we used to come and stay, and the memories cling on like cobwebs at the eaves of the windows. Visits to this house made me think of the Faraway Tree: each time I emerged through the branches of the journey here, a new adventure was waiting, the whole face of the house and the barns and the field and the garden would be rewritten by the weather and the gardeners and the people who visited. For Mum, as a child, it must have all seemed so much more ordinary, no matter how unusual it really was to spend time in a big house like this. It must have just felt like the way the world was supposed to look. What must that do to a person? How would that skew them away from seeing the world as it really is?

People's childhoods are the sources and centres of their lives, the frame of reference for everything else they ever do.

Every decision a person makes happens in the context of the world they've come from, the things they started out with, what it felt like and looked like to be them when they were young, and what that taught them to want. People are always working to tend the fires of their vanishing or vanished youth, to love the past back into being by always choosing whatever helps life seem more like it did at the start, when everything was still before them, waiting patiently in the future. That's how people hold on to their identities, and hold together their images of themselves, by remembering, playing out the feeling of their childhoods like a high clear note from a clarinet cutting through the hubbub of their buzzing adult lives. The world my mum longs for must be so very different from the one I know myself, no matter how much we think we share. The house I grew up in must have seemed shabby and small compared to a childhood spent running round this garden. Life, when it arrived, must have come as a disappointment for her. I used to think the house I grew up in was as big as the whole world, because of course there was a time when it was the whole world to me, and it filled the span of my imagination. It must have been just a starter home in Mum's eyes; a step along the way to other things that took her closer back to the feeling of childhood, even as she travelled ever further away from this place and the centre of herself through indifferent, relentless time.

I don't know what to do about Sam. Perhaps he's only a dream I've been having. Perhaps the whole world isn't really happening, but is only a fantasy I've spun out of memory to try and make sense of something else. Perhaps in my real life I'm standing somewhere in a long line of people. Or my teeth are falling out. Or I am running through the dark of a wood. Perhaps I've got lost in a forest and am scrambling for a way out here, through the clenched, splintering teeth of my imagination.

from Interview 23

So we flagged the bus over and got everyone out, and they all came quiet cos they were scared, you see, they weren't military, they had no weapons. We lined them up against the side of the bus, and none of them tried to run. Maybe they hadn't worked it out. Or just didn't believe it would happen, I don't know. We asked were any of them Catholic, and one guy put his hand up, I think maybe he was the driver, I don't remember so clear now. Maybe it won't surprise you to know I don't have so clear a memory of this; it gets blurred, it gets cloudy. But we pulled him out the line-up, the Catholic guy, and then we opened fire. Sure, it felt like a serious thing. But did I believe we were justified in what we did? Yes, I did. Afterwards, people had to disown us. It was seen as going too far. But we knew there were people higher up who were privately sympathetic. We had messages sent our way, some intermediary, a guy none of us had ever met. He told us no one was going to condone what had happened, but none of us was getting kneecapped.

Robert

THE HOUSE WAS built by the master builder Thomas Cubitt in the mid-nineteenth century. Another building had existed on the same site previously, but it was empty when Cubitt bought the land for what would become his family home. He pulled down most of the house that had stood there before and started again.

Cubitt had just completed his work building Buckingham Palace, and was therefore flush, and thinking about setting himself up for his old age. The work in London had been done so recently, in fact, that he used offcuts from the palace in his home – to this day, there are doors standing in the hall which were first made for kings and queens to walk through. People always seem to be impressed by that, although I never give it much thought, having lived here as long as I have done. And having seen enough of kings and queens at the dinners my work used to oblige me to attend to think little more of them than I do of other people. The only differences between kings and queens and anyone else being, I think, the scale of the responsibility they bear. Under all that, they're like anyone else. The most brutalised drunk and the Queen of England are the same inside, once you get past the skin of their lives.

It must have been a charged time to try to build a big house like this. I imagine the impact of the potato famine in Ireland and the failure of the crop everywhere would have been rippling black and livid across the country, as the age-old protectionism that had preserved this part of the world in its quietness was stripped away to solve the grain shortage in Ireland, and the sedimented rhythms of life fell apart for the people of Hampshire and the whole south – the whole country, I suppose. I can't speak for everywhere, only really knowing the south myself. There had been an explosion of violence bursting through those years, always the herald of change the world over, and Cubitt would have had to be wary of that. Machine wreckers had burned barns and smashed threshing machines when they saw what was coming: the move into the cities, the end of their world. Others had brawled against those rebels in turn, arguing the other case, demanding faster change. I read somewhere that Thomas Hardy remembered running round with a toy sword when he was a child, baying 'free trade or blood' to the terrified garden.

In the area around this house, the rioting saw some men deported to Australia, and others hanged for violence. None of their protests worked in the end. The poorhouses must have been booming in those years, and the farms packing up and caving in when Cubitt started hiring labour to build his house. The work would have been taken up with great resentment. The men who took it on must have known it would only sustain them for another year or so. They must have seen the day coming when they would have to move up and give in to the town. I wonder what that felt like. It is surely a strange thing to live to see the end of the world you were born into.

Although it's perfectly possible that old world hasn't ended at all, I suppose, but has simply gone underground for a while. For all that the history books record the flight to the cities as if they're telling the end of a story, I still sometimes feel that I see the descendants of those same workers in the village pub if I ever go in there for a drink. Men who believe things differently. In the White Horse, they still prop up the bar, people with bodies sculpted into distinctive shapes by the work they do, whose life is organised around a totally different way of thinking to my own. The men I say hello to in the pub seem to have no real feeling for progress, for comfort, recognition, gain. What matters to them above all, I've found in the conversations I've had drinking there, is that they will be able to keep living where they're living. Their existence is built around the idea of home above everything else, so they take whatever work's available to keep them in the right place, rooted like laurels in the soil they were born into. Perhaps you could say that hidden among these drinkers the pre-industrial poor have limped on into the twenty-first century, keeping their heads down so no one tries to stamp on them, riding out the capitalist interlude and living as people have always done in this part of the world, clear of progress, clear of change, waiting for their time to come again. Waiting for the day when the petrol runs out, and the nuclear rain starts falling, and everyone goes to market by horse and cart again. That might be how the whole long story of England finishes in the end, though I suppose that's romantic, I suppose that's fanciful.

I'm pontificating again. But just imagine it. Perhaps the whole world I've been part of, and tried in my own small way to prop up, the glorious world of London streets and speculation and concert halls, will be proven in time to have been an illusion, a dream, and a day will come when old truths, old ways will spring back up out of the soil?

I watch Kate walk through the gates at the front of the house and out into the road, taking her phone from her pocket as she goes and staring down into it like Narcissus into the water, like Orpheus losing himself in the memory and the dream of Hades. People move like drunks when they look at their phones while walking, I always think. It terrifies me to see them so hived off from the street and the day and the world around them, lost in fascination at the world behind the screen of their phone, mining narratives woven on the other side of the world for their sustenance while people who might have been their soulmates, might have been their friends, if only they'd looked up and talked to each other, have to sidestep round them because no one notices any more whose way they are getting in, whose car they are stepping out in front of. My old form teacher wouldn't have stood for it. I was always taught that people ought to look where they were going.

I suppose Kate must feel very isolated on her own here with me. It's a place for family, a house of this size; it's too big for two people to fill all its silences. Hattie and I thought it was paradise once, of course, our little island, our castle, our home, when we were bringing up Hannah here. Once it was just me and Hattie we were still all right, though I suppose we rattled round a bit, and heated more of the house than we really needed to, spreading ourselves across a lot of rooms. But two people who can only catch sight of each other across the distance of generations, and the distance of loss, as Kate and I do, will always run out of words that are loud enough to take flight through the different rooms and light all this house's darker corners. Kate is an angel for trying as hard as she does to make conversation with an old man like me. It can't be much fun for her.

I felt an idiot this morning at breakfast. I must be getting very old. Or going senile, surely. What was I doing, talking to the poor girl like that? Why did I ask her whether she wanted to come and stay with me? I felt embarrassed for her as soon as I spoke. Of course to her it would sound like a fate worse than death. How awkward it will be for her, having to say no or pretend I never asked. She looked at me then with kindness and, I think, with pity, too polite to tell me what she really felt, and then, horror of horrors, I was reduced to pulling the same silly faces that used to make her laugh when she was young, just to break the mood and the embarrassment in the room. She must have thought me pathetic, really. I saw in the way she looked at me that she felt sorry for what had become of us both, the warmth and laughter we shared when she was a little girl and came to visit on holidays only a memory now, receding.

I must make myself another cup of coffee.

The kettle boils, and I wait for the coffee to brew, standing in the kitchen looking absently through the window in the direction Kate went, out of the gates and up into the village where the magnolia is blooming. Then I pour out a cup, and head for the study.

I hear the phone start to ring while I am still in the hall, and hurry to my desk, sure I am going to miss it. I catch it on the fifth ring, just in time.

'Hello?'

'Robert?'

'Yes, who's this?'

'It's Frank Dunn. Long time no speak.'

I put my coffee down precisely and carefully on the coaster on the desk. 'Frank. A long time indeed.'

'I need to see you.'

'Do you?'

'Today, in fact. Put our old heads together.'

'Really?'

'I'm afraid so, yes. Look, we'll talk more later, all right? I'll pop by about twelve.'

'Is it really—'

'I'm afraid it is, Robert. Sorry. I'll tell you when we meet.'

I listen a moment longer as Frank hangs up, and stand there as the dial tone rings out, the sound seeming huge and long-legged at first as if it bounded the whole of the world while I held it to my ear, and then becoming distant, just a tautness in the room, as I drop my hand back down to my side, put the phone back in its cradle. I walk to the window and look out over the garden. The willow in the middle of the lawn is perfectly still; there is no breeze stirring.

Frank Dunn is an Honorary Fellow at a college in Oxford who has spent most of his career teaching at Queen's University in Belfast. He published a book in the eighties called *Nominal Identity*, a voyage through the shallows of Wittgenstein – as far as I have been able to make out, not having actually read the thing myself. The way signs are formed by things, the way things are formed by signs, or some such stuff.

It was not in an academic capacity that I got to know Frank, though. We were introduced, with deft delicacy, on the occasion of my first visit to Queen's in Belfast. I was taken to see the sights and break bread there a few weeks after I first took up my position at the ministry. All of us in the most hideous suits, when I look at photos from that time, though of course we thought they were just the thing back then. The visit was put into my calendar without my having much say about it, I remember, and so I went dutifully through the motions, exchanging platitudes with the vice chancellor, unable to discern any meaningful reason for my presence, only presuming it must be obligatory for whoever was in my position to take an interest in the life of the university. So much of my work used to be ceremonial, really, and done out of no real feeling beyond obligation. So much of what I did with my time was only the dry echo of the rattling of sabres, the changing of guards posted long ago, routines and traditions that had once been the backbone of a whole empire now played out by men in dull suits who didn't look the part any more, didn't know why they were doing it all, and would much rather have been back at their desks getting through their in-trays and filling their ashtrays up a little higher, finishing the sandwiches they brought from home for lunch.

At the end of the afternoon, I found myself being directed as unobtrusively as possible into the office of Professor Frank Dunn. My assistant made the introductions.

'Robert, I'd like to introduce an invaluable friend of the department.'

'Well,' Frank said, the smile fixed sharp as steel on his face, 'I don't know how helpful a term "friend" really is. But it's very good to meet you.' He extended his hand to me, and I shook it, watching his eyes carefully.

'Good to meet you.'

'How are you coping with the change of scene from Hampshire to Belfast?'

I remember feeling not just shock but the sudden coldness of anger tighten in my stomach when he said that, a kind of base longing to lash out or hide. Frank clearly knew the whereabouts of my home, where my family lived, my wife and daughter, the very house where I am now standing some thirty years later. This man, this supposed professor, was making a show of his knowledge because he wanted me to understand that there was a file out there somewhere that had my name on it. The reference to Hampshire was a pure and naked exercise in baring the teeth of my vulnerability, the threat that I and my family faced because of the job I had taken. It tasted like blood, like iron in my mouth, to hear the words spoken. And from an academic, no less – a crumpled little man in corduroy whose desk was propped up with books, not the wilder characters with handshakes like hornbeam I'd been led to expect this from.

When I returned to my office later that afternoon, the situation was explained to me. I had just got back behind my desk, and was steeling myself to wade back into the endless paperwork, disturbed and unhappy, when someone knocked on the office door. Ian Knight, my liaison in the intelligence services, let himself in, and stood with feet planted firmly on the carpet in front of the desk, as if he expected to be hit by a wave.

'I understand you met Frank Dunn today?'

Ian and I had only spoken a couple of times at that stage, and we were both still wary of each other. I stared guardedly at him, and I remember thinking that both of us were trying not to blink.

'I did. No one told me who he was. I wasn't briefed.'

'Yes, that's why I'm here.'

'Is it standard practice to send me into meetings with people I know nothing about? But who, apparently, know plenty about me?'

'Sorry, Robert. Every now and then things slip when you're bedding a new team in. You should have been told, but the briefing didn't happen.'

'So he's . . . what – a conduit for negotiations, is he? He's one of these people you've told me about who can pass on deniable messages to the Provisionals.'

Ian inclined his head in agreement. 'That's right. We've worked with Frank on and off for the last decade. He's a valuable contact.'

'He doesn't fit the profile of the men you told me about, though? I thought all these negotiators ran haulage firms.'

'We wouldn't use the term negotiators.'

'Well, whatever he is, he doesn't fit the profile.'

'That's why you were introduced to him. Frank is unusual, and occasionally very useful to us, because the nature of his work makes it easy for him to come up with pretexts for travel, and more importantly with pretexts to attend the kinds of meetings that might be a little conspicuous for other people. The people who run haulage firms, as you eloquently put it. So we always like to introduce him to whoever's in your post, in case you need to have a lunch with him at some point.'

'I see.'

'In reality, most of the business we've done with Frank is still run through the security services, but your having met him simply opens up another available channel. You'll probably never need to talk to him again; it's just about establishing the possibility. Then, if anything ever comes up, we can make the best use of you both.' Ian smiled broadly, determined to communicate to me that what he had to say made everything all right.

For all that I was angry at being ambushed by my meeting with Frank, I ended up glad it had happened. It meant the connection was there and waiting in the winter of 1987, when Frank and I found ourselves making unexpected use of it in the wake of the Enniskillen bombing.

Apart from that one brief period when we worked together in earnest, my relationship with Frank remained a distant one. We met at public events on a few occasions, during and after my time in Belfast, and I like to think we always got on well enough when we did, enjoyed each other's company, politely, even sincerely in the end, as well as any two people could in the strained and unnatural circumstances which were part of life in that country at that time. But that was a long time ago, and on this bright Hampshire morning, where I find myself standing at the window of my study looking out at the willow and the day, lost for a moment in memory, I realise it must be a decade since I have even heard Frank's name. On other days it might have been a strange ghost to rise up from the past. But perhaps it isn't all that surprising today. I look at my copy of *The Times* where it lies on the desk, the story on its front page, and realise I already know why Frank is calling me now.

I poured so much of myself out down the phone, over the years. It has drunk up so much of my life. Time after time I called this very house from the office in Belfast, or the house where I slept in the Belfast suburbs, to hear Hattie's voice, and ask her how her day had been, both of us knowing all the while there was no point going into any real detail, because we had missed it all, another gulp of daylight, another day done.

I picture myself with a drink at the end of an evening. 'How are you?'

'Oh, fine. I turned over the vegetable beds this afternoon.'

'All of them?'

'I'm very tired tonight.'

'I'm sure you are, with all that digging. Did you get out at all, or have you just been round the garden?'

'I've been in the village. I didn't go into town, I didn't need anything.'

Sometimes, when she and Hannah came to visit me in Belfast, or when I came home, it would be 'we' who didn't need anything, both of us together and gathering our lives into the one dance. But those bright times were all too rare, because Hattie never wanted to relocate to follow me, move away from this house and put a distance between herself and the life she had decided to centre here. The fact I had taken a post somewhere didn't mean she wanted to store away everything about her life and hitch her days entirely on to following her husband. The result was that much of my life was spent away from her. Of course, I regret that, but these are the compromises we make to pay the bills, and to be at peace with ourselves and our ambition.

The day is lost now, of course. That phone call has overturned all of my plans. I shall have to set my mind to Frank, put my own celebrations aside. Nothing to be done about it; the issue has to be dealt with now it has come up. A catastrophe, really, when so many people will expect things of me today. I look at the pile of unopened birthday cards on my desk, and imagine the lives that lurk behind each of them, the people who went to the trouble to pick something out in WHSmith or some other card shop, and buy a stamp, and take the cap off the pen and begin. It is dizzying to think of the latticework of stories that link their lives with mine, all the closenesses I have ever shared with these people whose thoughtfulness is laid out before me today on the desk, awaiting the blade of the letter opener, awaiting attention. With such ease, with such ignorance, I signed my life away to my country, back when the world seemed young. If I had known the sum of the things I would have to set aside, the things I would pass up because I was needed at work, if I had seen that at the start, would I forge ahead with all of it again? Perhaps the worst of it is that I think I probably would. Who knows what I might have missed out on if I hadn't lived as I did? I pick up the phone and dial a number I haven't used in years. A belligerent voice answers on the fourth ring.

'Hello?'

'Geoffrey, it's Robert Shawcross.'

'Robert, good morning. How can I help you?'

'I wanted to let you know about a little get-together I've got coming up. Thought you might want to come down, and we could put our old heads together.'

'I see. Hang on, Robert, I'll have to call you back.'

'Absolutely.' The line goes dead and I replace the receiver. A simple protocol, outlined to me on the occasion of my retirement. I have never had to make such a call at the weekend before. I am glad Geoffrey was in. I don't know what I would have done otherwise – Frank's message meant I couldn't have talked to anyone else. 'Old heads' is an agreed phrase – a code phrase, if you will, though that sounds a bit sensationalist to me – to be used if the parties making contact want to conduct their conversations only with individuals already known to them, rather than dealing with the entire security service, most of whom, these days, weren't born when the Sixty-Niners took up arms. It is a way of having delicate conversations. Everything is reported upstairs in the usual way afterwards, but for as long as any exchange is under way, the 'old heads' protocol is a method of ensuring the people involved have all been round the course together before. I would never admit as much to anyone, but it is a protocol that delights me. Thanks to the obsessive caution of the IRA, I don't have to spend today liaising with the children who run Britain now, only the men among whom I spent my working life. There is pleasure to be had in reconnecting the old links you forged in the heat of youth. The phone rings and I pick it up immediately. 'Hello?'

'Geoffrey here. Who is it?'

'It's Frank Dunn. Midday today.'

'I see. Makes sense.'

'I suppose it does.'

'Do you want anyone there?'

'Not yet, no. If you could just stand by?'

'All right. I didn't have much on today, hope you're the same?'

'Nothing very much.' There is no point saying anything else; it wouldn't change anything to admit how much trouble this is going to cause.

'We'll speak again when there's news,' Geoffrey said.

'Absolutely.' Then I ring off for the final time, and hear the voice of my sister-in-law buffeting through the house as she comes in from the courtyard. Her cry of hello seems to me in this moment, unprepared for it as I am, like the saddest sound I have ever heard. The closest I will ever come to hearing Hattie's voice again. And the sound is being made by a woman who frequently enrages me, indeed has been enraging me at intervals now for sixty years.

I never understood how Hattie could have such a sister. One day, a world will come into being where people will be able to be with each other without having to marry into one another's families. Alas, it will come too late for me. I head for the kitchen to greet Laura, who I know has been looking forward to this day all year. I will upset her more than anyone else when I disappear into the secrecy of my office, but there is nothing to be done. Laura is already washing vegetables under the tap.

'Hello, old thing,' I say, hoping to annoy her.

'Who are you calling old?' She turns to face me. We take

each other in for a moment. 'Happy birthday, darling Robert.' She embraces me and kisses me on the cheek.

'What are you up to here?'

Laura waves her arms at the sink in despair. 'Getting on with the veg. Can you get everything we've already sorted out of the larder and we'll see where we are?'

'All right.' I embark on the first of what I'm sure will be innumerable journeys from the kitchen to the pantry in the course of the morning, and return hefting a huge plate of salmon, which I deposit on the kitchen table. 'What they don't say in the Bible, of course, is just how big the fish were that Jesus had with him when he fed the five thousand. A few of these and it might not have been such a remarkable achievement after all.'

Laura laughs. I like making her laugh, because she always tries her best not to find my jokes funny. It's a small triumph to break through her defences.

'Really, Robert. It hasn't gone off, has it? I'm worried it will have gone off.'

'No, no, all is well. Have no fear. Today will go as well as it always does, thanks to you, Laura. All this is going to be hitch free.'

'Well, that's all right then. I see Kate's down already?'

'Yes, she came down last night.'

'How is she?'

'Oh, you know. Very subdued. And she's worried about today. She'll be all right. It will just take time and support, I think.'

'How much more time does she need, though?'

'I don't know. It's still very recent, you know. She'll get better.'

'I hope so. Does she talk about it?'

'Not to me, not yet. I tried chattering away this morning, but that didn't seem to open her up.'

Laura turns the oven on. I'm sure there's sweat on her brow already. She turns to look at me. 'But we're not worried about her, are we?' I suppose Laura must love Kate as well, no matter how fussily and impatiently she expresses it. The way a dog loves a chew toy, you could say.

'No, no. She'll be fine.'

'After all, bad things happen, don't they, it's part of life, and we all just have to come to terms with that. And people come through them, and after a while they get better.'

'Yes, I suppose they do.'

Laura takes down the chopping block and starts work on a pile of potatoes. I wonder whether there was more she wanted to say about Kate. She is angry about the whole thing, that was clear in the way she spoke; she disapproves of how it has been handled. She wishes Kate could have been compelled to keep speaking to everyone, rather than sealing herself off in the way she has. Perhaps she is right. Today, in the light of what has happened, putting mother and daughter back together again seems so much more difficult. I must keep Laura away from the sherry and the wine today, if that is at all possible. It would be awful for there to be any kind of confrontation. I remember having to practically prise her and one of my nieces apart five or six years ago, both of them slurring their words, having fallen out about car parking. She can be a belligerent drunk.

'You're chewing up the whole of this field. You don't have to drive so far down, there are spaces left here at the top of it!'

Laura had been clearly audible thirty feet away, and I hurried out to find her when I heard the argument start.

'I can't fit in there, that's not enough space.'

'It is enough space. The problem is whether you know how to park a car or not.' I came round the stables and saw Laura standing at the top of the field, red-faced, glass in hand, haranguing some poor distant relative I barely recognised, whom she could hardly have known at all.

'Laura,' I called to her from a distance, still making my way across the yard.

'But your side of the family never were up to much, were you, so why am I surprised that you can't manage this?'

'Excuse me?'

By now I had reached the scene of the altercation, so I poured oil on the waters, and led Laura away, and gave her a talking-to in the kitchen. She refused to apologise with a twinkle in her eye, knowing she was in the wrong, but determined all the same to enjoy the feeling of having got righteously, riotously drunk. At least until the following morning, anyway. While the party lasted, she was going to have her fun.

The secret of these days is that they aren't for me at all, really, even though it is my birthday we all say we are celebrating. They are days above all for the visitors. A few years ago, it became clear to me that I was now occupying a role as de facto head of my family in its diaspora, as the generation that had come before me fell slowly and finally silent. People started looking to me to make the speeches at special occasions. In part, this was an acknowledgement of the position I occupied during my professional life. The respect I gained among my relations was recognition of how I had risen to do something that I suppose you could say was important, depending on the way you looked at things. But in actual fact I suspect that it had a lot to do with the fact I owned the biggest house, and little else. People like a party. Perhaps the disparate, far-flung members of any tribe never have very much in common in the end, but I think people like to feel connected to where they came from, and all those who have come before them. It's nice to get together now and then and talk about grandparents, and call to mind people who are loved and missed. These parties are a chance to remember the departed, as much as they are for catching up with the living. For the younger people, I think perhaps the whole thing is frustrating, and seems like a hiatus in the year, but for my own generation it is good to keep in touch, and see what the nieces and nephews are doing with their one and only lives.

At least, it was like that once. But, increasingly, I find it all very sad. The rhythm of my meetings with the people who spend these days here with me, being kind to me, being polite and deferential, affords me a terrible clarity. When you see people day in and day out, the way their rhythms and ambitions change and fall away becomes somehow indiscernible – you find yourself too close to see the course they're taking. Like the collapse of a cliff path, which happens one stone at a time, you can get used to the gradual and ineluctable disappearance of the ground beneath your feet if it is simply a part of life. But to see someone once a year and every year, as I do with some of my more distant cousins, is to have nothing at all to talk about except what is happening to their dreams, whether they have hauled them any closer, whether they have fallen away for good. It is my fate to observe every diminution in the mobility and mental faculties of my oldest acquaintances; to hear about every job their children never got. It makes me feel far too mortal.

'Gorgeous day, isn't it?' I say.

'Oh, yes. Spring has sprung,' Laura says.

'And the sap is rising.'

'Yes, well. I read the most awful story in the local paper.'

'Oh yes?'

'About a woman who was trampled to death by cows. She walked her dog through a field, and they panicked, and ran right over her. The awful thing was, this other walker found her while she was still alive. The dog was dead, I think it was a golden retriever, poor stupid thing – they're such stupid dogs, aren't they? – and the woman was lying there next to it. She couldn't move. I think her back was broken – I think that's what they said. She asked the woman who found her to call for help, but there was no signal on her mobile, so she had to walk half a mile to make the phone call. Then she walked back, and the woman had died while she was away.'

'That's terrible.'

'That's what comes of the rising sap. All those frisky cattle.'

'I think it's more likely because they were scared of the dog.'

'Yes, probably. Still, all the same.'

'Quite.' I look around for something to do. That is the great lesson of life; always to look busy, lest someone should give you a job. 'I must just check something. Won't be a second.'

'All right.'

I leave the kitchen and head for the door under the stairs, descending quickly into the cellar. The memory comes of how Hattie used to worry I'd hit my head going down here, and used to call after me, her voice echoing through to where I stooped along. I try to stop the thought before the sadness of hoping to hear her voice takes over.

I am inordinately proud of the cellar beneath my house. The building itself is relatively new, dating almost entirely from the nineteenth century, but there is a section of the cellar that has been dated conclusively as having been built in the fourteenth, and that seems like grandeur to me. It feels extraordinary to walk hunchbacked into a room where men have probably been banging their heads on the low beams for seven hundred years. The greater part of the history of these islands had flowed over this place, the whole world has reinvented itself more times than anyone can count, yet here it is, the heart of the house, damp, murky, unaffected by any of it.

The house became the heart of my family as the passage of years built up memory on memory rooted in this building and the grounds around, life like a coastal shelf sedimented all around us, fastening us ever more firmly to the home we chose. Our child grew into the world here before setting out into it. We had hoped for more children to bring up here as well, both of us coming from big families, but that path wasn't open to us. After Hannah was born there were two miscarriages, and then Hattie never conceived again. Sometimes the world has plans for you other than the ones you thought you had embarked on.

I hope that when the time comes, another generation of my family will live here after me, and they might perhaps go on living here for a long time; that people born years from now whom I will never meet, all somehow linked to me by the long chain of the family tree I keep upstairs in the spare bedroom, will share the same hallways, bang their heads in the cellar. It gives me great pleasure to imagine so much life flowing out from the one place, all linked by the constant presence of the house, the backdrop to scene after scene, life after life. That's what I wanted to achieve when I bought this place, something that might be passed down through the family, give us a centre, give us roots. Perhaps it won't happen. Perhaps no one will want to live here when I'm gone and Hannah will sell it. But I like the dream, all the same.

I pick out the best whiskey I have to offer. I think Frank will appreciate this. I am certainly glad of an excuse to drink it.

I am pleased that Frank is coming to visit me, no matter how difficult the timing. I had begun to fear, in the few days that have passed since the story of the Boston Tapes broke in the press, while the phone did not ring, that the moment of my total irrelevance had finally arrived. A crisis had arisen, and no one had asked for me. I had started wondering whether I might at last have been consigned to history.

But even if the government no longer seeks me out, it seems the IRA still value my assistance. Frank will be coming to see me because someone within the IRA wishes to stress the risk to peace in Northern Ireland these subpoenas represent. Frank will tell me that the dredging of the river of history is a dangerous thing. He has asked to keep things among the old heads because his contact in the IRA has stressed that only those who have lived through the times recalled in these taped interviews now lying in wait in the dark of the library at Boston College can fully comprehend the buried violence that might be about to be unearthed, if things are not handled with the necessary delicacy. I can well understand the position; a politician in his forties now can talk with all the sincerity they like of the scars of the past, but I visited Enniskillen on the day the bomb went off. No briefing will convey what it was like to live in Ireland in the depths of the Troubles. It seems perfectly reasonable to me to mistrust the capacity of the younger generation to handle these old issues with the tact they require. The current lot have proved more or less incapable of handling any of the simpler tasks of government, after all; it's terrible to imagine what they might make of something genuinely challenging.

In the deep heart of the house, I drink in the smell of old damp, old silence, and wonder what it is like for a man who has killed other men to go back over the violences of his life, and lay them down on record. Do they feel proud when they remember, or are they desperate, and clinging to whatever was left of the memory of their lives, willing to tell any story at all, if someone would only listen to them? I think perhaps I know that feeling, that emptiness. I live with it myself; I cradle it more nights than I care to remember. In the dark of the small hours I find myself willing to recall any night, any story at all, so long as it will brimfill my consciousness so the memories spill over and flood me into a drugged-seeming sleep. Anything to shut out the silence that waits at the end of every sentence, the knowledge that my death is coming one day like Hattie's came to her. I remember the day she got her diagnosis, the doctor's appointment in the diary she wouldn't talk about when she got back to the house that afternoon.

'Everything all right, darling?'

'Nothing to worry about. Just a check-up, that's all.'

I didn't realise it was a lie for weeks. She kept on trying to hoard what was happening, keep any upset away from me. She bought flowers, filled the vases in the house. Daffodils and roses and tulips. She made a point of cooking my favourite meals, going through recipes like a singer through their repertoire, and I often walked into a room to find her furiously tidying, or dusting, or reorganising bookshelves. Letters started arriving from the hospital. She'd turn away from me to read them, then fold the letters up and put them into a pocket, hidden from me. I still don't know whether she was trying to protect me, or protect herself. Perhaps she just couldn't say it all out loud.

If I could only believe we'll see each other again. But I think that's just a child's illusion. All I can save of her from the fire now is memory. The two of us side by side in bed, both reading our books till we were ready to sleep, the pages turning like birds flitting over the coverlet. The sound of her breathing growing slower and deeper as she fell asleep by my side. Now she isn't there to lie beside me and save me from the things I fear, I feel mocked by the absence.

I want to believe life is about love. That was how we lived, Hattie and me. But that's such a difficult faith to hold to. What the world I have known really seems to be in love with, when I look back across the span of it, is death. So when these old, battered murderers speak into their microphones, what's driving them? I wonder. Do they believe their lives have been worth living? Do they love what they've done? Or are they really trying to kill themselves?

What story would I tell if they put the microphone in front of me? In some ways I am the least qualified person imaginable to answer that. I know I was a grammar-school boy. That was the engine that propelled me away from the lines of work the rest of my family always fell into before me. My father ended up as a chauffeur, if that wasn't too grand a word for what he did. He had travelled from north Wales to London as a young man, at a time when people were starving on the hills where he was born. He briefly found employment as a bus driver, until the first war broke out. Then he was chauffeur to a captain in Iran – it was still Persia at the time, of course – for the duration of that conflict. When he left the army, he moved to Rochester to try his hand as a taxi driver, but he was hopeless at timekeeping and always missed meeting the trains, the lifeblood of the taxi trade in a place like that. After a year or so he gave the cab up and moved to Wiltshire, where a man whose father had known his father in Wales had bought a farm and become wealthy when the army bought his land out in the war.

The Welsh connection between my father and his new employer was worth a job driving the farmer's Daimler on the rare occasions when he wanted to go anywhere in style. This car became the glory of my father's life, his great love. He would polish it till it shone, lavishing the thing with all his attention. To make up the rest of the income he needed to feed all our family, he farmed, much as his predecessors in among the roots of the family tree had always done before him. As a child, I loved seeing my father setting off down the road at a stately pace in the Daimler, or sometimes cadging a lift with him, because, back then, to be a driver always seemed to me like a holiday from the endlessness of the land, like a little escape.

Later, when I got into the grammar school and then went away to university, I came to see my father's work differently. Once I was out of the narrow context of the village I came from, I saw the social order I'd been part of differently, and realised my father hadn't been grand at all, he'd been a sort of servant. I became almost ashamed of him then, such was the shock of that discovery. And I suppose I was filled up with the snobbishness of youth, newly aware of the wealth in the world and the people who found their way in among it and never would have spoken to the kind of people who made up my family, my neighbours, my world. A long time passed before I brought Hattie to meet my parents. I thought she'd never speak to me again. Of course, when they did meet they got on wonderfully, and when I told her about my fears she laughed at me. She was never as paranoid and hung up as I was. But those are quite good qualities for working in the civil service, paranoia and an obsessive regard for propriety, so I can't regret them too much.

Now I am old, and older than my father ever lived to be, I am remorseful about the way he was diminished in my eyes back then, once I saw the reality of my family's station. I have tried to make up for lost time. I have made pilgrimages back to the childhood home, and on to where my parents are buried, time and again, to try and recapture the pride I once felt, when I used to see the shining Daimler eating the street as it shimmered past the house. And Hattie and I took an interest in family history, and she made the family tree and framed it, and hung it in the bedroom where it is today. I went to visit the poor scrap of field Dad and his own father once farmed, the steepness of the hillside my ancestors died on, and the cottage my father grew up in, still without running water even now, in the torrent-boiling flood of the twenty-first century. A poor life, that. Still, I am unable to resist the urge to romanticise it. Because things are undoubtedly beautiful in that country. Perhaps that's only the way I see things, of course. Perhaps I am in love with the idea of my father passing that way years before me, really the same man that I am, because he must have lived with the same heart beating in him that has driven me on. Our two journeys separated by the passage of years. That's a thought to cradle, to make you feel less alone.

I thought, as a younger man, that I might be starting something important when we settled into this house. I thought of all the children who would surely come after, the people who were going to inherit this place, the paintings on the wall that would steadily grow in number. Looking around me down here in the cellar I catch glimpses of the ambitions I burnished back then. There is a rack of bottles, dust-covered bottles of port, against the far wall, that a connoisseur would recognise as having some modest value. They were a little vanity of mine, a little extravagance: I laid them down at intervals to mark significant occasions. There are bottles there to mark the purchase of this house, the year Hannah was born, the year I took my job in Belfast, the year of my retirement, the year that Hannah married Michael and the year she had Kate. I gathered this collection together slowly, an alcoholic autobiography, always imagining days to come when I would have people to drink these with. Now I look at the bottles gleaming dimly in the dark, and I think I was just setting myself up for heartbreak. I can't imagine ever wanting to touch any of those bottles any more. It would be like drinking away the memories of the years they marked. And who would I ever drink them with, when I spend so much of the year on my own?

from Interview 38

My first gig for the IRA, I was a sort of messenger boy really, a runner. I just used to take messages through the streets. You can't imagine how much of it there was. With a guerrilla organisation, logistics and communication, that's most of the work, nearly all the activity that's going on is just passing word around because it gets so fucking difficult to do. And maybe with any organisation, I don't know. We must have been dozens of us out there every day, walking round Belfast, carrying our secrets, bumping into each other, never knowing. A lot of hidden currents like the sea.

Kate

I LOITER IN THE drive, killing time before going back into the house. Aunt Laura and Grandad have a way of winding each other up, and I think the mood will be a bit tenser now she's here. So I wait, scrolling distractedly through Facebook in the lee of the gates, and try to psych myself up to step back into the house and see how the two of them are getting on today.

I don't know what to do about Sam. He's let me down too often for me to feel sure he's really any good for me, but I can't help feeling there's still life to be lived between us. I'm too patient with him when he flakes out, really, too forgiving, but it's difficult to be anything else, because I owe him a lot, when I add it up. He's the reason the most isolated and frightened time of my life has started to recede.

When I first saw him I'd been out walking for most of the night before. A bad habit from the past I still hadn't quite broken, six months after going back to work. I used to walk whole nights sometimes after the accident, as if I was trying to be ghostlike, always lit by streetlight and moonlight and courting something terrible happening to me. I remember my first sight of Sam as a glimpse caught peering through the heavily caffeinated smog of a night without sleep. He walked into the call centre where we both worked, and smiled at me before he went to find his desk. As if he already knew there was a conversation we needed to have. He fancied me, I guess; perhaps there's no need to dress it up any more than that.

I asked around about him, talked to the boy who sat in the cubicle next to him. I found out we came from similar parts of the world. He'd grown up thirty miles away from me, in Salisbury, and it felt neat, like we were a story, to learn that about him. The place he came from seemed somehow important. To my mind, it meant he might understand me a little. I don't know why someone who lived near where you did would know you any better than anyone else, but that was what I decided all the same. I thought it might mean he saw things like I did.

He was a student, younger than I was, and working in the call centre at weekends to fund his drinking, as lots of students did. He was a funny-looking boy really, but he had a way of seeming to stand apart from everyone else, alone in the middle of everything, that meant he caught my eye. He seemed very solemn, despite his hair that stood on end, and his clothes that looked like he bought them all second-hand in charity shops. The long-limbed, hand-me-down graceless-ness of him should have made him ridiculous, but I thought it was pretty obvious that he wore his bad and brightly coloured shirts as a kind of armour, a way of deflecting other people's attention from the long hollow look he seemed to be taking at everything, and that didn't seem at all ridiculous to me. I understood what that felt like all too well.

I never used to speak to anyone at work, and would never

have spoken to Sam. But as I say, he must have liked me, because he made an effort, and tried to get me out of my shell. So we said hello when we passed in the corridor or on the street outside, and he shared a little of the news of his life sometimes, if we stopped long enough to talk for a minute. I stayed evasive about how little I had to show for living mine, how empty my evenings were. We would smile at each other when our eyes met, though I didn't think at the time that meant there was anything really between us. Our eyes didn't meet very often.

Then a day came when Sam tapped me on the shoulder just as I was about to go on a break. I turned round expecting to see my line manager, feeling hostile because my back hurt from spending too long in the chair. I was surprised to see Sam looking down at me.

'What are you doing for the next quarter of an hour?' he asked.

'Nothing. Reading my book.'

'Come with me. I wanna show you something.'

He led me upstairs to the abandoned floor of the office space above the call centre, and the noise of the day fell away as we stepped from the echoing stairwell into the long, bare expanse of carpet tiles, peeling walls and single-glazed windows drinking the day's light.

'Isn't this cool?'

I looked around the room where we were standing. 'It's an empty office.'

'Yeah, but isn't it weird that it's here above us, and there's nothing in it, and no one ever comes here? You'd think someone would use it for something. I sometimes wonder whether people don't know it exists. Come and look at the view.'

We went to the window and looked down, but there wasn't really that much to see. It was the same view as the room below, only seen from a bit higher.

'Cool,' I said, not knowing what I was supposed to think, but feeling underwhelmed.

'You think?'

'Well, not really, no. It's just Bristol, isn't it?'

Sam laughed, and I laughed with him, and that was when we kissed. I don't know who was responsible for that. I only know our lips met for a moment, and my eyes closed, and then we stepped shyly away from each other.

'Well, that's awkward,' I said.

'Is it? Why does it have to be?'

'I don't know. Perhaps it doesn't.'

He placed his hands over mine, stilling me. 'I wanted to talk to you. That's why I brought you up here. I wanted to say something to you.'

'All right. What did you want to say?'

'You always seem sad,' Sam said, 'and I've been wanting to tell you: I don't know what's happened to you. And you don't have to tell me. I wouldn't expect you to tell me; we barely know each other, do we?' He laughed nervously, and looked back out of the window as if something out there might help him get the words out. 'But the thing is . . . I've been wanting to say to you for a while, for what it's worth, that I lost my dad not so long ago, so I guess, I dunno – I think I kind of know what it feels like to be so sad that nothing can make it better. I do feel like I know about that. So if you ever want a friend

. . . I'm not saying I'd understand things, obviously, but I'm just . . . I'm here; no matter how useful I can actually be to you, I'm here if you want anything.' He stopped to catch his breath. Then he kissed me again, I guess because it seemed less embarrassing than either of us saying anything more.

For the rest of the afternoon I broke every sales record that I or anyone else in the call centre had ever set. Something had been unlocked in me, I think, and it seemed as if two years of silence and sorrow fell from my shoulders for a few hours. Someone had noticed me, seen the trouble I was in and wondered where it had come from. Someone had cared, at least a little. It lit me up to know I had been noticed. I completed survey after survey, charming the people I spoke to on the phone, amazed at how easy it all suddenly seemed, how difficult work and life had been for me just an hour earlier when there was no trick to it really; it just needed to be got through, one foot in front of the other, for ever, it was as simple as that.

What if you dreamed of your body as a leaf, the bud of a leaf growing riper at the fingertip of some branch in a wood somewhere, and gathering its strength until the day when it opened, sang out its colour and drank in the sun? What if you dreamed of your life as threads that would one day gather together into some greater garment? I had been living as if the world had ended, when it had been going on all the time. When Sam and I started spending time together, all of a sudden I saw the life still pulsing through the streets around me, and I started looking through Sam's eyes at the days I passed through, seeing things anew.

We hardly talk at all about our different darknesses, our

histories. We've picked up little secrets here and there. I know the brushes he uses for shaving were his Dad's, and he knows that I have a picture of Joe and Lizzy and me on the wall above my bed, but neither of us ever explains what mementoes like those mean to us. The past is an island receding behind us, and neither of us wants to spend our time looking back. It fell to us both, when we'd come through our trouble, to decide whether we wanted to live our lives as a continual farewell to what was passing, or face into the voyage and the future and snatch what was happening now. We've both tried to choose the latter, walking through the streets of Bristol together, drinking coffee in the cafés, drinking lager in the pubs. The place is really too busy for Sam, who's even worse around towns than I am. Bristol's hemmed in wherever you look, by cliffs, by roads, by flyovers, the river, and Sam will grab at any excuse to get out beyond it all, into real country, into the steep gorges of the surrounding hills, as often as he can.

'D'you wanna get on a train and go somewhere?' he likes to say.

'Where?'

'I dunno. I don't mind. Cheltenham. Bradford on Avon. We can go somewhere lame. We can go wherever you want. I just feel a great need to be speeding along at eighty miles an hour somewhere this afternoon.'

He's a dreamer. That's all right by me. I like sitting around and dreaming with him. We can share time in silence for longer than anyone I've known before. It's enough for the two of us simply to drink in the light falling over woodland, to walk alone together till we're out of breath and reeling, to try and recognise birds by their songs, a game Sam is quite good at which I can't play at all. He lived more of a country childhood than I did. He's tried to teach me, but I find it hard to get the knack. 'What's that one?' he'll ask me when we hear a call, and the gleam on him makes me happy as he falls over his feet, walking backwards so he can look at me, quizzing me.

'Easy. That's a collared dove.'

'Ding! What do we have for her, Johnny? And who's that?'

'That's a magpie.'

'Ding ding! And that?'

'I don't know that one.'

'Seriously?'

'No. Is it really easy?'

'Female blackbird, innit. That's dead easy. *Nul points*.'

There's no need, among the richness of our games and our time, to talk about the past. I don't know how close that means we really are, that we keep so much of our two lives secret. But it feels safer that way, not to risk too much of ourselves.

He makes things easier for me. Life isn't as empty as it used to be; time isn't as difficult to fill. There's less room in my head for the dark to flood into, and that seems to mean the wounds begin to heal. Or at least the waters start closing over everything that's happened, as I leave those memories ever further behind me, too far now for that life to hurt me as it did in the first few years. I've started sleeping through whole nights. I wake up in the same position I fell asleep in, and smile, because I thought that might never happen again, I'd become so used to my restlessness. Now I find I can go out, have a drink, enjoy an evening.

But still, there is a limit to the closeness I can find with Sam, no matter how much of a good thing he is for me. Very early in the territory we shared, we reached a precipice within us both that neither dared look beyond. There'll be evenings when Sam will come round and find me sat in my kitchen staring out of the window at the sun going down, mute and distant.

'You OK?' He fumbles for the right way to reach me. The language we have for making sure someone else is all right always strikes me as being so thin, so inadequate. There should be ways for Sam to come in and say to me: I know the things you're carrying, I know the paths you're travelling down, I know I can't do very much to help you, but if there was anything at all, you'd tell me, wouldn't you? Perhaps someone else would know how to say that. Perhaps all the silence around me is only spun from the threads of Sam's shyness, and someone else would have broken through. I don't know.

'Yeah, I'm OK.'

'Do you want to talk about it?'

'I'm OK.'

Sam will turn on the kettle. 'I'll make us tea.' I know in little touches like that what kind of family he comes from, the Englishness of him. No subject too big that it can't be avoided with a cup of tea, a chat about the football. All real speech can happen through the secrecy of those intermediaries, and the steam rising from a cup of tea is the mast all hopes are hoisted on.

And Sam is still a student, going through the mill of undergraduate life in Bristol, and sometimes, because of that, he forgets about me, and that puts another distance between us. There are nights when we arrange to meet, and he doesn't turn up. At first I'm angry, and then I feel afraid, convinced something has happened that's stopped him from coming. Then I call him, hating him because those calls remind me that no matter how much I try to keep to myself, I've ended up needing him. I call him time and again, convinced he's hurt somewhere, desperate to hear his voice no matter how angry it makes me when he finally picks up the phone and I can tell from the noise in the background that he's in the pub with his friends and not thinking of me. 'Where are you?'

'I'm out. Shit, were we supposed to meet?'

'Yes, but don't come round now.'

'I'm so sorry. I can come now.'

'I'd rather you didn't.'

'Please can I come over?'

Then I either give in, and he comes round half-cut, too tongue-tied to apologise properly, or otherwise I manage to keep him away, and then I feel more alone than I would have done if there had been no one to forget about me at all.

Dating a student means putting up with a lot of that kind of bullshit. I can't believe how easily all the things that preoccupy him bore me half to tears. It's strange how quickly I've left all of student life behind me. Just a few years ago, Sam's preoccupations used to be my life as well, the endless cyclical fallings-out with people you didn't actually care for anyway, the essay crises, the parties, the hangovers, the tears. Now I've come out the other side of all that, it seems so unimportant and so small to look back on, watching another person wading through the same distractions.

Sometimes he does all right at being strong when I need him, and sometimes he can't offer me much at all. It isn't really his fault. His ambition or his insecurity or the troubles in his own head get in the way of his noticing there's never really a day when I'm all right. There's never a time when I don't need his help. He doesn't always see that. When he does, he's kind. Or that's what I tell myself, when I wonder how good he is for me, and try to convince myself we're good together. In the last year, I've done so much that would have been impossible without him. I need to remember that, and be thankful.

We don't get to choose many of the tensions that form us. We're not in control of the lives we're born into; we're not really in charge of our dreams. And perhaps we only have so much choice about the person we choose to form the other half of our life, perhaps there are forces beyond us that affect that as well. All the same, sometimes it feels like choosing, to be with someone, and I do feel as if I've chosen Sam, for however long, the next little while, as long as we're good for each other. Perhaps not for ever but for now. And I really want to have made the right decision, so I try to convince myself of the goodness in him. In the fog of the world you find someone and cling to them. Once you've chosen, so much of your life will be made up of that other person, attempting to deserve them, interesting them, showing them what you really meant, if only you had the words to say it. They can shape everything you do.

Sometimes I wish we hadn't missed so much of each other's lives, Sam and I, and there wasn't so much to explain away between us, so much life that never seems possible to put into words. I wish we could have gathered each other up and away from the fire of it all a little earlier, and saved each other from some of the loneliness we've lived with over the years, neck-deep and drowning. But the world is as it is, and we all have to live with the damage that's been done to us. We have our walks through the quiet of the woods on the outskirts of Bristol, steep public paths, dappled light on our faces, and we hold them close, we cherish them. We have that moment of recognition shared in the room above the call centre, when Sam decided to take my hand, lead me out of the noise of the big room into a silence where we could stop for a moment and look at each other.

I suspected Sam wouldn't come today. He didn't want to risk himself amongst a garden full of strangers, another person's relatives, an afternoon of questions about how we met. He didn't feel brave enough for that. I know that's why he bailed. It's enough to make me wonder whether I should just forget him. It seems selfish to me, that he could let himself be overcome by his fear, and not realise how exposed, how alone I'm feeling. I'd been hoping we could rely on each other today, lean on each other to make each other stronger, two trees entwining in the storm passing over. I wanted to be able to rely on him. But he thought of himself, not me. And now I'll have to face the day alone. I'm not sure how I'm going to handle it. It's so casually and unthinkingly cruel of him. He's shown me that I am still on my own. No one is going to help me be brave when I see Mum again. I'll have to find that courage for myself.

I come back into the house to find Laura busy in the kitchen, windows fogged from the boiling of potatoes.

The smell of food is easing through the rooms all the way to the front door like heat through a radiator. Plates of salmon have been brought from the larder and placed bright and gleaming on the big table in the main room, their dead eyes open to the ceiling, their flesh sliced open to the air, staring back forever into the very last moment of their living, the river they had been leaping from, the hook that had snagged them, the net they had drowned in.

'Busy in here,' I say as I come in.

'It'll be busy in here all day.' Laura doesn't turn round to look at me, carrying on the dance of her hands with the knife she's holding instead, her body coiled over in furious conversation with the chopping board before her. 'I hope you won't mind lending a bit of a hand today, will you, my love?'

'Of course not. What can I do?' It's all so Sisyphean. All this work, every year, just so it can be finished and packed away, then got out once more and gone through again a year later. We all age and the work never changes. All the knives worn down little by little but the dance they were put through endlessly repeating.

'I don't quite know. I suppose the bar needs setting up – could you do that?'

'Of course. Under the willow again?'

'That worked well before, didn't it? And it won't rain today.'

'It's a bit cloudy.'

'Don't worry, it's not going to rain. Bit breezy, but we can put up with that.'

'We've got the marquee, after all.'

'Exactly. Now, if you could fill up the cool boxes hiding in the larder with a bit of ice, that can look after the lagers. Ale doesn't need keeping cool and we'd want separate ice for actually putting into the drinks, but that'll need taking out of the freezer over the course of the day, we can't take it all out now.'

'Or it'll melt.'

'Exactly. I'm sorry, you know what you're doing, don't you? I like to fuss.' Good of Laura to admit that she was treating me like an idiot.

'Where's Grandad?'

'Oh, rumbling round in the cellar the last time I heard him. Fetching something.' As Laura speaks, Grandad appears in the kitchen doorway.

'Rumbling around, was I?'

Laura jumps, her shoulders shooting up to her ears as she turns to see him, like an actor over-egging her way through a bad play. There are many things people do in real life that you could never put into a movie. No one would believe them; they would say people don't really do things like that. But then there are lots of things that happen in stories and on TV that never seem to happen in the real world, either. Perhaps the mistake is to assume the two are supposed to have anything to do with each other. Perhaps that isn't the point at all, and stories are supposed to be dreams, not realities.

'Robert, you'll give me a heart attack!'

'Sorry. Are you all right, Kate?'

'I'm fine. I had a nice walk. I feel awake now.'

'Clears the lungs out, doesn't it, stretching the legs,' Grandad says.

'I'm just going to set the bar up under the willow.'

Grandad makes sure Laura isn't looking at him, then rolls his eyes at me. 'Oh yes? Shall I give you a hand with the trestle table? They can bite your hand off if you're not careful, those things.'

Laura turns to look at him, frowning, as if she's been wronged. 'I need plenty of help in here.'

'I'll just help Kate with the table, then I'll come back. Only a minute. They're difficult to manage on your own. All right?'

Laura turns her back on us both in order to plunge despairingly once more into the work. 'All right,' she sighs, and it is clear no one has ever had to put up with more than she will have to today in the whole of the history of the world. Christ in his thorns didn't know agony like she is battling through.

'Come on then, Kate.'

I turn and follow as Grandad strides out of the kitchen and on through the main room, then opens the French windows and steps into the garden, stopping for a moment to drink in the light falling honeyed and gentle over his face. I did the same thing, half an hour earlier. It makes me feel close to him to see us moved by the same sensation. I notice the quality of the light has changed. But still we stand together and enjoy the day. These are the things people really share – the light, the weather.

'Still not very warm out here,' Grandad says.

'Aunt Laura says it won't rain though.'

'No, it won't rain. That's not in Laura's schedule, after all; we don't have time for that.' Grandad chuckles to himself.

There's a marquee on the main part of the lawn, put up

yesterday by a hire company who are booked to come back at the end of the day and take it down again. I think marquees always find a way of looking shabby, even the beautiful ones people hire for weddings. There's something self-conscious about a structure that's going to disappear again with the sunset, to last only as long as the light. I follow Grandad as he turns away from the lawn and crosses the mounting yard to unlock the big side barn, where the trestle table waits for us somewhere at the back in the smell of old straw and the dark.

'Are you sure you're all right about helping out with things?' Grandad asks.

'Of course. I enjoy it.'

'I don't know whether anyone can enjoy it all that much, pouring everyone's drinks all day, but it's such a help. We so appreciate it. I suppose you *will* end up pouring everyone's drinks all day, won't you?'

'I think I probably will, yeah. That's what I used to do.'

'Only till things are swinging along though. People can look after themselves once there's a bit of a crowd and everyone's happy.'

Grandad has succeeded in unlocking the barn door, and we step through into the cool of the cavernous space inside. He finds the light switch and turns it on, but the room hardly grows any brighter at first, as the bulb stutters slowly before starting to warm into life. It's a strange room, this one. A peace lies over everything. Somehow you can tell no one has come in here for a long time. The quietness has weight, it stretches back through time, you can hear the echo of it.

All around us lies old furniture in plastic sheeting – stacks of outdoor chairs, a table-tennis table, a lamp without a shade. I look up to the loft attics, which seem to hang above us either side of the entrance, propped up by the pillars holding the roof. The attics can only be accessed by means of an old wooden ladder, which is leaning now against the back wall. They were haylofts when the barn was first built. They haven't been used for hay since Grandad owned the place, but that undoubtedly was their first purpose. It was a way of keeping things up and away from the rats that must have once thronged in here, back when farmers all kept terriers. One of the attics used to be a sort of dangerous playroom in my childhood, where I used to find things to dress up and parade around in. The other was filled with the abandoned, forgotten and outgrown toys and clothes and cots and bedside tables of Mum's childhood, the sloughed skins of the years when she grew up here. None of that's here any more. Both are empty now.

Joe visited this house with me a couple of times. Once to come to a party like this one, and again the following autumn, when we stayed here for a night to get away from the city and catch up with my grandparents. He found the party easy. Knowing no one, he was able to treat everyone the same, and talk to anyone who wanted to talk with him, without having to wade through the secrets and old feuds that made up the politics of any family. I hardly saw him all day. He was whirled around between uncles and great-aunts, laughing at one story after another, loving the day because that was the person he was, happy, uninhibited. I never knew anyone before or since who seemed so confident, so young. When I'm with Sam, I swim in the shyness of both of us. But Joe used to be different. I used to smile so widely. He managed to draw me out of myself.

The time we came here alone was stranger. We sat with my grandparents, making conversation and drinking too much. Grandma and Grandad put Joe in a separate room to me, and we wondered whether to talk to them about it.

'Of course, it's not their fault for arranging things like this, it's perfectly normal to them,' I said. But obviously I was mortified. We sneaked off for a minute before dinner to sit down together on the bed in Joe's room, and work out what to do. He held my hand to show me it was OK, but I remember feeling sure I must be blushing, and Joe would look at me differently now, and think I came from some strange, old-fashioned family. I had been excited to show him some more of the world I thought I belonged to. Once we got there, I wasn't sure I liked what it said about me, after all, what the landscape of my childhood holidays might reveal.

'It's their generation, isn't it?' Joe said. 'This is what was normal for them. They probably didn't share a bed till they got married.'

We agreed that the adult thing to do would be to bring the subject up, and ask whether we could share a bed. They might respect us for asking. In the end, though, the idea of that conversation seemed too frightening to both of us. We weren't quite as grown-up yet as we sometimes liked to think, and a conversation like that felt like a cliff face too steep to climb. We waited for half an hour in our different bedrooms till we thought Grandma and Grandad were asleep, then Joe crept to me across the hall.

I remember the half-hour of waiting for him as clearly as if it was still happening now. Sometimes, you feel like you might be able to step back and live inside a lost moment for ever, holding on to it and drinking it in until the details rub off it and vanish, until the images get old and the sharpness of the colours and corners wears away. It was wonderful to lie in that bed and think there was someone so close by who wanted to be with me. A tender feeling. Sometimes if I think about Joe for long enough, I can still imagine that's where he is now, lying and waiting to come to me when the night is late enough, thinking of me waiting for him in another room. I can still imagine what he might think of everything that ever happens to me, and see through his eyes even though he isn't with me. Sometimes I'll be walking through a building or a quiet, empty street, and the thought will come to me that behind one of the doors I'm passing is my grandad's spare room, and all I have to do is open the right door and step through, if I only knew which one to open, and only had the key. Then Joe will be there for me again, and all the rest will be forgotten. It's dangerous to dream like that. It's too sweet a feeling to bear.

When I was fifteen I lost my spare house key in a pub where I was drinking, and got home to find my parents were already asleep. I was too embarrassed to wake them, so I broke into the garage, and lay down on the concrete floor by the car on an old cardboard box like I'd seen tramps doing, because it was supposed to keep you warmer not to lie directly on the floor. I waited like that till morning, freezing, wide awake. It feels like that to be me now. It feels like the key to my life is missing, and I'm waiting in the garage, and I can't get back in.

*

That's where I've been ever since the night of the accident, the hour when life went wrong, when my optimism ended. I had been seeing Joe for a year, and was wading through my degree, while he was coming to the end of a Teach First year in Brixton. Joe was living in a flat-share near Tooting, despite his mum's best efforts to persuade him to stay at home. One night he was driving back from a day by the sea catching up with university friends who'd dropped out and moved to Brighton, and there was an accident by South Wimbledon station. Joe seems to have tried to run a red light. There was no alcohol in his blood; perhaps he had been listening to music and wasn't concentrating on the road, or perhaps he just wanted to get home faster. He carried on over a crossing, and a lorry ploughed into him. The car hit a wall. In the windscreen, there was a perfect circle drawn where Joe's head cracked the glass into a whirlpooled spider's web. He had to be cut from the car, which lay on its side, mauled to death by the lorry looming over it. I learned later that it took a long time to get him out. There must have been a lot of blood. I saw what was left of the clothes he had been wearing; I knew he had lost a lot of blood by the time he got to the hospital. I remembered the sky that evening as I rushed to see him was alight with violence, red and glaring; I remember thinking at the time: Perhaps that's the heart going out of him. They carried him into a helicopter, and took him to Tooting, where they landed on the roof of St George's Hospital, one more sorrowful cargo, one more frail heart trying to carry on beating.

The call when it came was from Lizzy. I was eating beans on toast for my dinner, in front of bad TV, alone on the sofa, and my phone rang. I answered it still bent over my plate as I finished a mouthful of baked beans, knowing Lizzy wouldn't mind if I spoke with my mouth full.

'Heya.'

'There's been an accident.'

'What?'

'Joe. He's been in an accident.'

'Where is he?'

'They're taking him to St George's Hospital.'

'Are you there?'

'I'm going now.'

'Is it serious?'

'They've taken him in the air ambulance.'

I felt the fear like a punch in the gut. I remember noticing even then, in the first rush of panic, how simple people really are when you strip away the language we dress ourselves up in. What coursed through me in that moment were the same chemicals that had electrified me the first time a pet cat had been put down, the first time I'd ever been dumped. I felt terror in the same place in my stomach as the time I was nearly hit on a zebra crossing, and everything reminded me of everything else, and everything seemed to have been leading up to this feeling all along, all my life, because everything else was cast into shadow by this.

I left the plate of food on the sofa and went into the hall, and noticed as I did that I wasn't running, I couldn't move my legs right. The light from the hall lamp seemed to be lighting a dream. There was a knife sliding in between me and reality, I felt sure of it; this couldn't be real, I was trapped on the wrong, dream side of the blade. I put on my shoes, and picked up my coat and keys and purse, then went outside, and when the freshness of the night air hit me, I found my strength and started running. I went too fast down the road where I lived and round the corner out on to the pavement of the main road into the wraithlike ribbon of people passing ghostlike on their phones, boxed into themselves, far away from the crisis I was facing. Halfway to the station, by the entrance to the cemetery, I had to stop and walk for fifty metres, because I wasn't fit enough to run all the way at the pace that I'd set myself. I dragged the air into my lungs, and the air was cold in my throat. I felt like the whole of the city must be bathed in red from the spectacular light in the sky, the skein of red cloud scarring over everything. Red getting under fingernails and eyelids, red in our mouths and shining from belt buckles. Red in the sewer grates, gurgling to the rivers, red in the aisles of the supermarkets, red hearts beating. I got to the Tube and went underground. I wanted to scream but all I could do was stand and rock slightly, panic slightly, fear holding on to my gut. When I got to Tooting Broadway I ran out of the station again, across the mad blur of the road and the cars blaring at me and the buses huge and looming. I followed the map on my phone down hurried residential streets, certain I had done something wrong, taken a wrong turning, because surely there couldn't be a hospital down a street this quiet; then I saw the building looming in the distance and ran towards it, as if I expected an embrace. I went in through the main doors and ran to the desk.

'Where's A and E?'

'You need to go back out and it's along to the left.'

I turned again and ran. In A and E there were great lines of people massing with the evening's injuries. I blundered through them. I rushed up to another tired-looking woman working at another desk.

'I'm looking for someone. I'm looking for my boyfriend.'

The woman was clearly annoyed with me; I must have jumped a queue. I didn't care. 'What's his name?'

He had already gone through to surgery, and of course I wasn't allowed to follow him. They took me to Lizzy instead, Lizzy sitting with her parents, frozen in shock, the blood all drained out of their lost white faces. Neither of the women were crying, but Joe's dad had his head in his hands when I rounded a corner and saw them. Then they looked up and saw me, and all four of us collapsed into tears.

It was the end of youth. All of the plans Joe and I had both cherished were gone in a moment. The world grew colder for me from then on. I thought sometimes what a fool I had been for having thought so well of it till then. For having believed that things might turn out well, as if I was living a story. I couldn't help but look back on my dreams and see the absurdity of all of them after that night. The planning and dreaming and thinking of the future that everyone did, putting off one thing after another when they might have been living for now, when life could vanish from you as fast as one vehicle ploughing through another. It made all Joe's ambitions, which I had believed in and stoked myself, seem so small, so fragile, so unreal. Ever since then, it's been difficult for me to care about my own life, my own ambitions. What's the point of expending that energy if you can just suddenly die?

I never went back to university. I trailed the student debt along behind me, a reminder of all that had happened, a taunt. Sometimes I thought about trying to find a way to pick up what I had left off doing, and get through a last year of study somewhere, and find a way to graduate, just so the debt could be worth something to me, but I didn't feel brave enough to try. It would be like picking a scab, and I felt sure I'd bleed out under the pressure of it. I needed the wound to grow older before I tried.

The trestle tables are stacked against the back wall of the barn. Grandad leads the way towards them. As we lift one and start to make our way back to the barn door and the yard and garden beyond, he slows, and clears his throat.

'There's something I might need your help with today.'

'Oh yes?'

'I'm going to have a visitor. Someone rather unexpected, who's not exactly connected with our party. We're going to need some time alone, I'm afraid.'

I look up, but he's staring intently at the joint of the table, and won't meet my eye.

'Oh.'

'It's highly inconvenient, I know. But it's also rather unavoidable. However, that doesn't mean Aunt Laura would be likely to be very supportive, so I'd be grateful if you could try and keep her off my trail, if I do disappear for a while.'

'Of course. Is everything all right?'

'All absolutely fine, yes. Just a development I need to deal with.'

'A work thing?'

Grandad smiles. I guess he's never used that phrase himself.

'A work thing, yes, that's it. But don't say that to anyone. As a rule I'm not really supposed to have any work things any more. Not all that good for the heart.'

'No, sure. Mum's the word.'

We carry the trestle table out and put it up under the willow's branches, green and budding in the spring light.

'Are you all right lifting this?' I ask, worrying he should be taking it easier than he is.

'Don't you start. I'm quite all right.'

'I bet your doctor wouldn't like it.'

'But my doctor isn't here.' He smiles at me, looking a little tired, but I can see he isn't struggling. 'Not much further. Keep up.'

Manning the bar means standing out in the wind, if there is any, away from the shelter of the marquee. I resent that just as much as I resent opening bottles for people I hardly know who seem to think they have some claim to me, because of where we come from, because of the history we nominally share. The willow doesn't offer any real shelter from the elements, not this time of year, but it looks nice, and that's important, I suppose, so that's where the bar's always set up. No matter that it means I have to stand in the cold: it makes a pretty picture. I guess it would be wrong to complain though. If Grandad wants me to help him, I'll do whatever he asks.

'So you can't tell me what's going to be keeping you busy today, then. This secret project.'

He smiles. 'I'm afraid not, no.'

I nod. 'Or you'd have to kill me, right?'

He laughs indulgently, pleased to be striking a pose in my eyes as a geriatric James Bond.

'Is something bad happening?'

He shakes his head. 'The only bad thing that could happen would be for Laura to find out that I'm doing a bit of work, and then to spend the whole afternoon going on about the state of my heart. That would be a rather awful diplomatic incident; I don't know where we'd bury all the bodies.' He winks at me. 'It's all very dull and administrative; you mustn't worry about it, it's nothing. I'm just needed. Even now, every now and then, I'm still halfway useful for one thing or another.'

'I'm sure you are.'

'Speaking of which, I ought to go in really, lend a hand, so we don't fall behind. Do you mind?' He gestures to the boxes of wine already waiting among the roots of the willow.

'Of course not, no.'

Grandad stretches his shoulders, readying himself for the next thing. 'Won't be long before people start arriving.'

I watch Grandad as he walks away from me, then busy myself with setting up the wine on the table. I wonder why he mentioned his heart, if he's feeling pain somewhere today? Or is he always in pain, and I just never think to wonder about it, about how things must be for him now? He goes into the house, and I'm alone again.

from Interview 42

There were a thousand different scams on the go for getting messages in and out the prisons, out the H Blocks. Simplest thing everyone got up to was secreting written notes, of course, everyone knows about that. Most of the news coming out of Long Kesh prison had been up someone's arse before anyone read it. Which you might call ironic, because many would say the newspaper a lot of that stuff got written up in was only good for bog roll itself. I'm not telling that joke cos I agree with it, mind you, I just heard it, and maybe it's funny, I don't know. Sometimes things would get intercepted, there'd be a cavity search and something would be found. But not so often. And anything really important, we'd get a more respectable visitor. People are less likely to cavity-search some pillar of the community. Stands to reason, doesn't it? So we'd get folks from the church. Or there was this guy used to come from the university, we thought that was hilarious. Used to say he could correct our spellings as well, if he wanted.

Robert

In the memory it is Remembrance Day, a few minutes before eleven in the morning: the moment the nation I served gathers together to recall and reaffirm its central myth, and to express its truest image of itself, rendering the grey wet November morning into something suddenly, fleetingly beautiful. I have always loved the Remembrance service with the fierce passion I suppose can be expected of a man whose boyhood played out against a landscape of bombed screamings, shattered uncles, evacuations. But I can't imagine anyone ever attends those ceremonies and fails to be touched by what they hear and what they see, no matter who they are and what they've lived through. I can't imagine it's possible to absorb those days, and think of the millions of dead littered down the years of the last century and all the centuries vanished before, and not feel something for them.

I can still see the scene very clearly. I remember where I was standing when I heard the news. I was in my overcoat in Belfast rain, watching the laying of wreaths that glimmered weakly in the grey November weather. I can see myself among the assembly, one more pale and corpse-like face in a sea of solemn faces gathered together in the act of remembering. I had planted my feet in the wet, dead grass beneath me, and from my redoubt behind the shelter of the collar of my coat I watched children troop poppy wreaths up the central aisle to the memorial. I remember wondering idly whether snipers ever tried to get at events like these, in the minutes before someone brought me the news. The coincidence of that thought has lodged in my mind. I remember deciding that it would never be worthwhile shooting at a Remembrance Day parade. Every attempt to attack or apprehend people at funerals during the Troubles ended as a public relations disaster. If you shot someone while they remembered their dead, you were sure to end up on the wrong side of the story when it crawled through the next day's papers, and the consequences started to play out through the back-room meetings, the military briefings, the arms caches broken open and men tramping through grey fields to the murders waiting for them in the endless sucking hedgerows. History would end up casting you as the heel.

Miles from where I was passing the morning in Belfast, in the Fermanagh town of Enniskillen, there were soldiers parading towards another war memorial that Remembrance Day in 1987 when the wall of the reading rooms opposite the memorial exploded out into the street, killing eleven people and injuring sixty-three others. An IRA bomb intended for the soldiers had been concealed there the night before, waiting heavy with death in the dark of a sports bag. Bad intelligence meant it detonated before the soldiers had arrived, and its victims were civilians and a police officer. The targets of the bomb watched appalled from further down the street as a cloud of brick dust drowned the dying.

The day was a disaster for the IRA. It emerged that the bombing had been hurriedly sanctioned by a middle-ranking IRA officer as retaliation for the violent disruption of the funeral of two Republican gunmen the previous week. Police baton-charged the funeral of Eddy McSheffrey and Paddy Deery when someone fired a three-volley salute over their coffins. One of the coffins was knocked to the ground in the fight that ensued. Plastic bullets were fired into the mourners. So as Remembrance Day approached, the IRA transported a forty-pound bomb to Enniskillen, moving the parts piece by lethal piece in relay, using several cars, in order to avoid detection.

It was a day to turn the tide, and perhaps it sounds callous to say it now, but I saw the opportunity before me immediately, even as I hurried away from the service I had been attending and into the fogged, clammy back seat of a waiting car. Attritional, soulless conflict had ground Ireland down for long years. The sections of the general public sympathetic to the Republican cause held fast to their beliefs, but they were tired, they were demoralised, depressed. Their lives had been limited by what had happened around them in their name; low dark roofs had been put on their dreams. I was driven to the site of the bombing. It was clear as day what a terrible thing had happened. I listened to a man who had been trapped beneath the bricks with his daughter. He had held her hand and told her he loved her while she died. Later that day, he was put on television, and I felt ashamed to watch him speak of forgiveness while I myself still felt so angry at what I'd seen. The bodies were still being removed when I got there, loaded on to stretchers and then into ambulances to be taken away. The paramedics were gentle, efficient, their distress written clear on their faces, their training showing plainly in the precision of what they did. People were crying around them, yet they carried on. The police combed the area for further devices with grim, meticulous patience, the streets closed off, blood and brick dust on the ground around them, scorched into the memory of everyone there.

When I returned to Belfast, trailing that brick dust like guilt behind me on my shoes, I found a message waiting for me to say Frank Dunn had called the office twice. I returned the call, and within the hour Frank was sitting in front of me. He looked terrible. A man who hadn't slept, his face now mottled with what seemed to me like a sense of shame, a sense of urgency. He may not have been any part of the IRA, he may only have been a conduit. But he knew that in my office the shadows of their actions fell on him.

'We have to do something,' he said.

'What can be done?'

'That's what we have to discuss. We have to come up with a plan.'

'That's what your contacts want, is it?'

Frank raised his hand in an equivocating gesture. 'It's not about what those guys want. That's not the only thing that brings me here, don't you see that? I'm not just a messenger boy. I'm here now because I want to do the right thing. I've not been sent. You have to understand, Robert, I haven't even told my contacts I'm talking to you now.'

I ran my finger down the spine of the diary on my desk and wondered what I was supposed to say. 'I see. Are you offering me information then?'

Frank laughed, grimly. 'I'm not an informer. I don't know anything you don't and I don't go in for all that. I'm here because this has to change now; we can't be having things like this happen any more, and the community knows that, the community won't stand for it. I want to help to start a conversation. We can't be having days like today, Robert, we have to make a change.' Frank leaned forward in his chair while he spoke, his elbows on the arms of the seat and his eyes very blue, and I saw the sincerity there, for the first time, and the hurt and the fear roiling in him.

'I agree with you entirely,' I said.

'So I've come looking for assurances that dialogue is what your government wants as well. That's what I want to hear. I can bring you the people you need to talk to. So I want to take that message back, and let people know there's an ear to speak into, people are going to listen. Because today is a disaster and I'm afraid what it might lead to, if people head in the wrong direction now. If I can tell my contacts you'll solve this by talking and not by making arrests, they'll come to the table themselves.'

I listened carefully to Frank, and weighed my words. 'I understand. I can tell you, Frank, there is nothing I want more, and nothing the government wants more, than to facilitate that conversation. A conversation that might start to turn us in the direction of peace.' It was overstepping the mark, but I knew my staff believed Frank to have influence; it was too big an opportunity to miss.

Of course, I'm probably overstating the significance of that moment if I say that it changed very much. Across Britain and

Ireland on that day, conversations between intermediaries for both sides led to the same resolutions, time and again, and Frank and I were only one scene played out among many that all led towards the same resolution. That day we were part of a broad consensus, a wave of rare agreement. So in the end I risked very little in stating my opinion as I did. Nevertheless, I like to think that was a day when I took a stand. When I look back across the years, I think I see that what I agreed to on that day became part of a change in the history of Northern Ireland, the start of something. Frank did as he'd promised, and a series of meetings flowed from that moment that could be said to have made a difference. As a result, I've always felt that on that day I was part of something important. Something unusual, at least. I had retired by the time of the Good Friday Agreement, but when it was signed I still felt able to look at the way the tide had turned and recognise how much of that had started after Enniskillen. The decision I took that day, meeting with Frank Dunn and then ploughing on through the painstaking negotiations that followed, the messages he brought to me and those that I passed back through him, were part of that new chapter in the history of Ireland and of the United Kingdom. The years of meetings and negotiations, of ceasefires and brinkmanship and argument, the rest of my life's work unfolded from there.

Frank had risked more than me by speaking as he did that morning. By approaching a civil servant of my rank, he had effectively obliged his contacts to engage with any British offer of negotiation; to do otherwise would have been a de facto act of violence, a commitment to other silences and aggressions still to come. For this, Frank was later severely reprimanded by officers of the IRA. On the one subsequent occasion – after the talks we engendered together had taken place and our collaboration was concluded – when I found myself in the same room as him, he told me he had been kicked into the cold as far as those contacts went, and no longer considered himself to be a conduit for anyone.

'I was told in no uncertain terms I should count myself lucky that no more will come my way than an excommunication,' he told me over champagne, elegant in bow tie in the corner of some reception.

'I can't really believe you merit even that much censure.'

'It was embarrassing for them. I made decisions for them, didn't I, I forced their hand. I knew I was doing it, but I think it needed to be done. I don't regret it at all, I'm just glad I wasn't kneecapped.'

'I hardly think kneecapping was ever a likely outcome.'

Frank shrugged. 'You never know, though, do you?' And as he studied the inside of his champagne flute, I saw that he was serious.

Those had been almost the last words Frank and I spoke to each other. We were interrupted then by another guest at the party, who broke in to talk to us both about academic politics, never imagining for a moment, I suppose, that the two of us would have any other kind of politics in common.

I get back to work in the kitchen with Laura, trying not to get under her feet, lifting and stirring and apologising as the plan that has been mapped out in her mind is made flesh and revealed to me in increments. Shortly afterwards the guests start arriving. I take up my station by the front door and welcome the familiar smiles of my family and my friends as they come into the house, deposit their coats, put their heads round the kitchen door to say hello to Laura and make their way out to where Kate is manning the bar.

'How lovely to see you, Anthea.' I kiss a distant cousin on the cheek, a woman I remember once sharing a camping holiday with in west Wales, long ago when Hattie and I were young and newly married.

'So lovely to see you again, Robert, it's been too long.'

'Has it been two years?'

'Three, in fact.'

'Good Lord, isn't that extraordinary?'

Anthea is replaced almost immediately by a niece whose name I momentarily forget, along with the names of all three of her sullen, black-clad, greasy-haired children, who are sulking from the indignity of the car journey, I suppose, and won't meet my eye.

'How lovely to see you.'

'You too, Robert, so lovely. You remember Dylan and Chelsea and Ivan?'

'Of course, of course.' By a supreme effort, I manage not to laugh at their names. No wonder they look miserable. I hope they manage to steal some alcohol from the bar early enough in the afternoon that they can get drunk and enjoy themselves.

It is perfectly enjoyable seeing people and making small talk in this way, but I can't quite fix myself to the task. My mind continues wandering. In the wake of Frank's call I can't just live in the day around me. Wherever I look now, the events of that Remembrance Day are waiting just beneath the skin of the garden to draw me back into the labyrinth of memory. All the life and crispness of the moment I am in have been drained away by that call, and I hear the siren song that is the thought of being needed elsewhere, of still mattering in the way I did when I was younger.

Hannah and Michael arrive just before eleven. I take her aside before she can get as far as the kitchen to see Laura, and smile, and kiss her on the cheek, and fix her with a look. 'You know Kate's here, don't you?'

Hannah crosses her arms, appraising me, guarded. 'Dad, are you going to give me a lecture about behaving myself?'

'It might be very boring but the thing is that, as a rule, darling, you don't. Do you think it might be possible to be gentle around her today?'

'Mustn't embarrass the family.'

'No, actually, that's not the reason. The reason is that I want this mended, like you do, like we all do. All I want is to see you two speaking to each other again.'

Hannah puts her hand on my arm. 'I know, Dad.'

'She's been through a lot.'

A look of exasperation passes across my daughter's face, and I recognise her old impatience with me.

'I understand, OK? I think I know my own daughter. Michael and I talked about it on the way here.'

I suppose that is all anyone can do, in the end.

'All right. Come and say hello to Aunt Laura, then. Kate's running the bar outside.' I follow Hannah as she makes her way through to the kitchen, then find myself diverted by another tranche of guests coming into the main room, and have to welcome them and show them where to put their coats. By the time I look for her again, she isn't in the kitchen any more. I suppose she's gone to look for Kate. Now I will most likely miss the moment when my daughter and granddaughter see each other again for the first time since Kate went into the hospital, since the changes that have undone them. I feel my shoulders tense at the thought I won't be there when it happens, to try and keep them from hurting each other. But it is too late now: she's out of sight. They will find each other. I just have to hope they both feel ready for it when they do.

Those two women, with their whole lives trailing behind them, their rich lives, filled with talents, beset with troubles, would not exist if it weren't for me. Strange to think it. Turning to look for them, finding nothing, I glimpse instead the birthday cake that Laura has made me, waiting in the larder to be brought out at the end of the afternoon. She must have left it in the car, and only remembered after I took out the salmon. The cake is heavy with candles, a petrified forest of wax and years, enough to burn your eyebrows off. How can I have gathered so much fire so quickly, when it seems only yesterday that we looked round this house for the first time?

I remember the years when Hattie and I were young, when it used to be us who travelled together to visit Hattie's mother when her birthday rolled round. Everyone takes their turn at the different stations of a life for a while, as they barrel through it all. That time is still almost visible around me, it seems, if I let it all come, if I draw out the thread of that part of my life and let it run through me like electric current once again. The drive out to Devon, bare expanse of the moor as you crossed over, wildness of gnarled trees clutching the road-side. The peace and greenness, and feeling close to each other as talk flowed easily while I drove the car.

'I think your mother knows that she ought to downsize, but the trouble is the thought of what she'd have to give up if she did.'

'What would she have to give up?'

'Well, the memories in the place. The life that she's lived there. And everything she still has to remind her of your father.'

There was a musicality to those drives, and all the ritual pilgrimages home or back to the place of your graduation, or back to a town where you used to work, the journeys which seemed to pattern every human life. All those trips and returns formed a latticework of landscapes like refrains, calling you back to who you had been the last time you took them in, weaving together the seemingly diverse experience of year after year into something like a single and coherent dance, a set of variations always finding their way back to images which had assailed you before. The repetition of those journeys seemed to find expression, for me and Hattie at least, in conversational byways we would rediscover every time we made the same drive back down to Devon, subjects we never touched on in our ordinary lives but which we would dive into again as the affluent and cultivated slopes of the Hampshire countryside gave way to the wildness of Wiltshire, and the lush sleep of the valleys of Dorset, and the sharp green intake of breath that seemed to welcome you to Devon.

'I wish she'd let it all go and remember that she's not so

very old, and life doesn't have to be over for her, life doesn't have to be all about remembering,' Hattie said. In the memory we were coming to the end of our twenties, and bathed in the light of the years before Hannah was born. I remember the blue scarf Hattie was wearing, the deep red of the flowers that patterned it, her hair flowing over her shoulders and calling out an echo of the wheat in the fields we drove past.

'That's always going to be difficult for her to contemplate doing though,' I said.

'Of course it is. But we get one life, don't we? We have one opportunity to get a few things done, and see things, and to experience. And getting all that done will sometimes mean doing the difficult thing, and getting on, and putting a stop to all this remembering she's mired in. Because it holds her back. It will stop her being happy.'

'Unless it makes her happier to remember the years of her marriage than it does to be in the years she has now?'

Hattie sighed in exasperation. 'If I go before you, I expect you to remarry, you know.'

I felt my heart quicken. I had never heard Hattie say anything like that before. It made me feel shaky and electric, to let in the alien thought of our lives ending. 'Why on earth would you want that?'

'It's what I'd do,' Hattie said. 'Not because I wouldn't love you any more, but because I wouldn't be able to have you back. What pleasure is there in pining for something you can't have back? Why not just go and hang yourself there and then, if the world offers so little?'

'I'm sure you don't actually think your mother should hang herself.'

Hattie laughed. 'Sometimes I wonder.'

'Hattie!'

'No, sorry, you're right, I'm being silly. Of course I don't. It's just she frustrates me. I want her to be happy and she won't be.'

'You'll make her happy by being there this weekend.'

'Perhaps. But she'll make me sad.'

'Why?'

'Because she'll just want to talk about Dad like she always does, and it makes me sad to think about him.'

For the rest of the year, we would never discuss the emotional state of Hattie's mother. We would talk about work and what was for dinner, because those were the conversations life was made out of, that was what people did. But in the car on the drive down to Hattie's mother's birthday, in those years after the death of her father, the talk always led back to him. The distant and emotionally crippled man Hattie had grown up keeping clear of, in case he lost his temper and clipped her round the ear. The man she had loved with the whole of her heart, and could not bear having lost.

'Do you think what you really want is to not have to visit the farm any more?' I asked.

'Why?'

'Because it hurts you to think about him. And that's why you don't like her thinking about him all the time. Perhaps it would feel easier if it seemed like he'd never existed at all.'

'Oh, I don't know. Let's not get too psychoanalytical about all this. I just want her to set her face to the future.'

Silence fell then, loud as mourning. Hattie turned to look out of the window at the wheat fields blurring by. I didn't know what to say to break the mood, to cheer her up. I remember the shame of that moment. The feeling that a better man would have known how to make her smile again. Sometimes I think I never quite solved the light that went out in Hattie when her father died. She carried that sadness with her to the end of her days. And she only ever really talked about him on those journeys spent westering home, trundling to Devon and another clutch of candles blown out on the top of another cake her mother had baked for herself. I used to long for those journeys, weeks before they rolled round. I think I looked forward all year to the chance to feel that close to her, when she would allow herself to talk for a little while about what mattered to her most. Her family, the roots of her life.

The crowd under the marquee grows, and now there are fifty of us milling. I move among them, thanking people for coming, asking those I haven't seen all year what they have been doing since we were last together. I can't quite commit to all these questions, though, I can't quite bring myself to care about it all. Ireland is in my mind. But that isn't all of it. I can't quite care about any of it, now Hattie isn't here with me.

For sixty years, the other half of the ribbon of my life was her. Try as I might, I can't understand what it means for me that her voice has fallen silent now, while mine is still running on. We never thought of ourselves as separate beings in all the married time we had together; we always saw ourselves as half of two, indivisible, interdependent. We had taken on the project of our lives as a partnership, and always believed each of our achievements had been dependent on the presence of the other, that we wouldn't have achieved anything on our own. It was, in other words, a good marriage. So what am I now she has gone?

We met at Oxford, in the spring of 1956, the first Hilary term after matriculation. The romance of thinking back to that time now is irresistible, of course. It astonishes me to recognise how much wonder has been granted to me in the course of my life, and my years at Oxford were among the best that were given to me. In the memory, the Oxford of that time is bathed always in spring sun and shining, not unlike the cool light of this day I'm standing in now. And there used to be bicycles, long walks over Port Meadow, and the glare of glass and the clatter of glasses in the King's Arms and the Turf Tavern. And there were cellos playing in the Holywell, punters circling the river round the deer park in Magdalen, the rawness of tired lungs flung into rowing practice at dawn on the year's coldest mornings. And there were long, wine-dark nights, and having to climb out of the women's colleges after dark when the gates had been closed, and having to break back into your own college over the back wall. And then there was Hattie, and the feeling of fainting that was falling in love.

I had done my national service before going up, and Hattie had come straight from school, so she was two years younger, and I fancy that she looked up to me at first, she thought because I was older I might perhaps be wise. That didn't last long, of course. Once she knew me properly she learned that I needed her guidance far more than she could ever benefit from mine. But by then there had been time enough for her to come to care for me. So we did what was natural at that time, and married in the summer of our graduation. I wish I could still feel that I belonged in Oxford. The thought of the place still feels like home when I call it to mind. The memory of youth is always like harking back to home, after all. I envy Frank his position with a college and access to lunches and conversation. There was a time when I could have become part of that world myself. A headhunter approached me to ask whether I might consider applying to become the head of an Oxford college at the time of my retirement, and I examined the possibility for a while. It was flattering. It might perhaps have proved enjoyable. The trouble was that I never felt comfortable visiting the city, never felt satisfied by going back ever since I had graduated and left my digs. It had always felt like a lost domain. I see now that the only way I would ever have been able to shake off that sense of loss would have been by plunging back into the place and making new memories. I should have taken the job. But I didn't realise that was what was being offered to me at the time, so I let it go. Now it is too late, it is long vanished.

I met Hattie while we were doing a production of *The Cherry Orchard* on a college lawn, the only play I ever appeared in. I wasn't there because of any talent. The play had a lot of parts, and bodies were needed to fill the scenes, and I must have been in the room when the rallying cry for actors went out. I don't quite remember how it happened that I ended up on a stage – I never liked being looked at.

I felt I loved Hattie the first time I saw her. We auditioned together – I was tried out for several parts, despite my evident lack of ability, there being a general surplus of women and a shortage of men available for every theatrical undertaking at Oxford since time immemorial. I remember she walked into the room, and our eyes met, and I couldn't look at her again for the rest of the time we were in that room together, I felt so afraid of her, and so alive. I suppose that attraction must have been part of the reason I only got a part with seventeen lines, along with my abiding lack of talent, as not being able to look at the girl you auditioned with was always going to be a significant impediment. But I couldn't help myself. The world had become huge and wonderful and terrifying, transformed utterly in the space of a breath, because I had learned that she was in it, and I had never known how much life was lying in wait to amaze me. I had never known till then that I wasn't awake. I had never known it was possible to feel the blood that coursed like music through your own body as the adrenaline sang.

It might have been only the charged sexuality of any rehearsal room that meant I was struck by the thunderbolt, but it did the trick. We didn't do anything about what we were feeling till we came to the party on the last night of the show and started to drink, as was traditional with these affairs. Then, in a far-flung, unfamiliar common room, I found the courage to speak to her, and we kissed, and that was the start of everything, or the end, depending on how you looked at things. She sat on my lap, and cocked her head while she looked at me, smiling.

'Well. What are we going to do about this then?'

I knew I was done for the moment she spoke – I felt sure that this was fate reaching out to claim me. She wanted to smuggle me back to her rooms that night, but I wouldn't go with her. 'Not tonight, Hattie.'

Her cheeks flushed, and she drew back from me. 'Why not? Have I said the wrong thing?'

'No, nothing like that. I just – I don't want to do things wrong.'

'What do you mean?'

'I don't want to just be a night without sleep for you. I'd like to be someone you wanted to know.'

She seemed too important to me to just go home with, to dive in at the deep end. She was something I felt suddenly sure I wanted to last for ever. So we went home to our separate beds, and met the next day, and nursed our hangovers together.

I have always thought finding Hattie was a little like an ending, the conclusion of an interval of loneliness. In the right light the whole of the rest of my life could be read as a postscript to the first time I told Hattie I loved her. No matter how difficult life sometimes seemed, nothing really frightened me again once I knew I would journey through the world with her. Until the time came for dying, that is, which is why all this comes back to me now. I should try not to let all this in today.

I proposed a few weeks after we finished our finals, in a rowing boat on the Thames above Henley. I had champagne there with me, waiting for her reply. I was trying to construct a romantic scenario we'd be able to tell friends about later. In the event, whenever we talked about the day we got engaged, we always ended up laughing. I nearly overturned the boat when we climbed back on to the bank, shaky from the emotion of the day, shocked by the gravity of the question, never having guessed how momentous it would really feel in the moment of asking. I had to catch Hattie as she started to pitch over into the river. We married later that summer. Neither of us knew what life had in store then. I hadn't yet secured my first position in the civil service. That came a few weeks after the breathless days when we gathered both our families into the same place and celebrated the engagement all together.

It all unfolded endlessly from there. We rented a flat in south London and moved in together after the wedding, and I would catch the train in from Earlsfield in the mornings, then walk the rest of the way from Waterloo through all the picture-postcard views that sprang up one after the other as you crossed the Thames. I liked Earlsfield. Edward Thomas had rambled through its streets as a boy, and Hardy had lived there as a young man. I liked to stand under the older trees and imagine those men resting under them, standing just where I was, staring at the same branches, different leaves falling.

We spent our leisure hours walking over Wandsworth Common, Wimbledon Common, Richmond Park, and going to cinemas and the theatre and to concerts, weekends filled with picnic hampers, disbelieving happiness that always seemed to hang suspended in the air between us because we both always felt lucky to be with each other. When you finally find the person you need, and find they need you too, things can come to seem absurdly easy. Work came to us when we needed it, and we had a place to live, and when we decided to have a family we bought our first house. Life opened up for us as lilies do in the light of summer.

Buying this house came about by chance, a risk we decided to take because those were the days when the world lay all before us, and if we were brave enough we felt we could do anything. We had gone to spend the weekend with my family in Wiltshire, and driven past this house on the way down. At that time it was a ruined, tumbling heap of ivy-choked brick-work with a 'For Sale' sign in the driveway. It had been occupied previously by a religious order who had run out of money, or otherwise died out and moved away. The story was never made absolutely clear to us, but we knew they had been there, carving up the house to suit their own purposes, to tell their own story through its rooms. When we first moved in there were still locks on all the doors.

'What a wonderful project that will be for someone,' Hattie said, smiling at me as we passed the house. 'Giving life back to a lovely old place like that. It'd be just like building a life, wouldn't it? Working on a place like that.'

The following Monday, when we returned to London, the vision still lay there before us, calling. So we made enquiries, and found we could afford to do it if we wanted to commit ourselves to a different life with a different centre. And we decided that we did.

When we had decided we wanted a child, both of us experienced the sensation of vertigo. It was extraordinary to us to think we had been children ourselves so recently, and then suddenly to be contemplating the realities of bringing a new life into the world. It seemed extraordinary that we were allowed to do this thing, which would make our lives so very different. It was as if we were missing a catch. The same feel-ing came to us again when we decided to move out of London, to take on the house. It's frightening to think how many decisions we make that change our lives just as decisively, every week, every year, without realising. All my life, I must have been shaping and limiting what was possible for me, and only seeing the tip of the iceberg of the choices I made.

The source of the love I feel for this house now is the work we did together to restore it. I see all the beauty and all the life I shared with Hattie reflected in all the rooms around me.

I glance towards the mounting yard, packed tight with cars, and see Frank driving in through the gates. I will need to explain to him why there are so many people here, and put him at his ease a little. The man will surely be alarmed by the crowd. I separate myself from my guests as carefully as I can, and watch as Frank parks in what little space is left. Then I cross the lawn to Kate where she stands among the wine and lagers and the old men topping up their glasses as they bathe in memory and spring sun.

'Kate.'

She looks up, knowing already what I am going to say, it seems to me. 'Yes?'

'The gentleman I need to speak to has arrived. Will you be all right to cover for me here for a little while?'

'Of course.' Kate's eyes flick across to the cars where Frank is emerging from his faded grey Corsa. No trace of understanding or dawning realisation is visible on her face as she takes him in, the old tweed, the lined face, the last of what was once a great thick mop of unruly hair, like fog coming over a hill. I feel sure that this will all be all right. Things will be secret and safe; no one but Frank and myself will know what happened between us today, because no one is going to suspect anything, ask any difficult questions. How could anyone possibly work it out just from the look of him?

'Thank you.' I turn on my heels as smartly as I can and make my way back over the lawn towards Frank. I wonder what Hattie would have said if she had seen me, making tracks like this. Most likely she wouldn't have let me get away with it. Whether she was at the front door greeting guests, or in amongst the middle of the party, she would have seen me and come over and fetched me, and made sure I did my duty as a host. I know as I walk away that I am letting her down. Perhaps she would have understood. She always knew I liked to find moments of quiet in the middle of these kinds of days whenever I could.

We meet by the mounting block in the shadow of the house. Frank's face is ashen and, of course, he has changed: he is older. I take in the alteration, surprised to find it falls on me like a blow, as if I am losing a friend, not an old, uneasy acquaintance. Perhaps my appearance unsettles Frank as well. He speaks first.

'Robert, I had no idea. You should have said. I'm so sorry to be calling today. What's the occasion?'

'My eightieth birthday, in fact.'

'I'm sorry that I'm taking you away from it all.'

'I'm sure we won't be all day, will we? It's been a long time since I heard from you.'

Frank looks down at the gravel beneath his feet, nodding, grinding idly at the stones under his right heel. 'More than twenty years, I think.'

'Indeed. Is it too early for a drink?'

'Not today, I don't think, no.'

'Why don't you come with me to the office then, and we can carve out some quiet for ourselves.'

I lead Frank across the lawn and through the back door into the house, then pass quickly through the kitchen, where I am glad Laura doesn't turn round in time to see us. Once Frank is inside the office I close the door behind us, and feel relief. Perhaps that will be the hardest thing I have to do today, getting past Laura in the kitchen, and it passed off without incident. Now, Laura having been evaded, no one will notice my absence for a little while. Once they do, it will be some time before anyone finds the courage to knock on this door.

I feel again the weight of what it means to commit one's life to public service, and accept that one might be called on for help at any moment, for any reason imaginable under the sun, right up until the very last day of one's life. That is a responsibility you never quite understand, unless it happens to you. How much you give away to join the club.

I gesture to the tray on the desk I prepared this morning. 'Good whiskey. I thought you might appreciate it.'

'Wonderful. Thanks.'

We make our way to the desk. I feel the ghost of friendship standing at my shoulder. It's strange, because Frank and I never really knew each other, and I have no idea even now whether we were really on the same side, when you get down to brass tacks. But it is so difficult not to become sentimental once the past is involved.

'I hope you'll understand I felt I should alert Geoffrey to our meeting. You remember Geoffrey? He was very junior in

Dublin, but he's now very important in London. The days are gone when I can be of any use to you, Frank, if someone else doesn't know that we're talking.'

Frank nods. 'I thought you would. Glad if we can keep this relatively private though, for the time being.'

'I've told Geoffrey as much. Now. I assume this is about these tapes they've made in Boston?'

Frank takes a first sip of his whiskey, watching me carefully. I watch him in turn over the lip of my glass.

'That's right.'

'I was surprised to hear from you, Frank. I'd wondered whether someone from the old days would be in touch, but I didn't think it would be you. I thought you were out of commission.'

Frank sighs, and holds up his hands. 'It appears this is a moment for bringing all kinds of people out of retirement,' he replies. 'I've been contacted because people thought I'd still have your phone number, really. Or that's my reckoning, anyway.'

I feel a momentary disquiet at the thought that I might have been asked for by name, sought out by some faceless stranger far away among the old days and over the water. 'Why would I be of any interest to anyone?'

'Anyone who ever stated a preference for dialogue between the different sides is of great interest right now. People need to be talking. We need to sort this out.'

I nod. 'You know I'm retired, Frank? You know I'm out.'

Frank smiles. 'Of course. I've always followed what you've been up to, Robert. Kept track of things. In case we were needed again. And out of respect, I suppose, for what

I feel we achieved together. We have a legacy to protect.'

'I think that would be overstating things,' I say abruptly.

Frank holds up his hands again in concession. He looks like a man at gunpoint. 'Forgive me. I don't want to overstep the mark. I just want to have a conversation. Because you know, for all that you're not in the swim any more, Robert, everyone knows how it works. You're a respected individual. A phone call from you might still go a long way in clarifying what the hell is going on.' Frank frowns deeply as he speaks, an attempt, perhaps, to look angry, though it seems somehow his heart isn't quite in it.

'You make it sound like something outrageous is happening,' I say.

Frank shakes his head. 'I have no opinion of these testimonies. I'm just passing on what I've heard.'

I steeple my fingers in front of me, as if I am praying to something. 'So what have you heard?'

'My contacts are alarmed that the British government are going after these tapes like this, with such determination. Surely you understand, Robert, this could be seriously destabilising. There are things in the world which were understood to have been buried. And now there is a project to unearth them.'

Can that really be all that Frank has come to say; surely he knew the answer to that? Surely it can't be so empty as this, the dialogue between us?

'The thing is, Frank, that a group of individuals who are very well known to the police service in Northern Ireland appear to be confessing to serious crimes on tape. Crimes which have cost lives. British lives, Irish lives. How could we do anything other than pursue those confessions? At the most fundamental level, that's what everyone involved in this is paid to do.'

'But this isn't only a matter of law, Robert, it's politics.'

'And can you imagine the political ramifications of being seen not to pursue these tapes? What would that look like, at home and abroad, to our people and to others? Legally, politically, however you want to look at it, it's essential for us to go after these confessions.'

Frank raises a finger in warning. 'They're not confessions in the eyes of those making them. They're statements of record by men who believe they were combatants. Not criminals. And they've been given on the understanding they'll stay private for the rest of their lives. A trust was established. And your government is undermining that trust. So I need you to do something about it.'

'What do you expect me to "do about it", Frank? What on earth do you want us to do?'

Frank leans forward in his seat. 'I need to know the agenda. That's all. If this is just people following protocol, and we're not expecting any consequences from all this palaver, and all of it's just a sort of show, all right then. I can take that message back. But I've been sent because people wonder whether there isn't some intrigue. People wonder whether the whole thing wasn't set up from the start. All these old soldiers lured into talking just so the coals can be raked over by lawyers a few years down the line. And a few key people embarrassed or even charged with things we all thought were best forgotten.'

I incline my head gravely, but I am glad. I don't have the authority to give real answers about any manoeuvre my successors might make, but I still know how things work. 'The most likely story here is that there's no intrigue around these tapes at all. Come on, Frank. The British don't care about Ireland, that's the truth. They don't think about it at all, you know that. But the police are obliged to investigate things like this, so they're doing it. So probably there's no great conspiracy, no.'

Frank slumps back slowly into his chair. I wonder whether he's reflecting now on how old he has become, the way being at the centre of things has passed him by, the same way that I have been all the morning. I can feel all of that, heavy in the room, so Frank surely must be able to taste it as sharply as I do.

'You don't think it's anything more?' Frank asks.

'I can't be sure, of course. I'm retired, I don't know what's going on. But I can tell you what's overwhelmingly likely to be the case. The whole thing hasn't been a trap ten years in the planning – of course it hasn't. If it had been, I think it would have been planned better. It's just noise, that's all.'

'You can't say the arrest of Gerry Adams is just noise.'

I nod. The news of that arrest was what really led me to expect I might receive some kind of contact from someone. It was undoubtedly an escalation. 'That arrest will have no meaningful impact on anyone whatsoever. There will be no charges. There is no real proof. It's one word against another, Frank: we won't get any convictions out of that. It's probably just police officers being bullish.'

Frank shakes his head. 'But surely you see that this is still a disaster in terms of what it means for all of us.'

'The disaster, Frank, was the catalogue of murders that are

now being itemised on these tapes. We can't do anything about that now. The police are aware of alleged confessions. They are obliged to investigate.'

Frank holds up his hands in concession again. 'I hear what you say.'

'Do you need something to take back with you?'

Frank stirs, uncomfortable, and studies the carpet. 'Well, look, it wouldn't hurt. The man I heard from this morning – we've not been on each other's Christmas card lists for quite some time, you know? I'm here sitting and talking to you because a man who once told me he'd like to see me shot called me up today at five in the morning. And he didn't sound all that much warmer to me now than the last time we spoke, and it's not a nice feeling, to know they still know where you are and what your phone number is, you know? It's an unnerving feeling. So it wouldn't hurt if I could do a bit of a job on this, and have something to tell him when I call him next, because at the moment I'm feeling quite far out on the limb.'

I suppose I should call Geoffrey now, and find out what exactly I am supposed to say. I have no information to work from, only instinct. Who knows, perhaps the whole thing really is a plot and I am wrong? But I think not. They used to have a phrase for these situations. In Whitehall they used to say the system operated on the principle of 'autonomous wankerdom'. Things were separated out into different jurisdictions and it wasn't possible to pull enough strings to cause an intrigue like this, it was just some autonomous wanker doing his job. 'Perhaps I might make a phone call in order to seek a little clarification? Would that be all right?'

'Of course. I'd be grateful to you. I am grateful to you, Robert.'

'It would be good if I could speak with Geoffrey privately, as in all honesty I don't know what he's going to say.' Perhaps I should suggest Frank wait in an upstairs bedroom for a few minutes – but he speaks before I can continue.

'I don't mind exploring the fauna on the lawn for a bit, that's fine.'

'Good.' I had hoped to keep Frank from meeting anyone else, but perhaps that was unreasonable. It certainly seems too abrupt to ban him from going out there, so I shall just have to stop myself worrying. He is unshakeably discreet, after all. It will be all right; he won't talk to anyone.

'I worry that it could have implications for me, if all of those tapes are seized,' Frank says suddenly, halfway to the door, as if he hadn't meant to speak.

I frowned, surprised. 'Oh yes? In what way?'

Frank shifts uneasily. 'I'm not saying I've ever been party to anything criminal. But there are men that I used to deal with who've given interviews to these guys. God knows why they felt the need to give an interview; it's madness really, it's madness. They must have known the law would get after them.'

'Perhaps they miss the adrenaline,' I say.

'Perhaps they do. Anyway, I'm worried some of them could name me. As someone who used to help pass things on. That's all anyone could say, mind, I've never been involved. Just passing things on. But it could be compromising for me, if that ended up being said in open court.'

'I understand, Frank. No one wants to be named in court proceedings against suspected terrorists.'

'Suspected terrorists is one thing. If you grew up in Derry when I did, of course you know a few of them. But setting up meetings with the government of this country's something else, you see. It could look an awful lot like collaborating, to some people back in Ireland. And there was a time when I was doing that and it wasn't exactly universally popular. Back when your lot were the enemy.'

'So what you're worried about is being too closely connected to us, then.'

'No offence, but yes, that's the way of it.'

'I understand. I don't know what can be done about it, but this country owes you a debt just as Ireland does. So if ways can be found to make sure your privacy is respected, of course they'll be found. We could look after that.'

'You think that could be done?'

'We wouldn't allow the naming of an agent in the field. You were never quite that, but the principle holds, I think.'

'All right then. That's a great reassurance, I must say.'

Am I imagining it, or do I see in Frank's face the relief of a boy who is going to get away with a bad school report? It's affecting to see him as vulnerable and as worried as this. It deflates me slightly to know Frank was so anxious to keep the history between us secret. His anxiety reminds me of how grubby the whole thing always was, our work, all my relationships from back when I was in Ireland. All of it was muddy and uncertain and mixed in its motives. I thought I was doing good work when I sat down with him, after Enniskillen. The few occasions we drank whiskey or wine with each other, and shared a smile and a guarded joke or two. But to Frank those conversations are something that need to be covered up.

There is nothing ever to be really proud of in a world like this one. Someone else is always compromising themselves, even in the very same moment when you believe you are at your best, you are making a difference, you are getting something right.

Frank smiles. 'It feels a bit like something real is happening again, doesn't it?' He lets a silence grow before he speaks again. I carefully avoid filling it. 'It's good to be needed. Almost like rolling back time.'

I shake my head. 'But I think it's a phantom, I think we're like those people who feel things in limbs they've lost, you know.' Frank's face becomes sadder, and older, as his smile ebbs away, and I know we are in agreement. I gesture to the phone on my desk. 'Give me ten minutes and I'll have something for you.'

from Interview 60

I got six-packed in 1992. That's when someone shoots you in your knees, elbows, ankles. That's why I'm in this chair, see, the shatter never healed so well. I can see now that I brought it on myself. I was a drinker. I mean I still am, but those days I was a real drinker, and I used to get a bit rough, you know? I'd start fights. And I picked on the wrong guy, who was IRA, and that's what did for me. Even though I was IRA myself. It was decided that I was out of control, and something had to be done. So I got a knock on the door one night, and they took me outside, and I got my six pack. At first, in hospital, I was angry. Raging. I was gonna find a way to kill the people who'd done that. Then I had a visitor. I didn't know him, no one from the usual crowd. Well spoken. Not a man I thought knew his way round a gun. They'll send a mate to give you a message sometimes if that's what they think's gonna work, and other times they'll send a stranger. There's a lot of thought goes into how things get passed on. This guy sat down and started me on the road to seeing that being angry did no good. He told me: The IRA will look after you, they'll look out for your family. You'll have that protection like you always did. So there's no use being angry, in the end. You'll end up losing the safety you have. He said to me: Armies have their discipline, they have to keep their discipline. That's why this had to happen to you. And have no doubt, it did have to happen to you. I didn't accept it at the time, of course. But eventually I saw the wisdom of what he'd said. Because I was out of control with the drinking. And armies need their discipline, you know?

Kate

It's like doing the Twelve Steps Programme, coming back here today; Re-engaging With the Ones You Shut the Door On. I hate it. All these people who know what happened to me, all these people whispering behind my back. But I decided I had to come here after three years away because I felt I was letting people down all the time I didn't take part in the life of my family, and so here I am, and now I have to deal with it.

I thought people would start to hate me if I didn't come back to them. They would say I didn't want them any more. The real problem is feeling like I don't deserve to be here with the living and the smiling. I thought I couldn't put it off any longer now the new year is starting to bloom, but that doesn't mean I'm ready; I don't know whether I would ever have been ready for this, whenever it happened.

Now I'm here it feels harder and more frightening than I expected. But I thought I'd be facing the day with Sam, and once again he hasn't turned up for me. Maybe that's what's shaken me. I knew what the day would entail, after all. That I would be out of control of my environment, and might well end up seeing Mum. I knew all that could happen, but it seemed less overwhelming from the comfort of my room back in Bristol. Now I'm surrounded. I gaze out over the lawn as it becomes busy with bodies, in outfits that range from jeans and T-shirts to pearl earrings and light suits, and remind myself: You asked for this, so there's no use complaining.

The sound of fifty people rushing to get drunk. I hear the lilting music of their voices dancing, beating at my eardrums. For a while, Grandma used to put up the framed family tree she had put together by the front door to welcome the guests on these days, so people could see what they were part of – and perhaps what they were letting themselves in for – when they arrived. But my second cousin Neil, who rather regrets the three divorces inked by his name near the bottom of the tree, objected to its presence, so it's no longer brought out and displayed. I learned enough from it before it disappeared back into one of the upstairs rooms, though, about how my family fitted together, to be able to make a fair amount of sense of the Brueghel-like throng chattering around me.

'Of course, you know why the trains run so well in India, don't you?' I make out the voice of Cousin Neil himself, holding forth, puffed up with certainty of his own brilliance.

'This isn't going to be a joke about Hitler, is it?'

'Certainly not. The trains run on time in India because our great-grandfather used to run them.'

'Of course, I'd forgotten that! He worked on the railways, didn't he?'

Neil scoffs. I don't think I've ever actually heard anyone scoff before, but Neil's intention is clear and unarguable. 'I wouldn't quite call it working on the railways. He had a staff of about two hundred, June, that's not what's commonly understood as working on the railways, is it?'

'Of course,' says a chastened June, a small woman I can't remember anything about except that Aunt Laura thinks she's a wet fish, 'he was a high-up, wasn't he?'

'I have in my possession, back at the house, a photograph of him on the day before he came back to England to join the Engineers at the start of the first war. He looks like a great fat walrus.' Neil says this with a tone of fervent approval, possibly because it isn't a bad description of himself. 'He's absolutely surrounded by Indian faces, all his boys saying goodbye.'

'You can't say that any more, Neil,' says Megan, Neil's harassed-looking fourth wife.

'Why not? What's racist about that? They're Indian. They have Indian faces.'

'Yes, but you can't call them boys, it's derogatory.'

Not so long before today, I would have found it unbearable to stand here listening like this. I lost the trick of being able to cope with the rough and tumble of human boringness, insensitivity, boisterous enthusiasm. Now, I'm learning to bear it all little by little, I'm trying to come home to myself.

I've built up the walls of my life so the world around me is – usually – a lot quieter than this party, this scene I'm in. I live most of the time in the company of Sam and a few friends who are gentle with me without making a big deal of it, and the flat I like being in, and the pages of books. I only venture out into the bustle of the city where I live, or any of the world's loud places, when I feel able to, and hide myself from the sharp elbows and callousness of strangers the rest of the time. But I feel I'm able to do it more often, these days. I'm learning to carry the quiet I've woven into my life at home around like an escape route, a trapdoor, and dive back into the memory of it when things get too much.

From the vantage I've fashioned for myself, the quiet isolation, Neil doesn't really depress or upset me, as he might have done not so long ago. Part of me finds him funny, in the way that anything ridiculous is always funny; part of me feels sorry for him, because he'll never realise how silly he looks, with his belly and his opinions sticking out a foot in front of him, preceding him everywhere he goes; and part of me loves him, for being just as unusual, in his own way, as I am – as anyone is, for that matter.

I look across the busy lawn at the people talking, the nibbles being nibbled, the glasses emptied and refilled, and for a moment the image comes of jigsaw pieces thrown into the air. Every personality bristling across the waking garden, like hedgehogs snuffling through flower beds, pigs hunting apples out of the mud, each of them sticks out in their own way at odd little angles, elbowing each other, finding new and ingenious ways to not quite fit, because that's what people do. Today we're doing our best to piece ourselves together. Perhaps if we ever pull off the trick, the image revealed might really become something beautiful. The picture that has been cut up and hidden in little parts carried by every disparate one of us might be a wonderful thing to make out, just once, even if only for the duration of an afternoon.

'Would you like a vol-au-vent, darling?' One of Grandad's neighbours thrusts a plate under my nose. 'Cheese and tomato. I think they're called vol-au-vents, aren't they? Or is that just what you call pastry parcels? Anyway, never mind, have a thing.'

I smile, weakly, and pick up a mouthful of feta on a cracker. 'Thanks.'

The woman sweeps on, radiant and ludicrous in her conviction that she's being helpful to everyone. I examine the thing, put it in my mouth, bite down, start to chew.

I was funny about food when I was barely out of primary school. It used to be my mum's habit to make all my sandwiches for the term ahead in a big batch at the end of the holidays, setting aside an hour and a tub of Flora and several brown loaves and a stack of cheese and pickle and tomato and tuna and ham and boiled eggs and mayonnaise, then sitting with me and the radio playing around us while the two of us made enough sandwiches to get me through all the weeks ahead till the next school break. The idea was that it took less time, doing it all at once; and of course, there was the question of money, how much she saved by buying things in bulk and how she saved even more by making sure I never needed to buy things from the school canteen.

Mum and I would fill several carrier bags with these sandwiches, and put them in the freezer. Each morning through the term, I would take pot luck, and draw a sandwich bag from among the others. It was a lottery. Tuna and tomatoes never defrosted by lunch, so quite often I had to eat frozen food. It wasn't long before I decided I'd rather not eat those. I wasn't even sure it was safe to eat frozen tuna. So I started skipping lunch on the days when I picked the wrong sandwich, and hiding the sandwiches in the clothes cupboard in my bedroom. I knew it was stupid, and wouldn't solve anything in the long run, and that the food I hid would only rot and start to smell, it wouldn't go away. But it wasn't a decision I took with the whole of my mind, I don't think. What I was really doing was trying to block out the thought of the lunches I hated. I used the cupboard as a place where I could put things so they didn't exist any more, and I didn't have to think about them. A way to keep out the light.

This policy worked for a couple of months, until one day I came home to find Dad waiting for me in the kitchen.

'I need to talk to you about something I found in your room.'

'OK.' I knew at once what it was, of course. Perhaps I had been waiting for the day when someone would discover what I was doing, and the loop I was trapped in could be brought to an end. All of us like to be saved, after all. When we were children, all of us liked to be picked up and held. But still, I walked over to the kitchen table with a feeling of dread for the shame I knew I would have to face in a few seconds. I thought Dad had seen something weird about me, a secret thing; he knew something was wrong with me; he knew I wasn't normal like everyone else.

'I wouldn't ever go searching round your room, of course, but I've been noticing a smell in there recently when I've been hoovering. So I tried to find out today where it was coming from.'

I realised then that he wasn't going to say it outright. It was too embarrassing a picture for both of us to confront. But those festering sandwiches sat smugly between us, just the same.

'I'm really sorry.'

'What have you been doing, darling?'

I felt a strange light-headed sense of unreality about actually saying this out loud to Dad, as if this was happening to someone else, or that I was watching myself from across the room. 'I just hate my lunches.'

'But didn't you think you could tell us about it?'

'I didn't know how.' Stupid. I had been so stupid. I hadn't thought things through.

'You just needed to come and talk to us.'

'I just didn't know how to.' Now I was whining, I could hear it in my voice, and the tears came in earnest. I knew he would be gentle with me, but I wished more than anything that he would just stop talking and we could pretend this had never happened, and I could bin all of the mess, and go on.

'OK.' Dad got up from his chair then, and crossed the room to hold me in his arms. 'You can't have been eating enough for a long time.'

'No. I get hungry at lunchtimes.'

'Will you promise not to do that any more? No more hiding?'

'Yes.' I would have promised anything just to end the conversation and get upstairs to the solitude of my room.

'I don't understand what you thought you were doing. You must have known it wouldn't go away like that, just leaving them all there?'

That was the worst of it, being asked why. I didn't know what I had been doing. It had simply been instinct. Something beyond me that made me try and hide away the things that made me unhappy, the lunches in their little plastic bags.

'I don't know what I was doing. I just didn't like my lunches and I tried not to think about them.'

Dad looked nonplussed, exasperated. 'All right . . . well, I suppose we'll have to make you better lunches now.'

In return for putting a stop to the hiding away of things, I screwed a promise out of my parents that I wouldn't have to eat tuna ever again. Mum wouldn't back down on making all my lunches at the start of term, she said she didn't have time to do it every morning, but that was victory enough to me, an end to chewing on frozen fish. After that, I still didn't always feel able to eat the sandwiches every lunchtime – bread that has been frozen, and was cheap in the first place, is a very sad meal to try to eat – but I used to throw the food I didn't want into the hedges between the house and school, rather than hiding it in the bedroom, and there was never any trouble about it ever again. With hindsight, it might have been better if I had talked more about the strange difficulties that seemed to assail me at lunchtime when Dad sat me down. But I was only a child, and couldn't see the dangers I was playing with then. I thought things that had been thrown away simply didn't exist any more. I wish all the instincts of our childhood were right. I wish I had got that right, at least. Life would have been much easier if that were true.

The episode with the sandwiches came back to haunt me later, in the months while I was settling into Bristol. Remembering it all now, standing on Grandad's lawn in the midst of a mild May day, I can hardly believe it could all really have happened.

It started with restricting in the months after what happened to Joe, and with exercising too often. I would walk for hours, go out and run, do workouts following the instructions of smiling American women on videos I watched on YouTube. Anything to stay busy, anything not to be still. I wanted to pay attention to every small and seemingly unimportant element that made up who I was, and decipher the sum of myself, piece my real life together out of the senseless algebra of experience. I didn't want to just eat any more, but instead to always know what it was I was eating.

It was a year after Joe's accident before I went to a doctor. The GP didn't look up from his screen while he spoke to me, typing up the previous patient's notes. I told him that my periods had stopped, and he asked me a few cursory questions. Then he asked me about my eating.

'I struggle to eat as much as I suppose I should, sometimes,' I said. 'I obsess over what I'm going to eat. I'll spend a whole day thinking about what I can have for dinner. Then sometimes by the time I get home, I've built it up too much, so I don't have anything.'

'So how much of the day would you say you spend thinking about food?'

I'd never asked myself this question before. I thought about it for a moment. 'I think about food all the time.'

The GP nodded. 'I think you have anxiety, and an eating disorder. I'll need to refer you for specialist assessment.'

Hearing those words spoken about me shocked me out of coping. My eating collapsed away to nothingness. I was racked by a fear of eating all the time, and woke with a sore jaw from clenching my teeth, with nail marks red and livid in the palms of my hands.

I started stripping my meals away to nothingness. Cutting out carbohydrates, fatty foods. One by one, the staples of my old diet were rendered out of bounds, and there was no one around me who stepped in and said anything. I stripped away potatoes and pasta and curry and pizza and bread and cheese and milk and eggs and sweet potatoes and chickpeas and lentils and Ryvita from my diet. The foods I had once enjoyed became mountains I could no longer climb, triggers, fear foods, ideas to scare me, make me start to sweat and shake, make my heart beat out of my chest. I was reduced to porridge and soup and salad. I was reduced to bananas. I told myself I didn't need food. I could get on better without it. I would eat once every four days, when I felt too faint to go on, and suffer agonies of guilt and blame for days afterwards because I'd put something into my body. When things came to their worst, I went whole weeks between eating anything. I could only walk very slowly. My heart stopped working as it should. When I became desperately faint, and thought I couldn't stay on my feet any longer, I would have a carrot, a banana, force something down and then have to curl up for the rest of the day, the pain of having eaten, the anxiety attack that came from having put food in my body overwhelming me.

For a long time, as my referrals were lost or rejected and my weight dropped, I averted my eyes from the truth of what was happening. I kept going to my appointments with the GP, and told myself things might heal, the end might still be just around the corner. When the doctor suggested he might need to take more drastic action, I ignored him. I chose to evade treatment while I still could. I didn't want to put my life on hold, and go into hospital. I didn't want to be fed through a tube, or put on a drip, even though I couldn't find the strength it would take to eat enough to keep living. So I blocked out those thoughts from my head, refused to entertain the possibility of a collapse. It wasn't difficult. It was all too easy to pretend around other people, and after a while I got so tired I would sleep for twelve hours every night, so there were no lonely evenings to fill with thinking. Anorexics, I found, sleep very easily. They don't have the energy for dark nights of the soul.

What I had for company instead of sleeplessness was an insistent screaming inside my head, like a face that was watching and shouting just the other side of a window, a face that was always there that I tried to ignore, not to look at directly. I knew all the time I was awake that it was there, it was happening. I didn't let myself think about it until things had become very serious.

There were two selves living in my body, two people fighting for the right to claim my name and take possession of my life. I still struggled for breath in there, hidden behind my eyes, drowning, staring out from the wreckage of the person I had been, still able to make myself heard in some situations. But the other self sprang up within me and fought to speak and drown everything else out, a voice like my own voice but separated from that real self like the two sides of a blade. A malignant intelligence waiting exiled at the edge of my subconscious. It raged around the walls of my mind, a wolf that longed to drag me out of the shell of myself, tear at my windpipe, put an end to me. The wolf would speak for me in some things. It took me over. And it stopped me seeing what was happening to me till very near the end.

In the end, Dad came to visit me, and that was the start of

the change; it was having someone step in and react to my situation with terror that began to prise open the trap closing round me. I had been keeping all the distance I could between myself and my parents, trying to keep myself away from them, safe in my isolation, but Dad kept calling to ask how I was and where I was, tried to keep up with what I was doing. I would tell him I was all right, and that I wanted to be on my own, and for a long time he respected that. But he must have realised something was going wrong. He decided to get himself a Facebook account – perhaps he was looking for ways to be closer to me – and I suppose he must have seen the few photographs of me that people had taken, as I grew thinner and fell deeper into sickness. One day he turned up in Bristol, calling to tell me he was in the city and needed to see me straight away.

'Is anything wrong?' I remember asking.

'Nothing's wrong with me, I just need to see you.'

We met when I finished work, in a café near the call centre. I guessed he had already been there for hours when I stepped in off the street, stirring the quiet air of the nearly empty room so that he looked up and saw me, feeling the draught from the door, I suppose. There was an empty cup next to him, and I thought he'd probably found the café as soon as I gave him its name, and sat there waiting for me ever since. I could see the tension in him. He looked like someone who had been coiled up with their worries for a long time. He must have been able to see the same in me, the fear in me as I walked in to see him and knew that I'd been found out again, just like the time he found the sandwiches hidden in the cupboard.

'Hello, darling.'

He looked tired, a darkness round the eyes, a tightness round the mouth, and I wondered whether he had lied to me on the phone, whether there was anything wrong with him. I still didn't think how my condition might be affecting him. 'Hi, Dad.' We hugged, and he held me very tightly.

'Shall I get you a cup of tea?'

'Yes, please.' I sat down and waited, looking at his empty coffee cup while he paid for more at the counter, then brought our drinks back to the table one balanced in each hand, folding himself over slightly because he was concentrating on not spilling anything. He stooped over the drinks as if he wanted to protect them. He sat down and reached out with his right hand and placed it on top of my left, and was still for a moment, looking at me.

'How are you?' he asked.

'I'm OK.' All I could think was that there was milk in the tea, and that I didn't think I was brave enough to drink it. By then I could only drink tea if it was black. Allowing myself milk would have left me disgusted at myself, my greediness, my need.

He nodded, slowly. 'Good. I've been thinking about something, and I wanted to bring it up with you. Is that OK? I don't want you to get upset.'

It wasn't so different from the time he sat me down to talk about hiding my sandwiches. I don't think I felt hostile towards him. I was upset and angry – distraught even – at what might happen now someone knew, but there was also a sense of relief. I had been waiting for someone to come along and take all that secrecy out of my hands, because I still didn't know how to talk to people about what was going on.

'What's the matter?' I asked, and he smiled, and his eyes filled for a moment with tears. I felt dizzy, as if the room had moved. I had never seen Dad cry. He was always so calm, so grown up about everything. I had never seen him share his vulnerability with anyone before, and I didn't think he wanted to share it with me now; it seemed like he was simply breaking down. He was afraid for me, and that shook him out of the calm that had always defined him.

'Kate, I think . . . you've got very thin. I think you've got quite a lot too thin, and I wondered whether you were aware of it.'

I started to reply, then felt a catch in my throat, and looked down at Dad's hand where it was cradling mine. My hands were already thinner. Even my feet had got thinner; my shoes were all getting too big. Dad's hands were old, but the veins on mine stood out bluer and clearer. I didn't say anything then, just thought about how different our hands seemed now from when they used to hold each other.

'I think you are aware of it. I think you're not eating. And I've come to ask whether we could make an appointment for you to go and see a doctor about what's going on?'

I told him then that I'd already been seeing doctors for a little while, that I had a name for what was happening to me, that people were aware of the downslope I was on, the black run. As I talked I started to cry, my hands shaking, and couldn't get the words out. He gave me a hug and I tried to get calm again.

'Can I come with you to an appointment, Kate, would that be OK?'

'Why do you want to?'

'I just want to make sure you're getting all the help you can. I want to talk to your doctor. Would that be all right?'

We booked an appointment on the phone there and then, and he travelled back to Bristol a few days later, and we went to the surgery together and sat in the plastic chairs, and listened to the GP warning me that I needed to change, as if I didn't know that already.

After we'd come out of that appointment, Dad tried to take the problem off my hands, but I wouldn't let him.

'I think you should move home, while you're ill,' he said. 'This is a very serious problem, Kate, more serious than work, or paying your rent or anything like that. It's your life. Why don't you take a bit of pressure off yourself, and come home for a while, and we can look after you?'

'The trouble is I think moving home would do the opposite.'

'How do you mean?' Dad tried to act puzzled, but I guessed that he knew what I meant.

'I don't want to upset you, but I feel like Mum's part of this, that's all.'

'I see.' He couldn't look at me for a moment then, and I felt guilty and ashamed. I wished I could explain it to him. But he had never seen it, all the years we had lived under the same roof, he just hadn't got it. The way she made me feel like I wasn't really worth anything. The way she made me feel as though there must be something wrong with me, some secret I didn't know about yet. All my life, that unspeakable shame, and he had never noticed, he didn't understand.

I had convinced myself that this had always been in me, ever since childhood. There had been some trouble planted deep within me, right back at the start, in the years when I didn't know how to love my mum. All I had ever been waiting for was a wound deep enough to bring this out.

Dad paid for private therapy, but it didn't really help. I suppose I had started giving up. I had decided I would never eat again. My energy levels dropped, and my speech was slurred, and I often became dizzy and faint. I took laxatives to try and purge my body of all the fat I could feel, even though it wasn't there, even though I wasn't eating any more. I cried myself to sleep night after night, alone and terrified and exhausted.

'If we're going to be able to work together, I need you to commit to eating three times a day, Kate.'

I couldn't even tell you the name of the therapist I saw in the last few weeks before my admission. A kind woman, she hugged me at the end of our first session. She knew it was too late for her to have any effect. Dad told me later that she tried to help by writing urgent letters to the GP, telling him to do more, to step in, take action. I barely had the energy to speak back to her when she spoke to me.

'Right.'

'Can you do that?'

'I don't think so.'

'Can you commit to trying, at least?'

'I don't know.'

'We're not going to be able to do anything together if we're not committed to a common goal.'

'Yeah.'

On it went, for an hour. Dad could tell when he talked to me afterwards that it hadn't done any good. He used to plead with me, hold my hand and demand that I eat. But I had decided I just couldn't do it any more.

Then a night came when I was woken at half past one by the ring of my phone and someone leaning on the buzzer to the flat. At first I ignored all the noise, but whoever was downstairs kept buzzing and buzzing, and after a minute or so, one of my flatmates got up and answered it. I lay in bed. A premonition crossed my mind that something terrible was coming, but I didn't know what. I just knew the person at the door had come for me, because my phone had been ringing as well. Then there was a knock on my bedroom door, and Dad looked into the room where I lay in the soft dark waiting for death or the ease of my suffering, and I saw two paramedics dressed in green and unfolding a wheelchair behind him. And I felt like the world had ended. I hated Dad in that moment with a burning certainty I'd never known before. I knew what was going to happen: I saw all of it. The degradations and humiliations of the hospital, no privacy at any hour of the day, the shame, the fear, over and over again.

'Darling?'

'Oh, no no no.'

'I'm so sorry, my love. But it's time.'

'I hate you.'

'I'm so sorry.'

'Why now?'

'I've begged them every day for weeks, Kate. I've been asking for weeks. Tonight is just the first night I've got through to someone who agreed with me. It's going to be all right, my love. They'll save you now. It's going to be all right.

'I hate you.'

'I'm so sorry. But I can't let you die, my darling.'

Dad got me sectioned by calling 111 again and again, behind my back, despite my insistence that he mustn't try and take that step, calling day after day until he got through to a doctor who backed up his instinct that I was in grave danger. That doctor called an ambulance, and came to the flat to talk to me before I was taken into hospital. Dad told me afterwards that for a long time no one had listened to his opinion at all, whoever he tried to speak to. Half the time, when he called, they wouldn't put him through to anyone because he wasn't with me, so they couldn't speak to me to make their diagnosis. When he did get through to a dietician, they would tell him there was nothing they could do; that it was the choice of the patient whether they started treatment or not. And then they would tell him that people could become very upset and angry with their loved ones if they took these decisions for them, that the blame and the hatred could be very difficult. As if they were asking Dad to give up. I always wonder what happens to the people whose families give up trying when they're told that. I can't help but think they all die.

When I saw the wheelchair I sobbed and hid deep in the burrow of the bed as the paramedics came into the room. Till then I'd found ways to keep walking despite how weak I felt, but the strength went out of me when I knew I was going into hospital. I thought my life was ending. I thought I was going to die, now there were going to be machines all around me, now there would be drips falling endlessly, nurses staring into my eyes. They put me in the wheelchair and took me down to the ambulance. Dad followed after me, but I wouldn't speak to him. All I could say to him again and again was 'I hate you, I hate you, I hate you.'

He watched me, helpless. 'I know,' he said. 'I'm so sorry. I'm so sorry this happened to you.'

I had lost the strength to think clearly, and believed that because I hadn't died yet, what was happening to me wasn't going to kill me after all, despite what the doctors had been saying. In the heat of my malnourishment, my mind had stopped working. I had started to believe I was going to be able to go on for ever without eating a thing. When that faith was taken away from me, it was the biggest shock, a terrible crumbling of the world beneath my feet. But in the middle of the horror and defeat of that discovery, I saw something I hadn't been able to make out before, and that clarity probably saved me in the end. I realised that what I'd been trying to do was to be more like Joe. I had been trying to find my way into a hospital bed because Joe was gone from me and I couldn't bear it, because I wanted to show him that I still cared. So when I was laid out on the trolley in the ambulance, and the paramedics were studying the way my heart had started failing, a secret, silent part of me felt this was victory, this was mastering something. I hadn't been good enough for him, but I could be good enough at this. I had thought at first that I wanted to live, but that had only been fuzzy thinking. Now I was seeing things clearly, right at the end, by the river that had beckoned, the place of forgetting. Now I was learning the role and the act of dying.

'Hello, Kate, you're looking well.' I turn, heartsick because I don't want to look well, I don't want anyone to tell me that, and see my uncle Owen. Owen's actually a cousin, Grandma's brother's son, but those kinds of people always prefer to be called aunt and uncle, I find. When I was younger I thought Uncle Owen was cool, because he was an opera singer, and had done *Don Giovanni* for the Welsh National Opera, and there was a poster from the production in the hallway of our house.

'Hi, Uncle Owen. How are you?'

'Not so bad, thanks. Intimidating seeing all these people, isn't it?'

'Do you think so too?'

Owen laughs. 'Of course. Everyone does on days like this. You're always terrified you won't remember someone's name. That was why I was excited to see you, you're someone I can definitely say hello to.'

I think it's just possible that Uncle Owen is sufficiently distant from the rest of my family that he isn't aware of my illness. He lives in Lincoln, after all, which is miles from anywhere, and like many of Mum's relatives, he doesn't get on with her at all. Perhaps no one told him what had happened. I feel a momentary lifting of the darkness that has been assailing me as the thought crosses my mind. It would be good to pretend to be someone else for the duration of a conversation. I thought everyone I saw today would be staring at me, checking for signs.

'How are you then? What are you up to these days?' I ask.

'I'm actually looking to do a bit of directing.' Owen bites down on a vol-au-vent, spitting puff pastry in a gentle cloud as he speaks.

'Oh, right?'

'Yes.' Having finished his mouthful, Owen pauses to wash it down with the dregs of a glass of Prosecco. 'The lungs go as you get older, you see, and the work dries up, so it's important to diversify. I'm doing a *Rigoletto* in Ludlow in the summer with a view to making my name and my fortune.' He chuckles as if this is very funny, and it strikes me how much more exciting everyone seems when you're a child, and you haven't learned yet how to spot the flaws in people. Even the most glamorous lives end up looking ordinary, if you watch them for long enough.

'That sounds brilliant.'

'You must come, if you're free. It's on for a week.'

'I'll definitely see if I'm around. That would be great.'

'All right. I'll find you a flyer before I go. Speak later,' Owen says, and walks away, and for all that I think he seems ridiculous and sad wandering round a family gathering trying to advertise his show, I love him in that moment for having no idea what happened to me, for talking to me as if I am purely and simply myself. It's rare, these days, to be addressed like that. As if there's no thin ice anywhere that someone might tread on, no past to fall into and drown.

Once I was in hospital I refused fluids for the first twelve hours. I wanted to show Dad how much he had betrayed me. The only thing I still knew how to do was try and die, so I threw myself into it, desperate, aching. The medical team couldn't compel me to take anything until I was formally sectioned, and the relevant forms had been signed. I was angry that I had been brought there, and the only way of showing that was hurting myself a little further. Dad sat with me, bowed over with his elbows resting on his knees, all the strength gone out of him while he begged me to live, and I refused to speak to him. The doctor told me if I kept trying to go without a drip, I'd most likely die later that night.

'I've already lost three patients tonight in the same condition as you. You have to take on fluids or you will die.'

'But how much longer could I go without dying? Couldn't I stay out until I absolutely can't any more, and then come into hospital? How many more days could I have gone? A week?'

A look passed between the doctor and Dad, tired and defeated, heavy eyes snagging each other. The doctor looked back to me, dragging the same heavy look like a body through undergrowth.

'I'm afraid we've already reached that point where you'll die if we don't help you. Tonight is that point. We have to get fluids in now.'

I found it was easier to accept things when it felt like there wasn't a decision to be made, or someone else was making the decision. So I let them put in a drip, sobbing so hard that I couldn't breathe properly, because I thought they would find a way to get food into me through it. And then I decided I had to get away from the place. I tried to get dressed and leave, but Dad wouldn't let me. He held me in the bay and I fought him, battering at his chest, his arms. I barely had the strength to stand but I found the strength to fight him. He told me later that I seemed like a bird held between cupped palms, it was so easy to keep me still. He could feel my wings beating but they had no real strength. I screamed and cried at being so trapped. I had to lie down again because my heart wasn't strong enough to pump the blood through me, and I started to faint. Dad cried, and I offered him no sympathy. I told him it was his fault. I told him I hated him for what he was doing to me. For the whole of that first night I sobbed, and felt as if I was filled with so many different people, all these voices screaming, wanting so many different things. They came like waves in and out of my consciousness. The determination that I didn't need this help being forced on me, that I was being kidnapped, that I needed to escape. The determination that I had always wanted to end up here, and be like Joe, and feel closer to Joe because I was almost as damaged now as he was. The terror that I was going to have to die, because I didn't want to live. The terror that I was going to have to live, because I didn't know how I could bear dying either.

The next morning, the first of my minder nurses turned up, the noise of their arrival waking me from an unconsciousness that couldn't really be called sleep. Dad, who had sat awake next to me through the night, tried to hold my hand and make me feel safer while I stared in fear at this strange new face sitting beside me, not understanding what he was going to do, whether he was here to hurt me or force me to eat.

Registered Mental Health Nurses, as the minders were properly called, were detailed to sit with patients under section every hour of the day and night, dividing the day into two twelve-hour shifts, to ensure the terms of the section were enforced. My first RMN was a thin black man with an accent from somewhere in Africa. I couldn't narrow it down any further, being delirious and barely listening to him anyway. He worked, it transpired when Dad tried to talk to him, as a lecturer in postcolonial history at the University of the West of England, and topped up his income with nursing. He said very little to me, but talked to Dad all morning about mindfulness. He wouldn't listen to Dad when he explained the severity of my anorexia, and believed it was good practice to keep offering me food in case I felt able to accept some.

'Whenever they come round to take orders for meals, I'll just order some food, OK? Then if the patient wants to have some of what I've ordered, they can, or if it doesn't feel possible still, they can leave it.' He beamed reassuringly at Dad.

'Dad. Tell him.' I had wanted to never speak to him again, wanted to never forgive him. But now he had put me in this place, there were new horrors I couldn't face on my own. So I bit down on my pride and accepted I needed him, clung to him for help like I was a child again, and saw he understood what had happened, the modicum of forgiveness he had been given, and the chance he had to protect me from this place.

Dad tried to explain as gently as possible that this tactic was unlikely to succeed. 'I don't know how much experience you've had with anorexic patients. I admit I haven't had much experience myself. But my daughter hasn't eaten anything at all for several weeks. The likelihood of her feeling able to eat an ordinary plate of hospital food right now seems quite low to me, so I wonder whether what you're proposing is going to just cause more distress?'

'It'll be all right. I'll order some fish.'

'But I really think it might be better if we allowed dietary decisions to be led by a qualified dietician, rather than yourself?'

The RMN smiled, as if he'd heard all this before. 'You have to be calmer about things, Mr Edwards. It doesn't do to get emotional in front of the patient. It's OK. I'll just order something nice.'

He ordered me a plate of salmon at lunchtime. When the salmon came, I lost control, terrified at the smell of the food and the thought of the thick, cloying taste of it, blind with panic at the thought of any energy going into my body, poisoning me. I forced my way out of the bed and into the hallway, then collapsed sobbing on the floor because my legs wouldn't carry me any further. Dad screamed at the RMN and picked me up like an infant in his arms, then carried me into the day room, away from the food. We buried our faces in each other's shoulders and cried then, for a long time.

Mum wanted to come but I told Dad I couldn't see her, and he called her and asked her not to come, because he knew I was serious, and knew I had grown very weak, and the distress of what was happening was dangerous to me. For the next two days, every time food came on to the ward I believed it would be forced on me. I would hear the trolley approaching, its death rattle growing louder on the other side of my frail blue booth curtain, and I would start to scream. I would try to escape, and become violent, biting Dad as hard as I could, scratching at him, kicking. On the third day, after he had stopped me trying to jump out of the window, we made a deal together.

'You have to be calm, Kate,' he told me, while I collapsed in his arms, too weak to stand, almost too weak to stay conscious. Another RMN watched on, an older woman who told us she had grown up in Nigeria.

'But they're trying to get food in me.'

'No one's going to do anything secretly. No one's going to do anything you don't know about.'

'They can't do it, they're not allowed.'

Dad held me up then by my shoulders, and looked me in the eyes. 'Why don't we make a deal, darling? We can't keep doing this every time the food comes. Because the other patients have to eat. It's not fair on the other patients to have you screaming, is it?'

I shook my head. 'No.'

'So why don't we make a deal that if I promise no one's going to try and get the food into you through the cannula, you promise to stay calm when it comes?'

It's strange to think of the way he reasoned me back into life, weaving the world into a different order for me, so I could accept things that had terrified me till then. He made it all right when the problem wasn't about food any more, when the problem was about helping other people. He took me out of the minefield where I was trapped, and into a place where I could make decisions.

'OK.'

'Do you think you can do that?'

I was so afraid, so very afraid of letting food near me. I thought if I could only go on a little further, and last for a little while longer, people would see I was right, I could be OK, I would love Joe enough and the guilt might be over.

'I'll try.'

'Because it'll be fairer on the other patients, won't it? And you can't keep being this afraid, my love, it's going to wear you out.'

I still refused to take in anything but water. Nothing else, nothing to pollute my body with calories. And that meant I continued to die. When I went into hospital my blood results were those of a coma patient and I heard the doctor who first examined me compare my physical state to that of an Auschwitz survivor when talking things through with Dad. I would only allow water and vitamins through the cannula. Vitamins wouldn't make me fat. And I didn't want to die, I wanted whatever the doctors thought the vitamins could give me. This wasn't all happening because I wanted my life to be over. I just wanted to get all the fat out of my body. On the third day after I went into hospital I was pushed on a wheelchair through to a side room at the end of the ward, where I started to shake with the cold, although everyone else had taken off their jackets. Without the additional heating of the main ward the temperature was almost unbearable to me. There were three people waiting there – patient and calm and expensively dressed, their smiles so full of understanding, with the light of the day in the window behind them. They had put out a plastic bucket chair for me, but when I tried to sit down it hurt too much, the bones of my legs cut too sharply into me, so Dad helped me down on to a sofa at the corner of the room instead, and the psychiatrists all moved their chairs.

'Sorry about this,' he said, lifting me across to the new seat like a dog being carried into the vet's.

'That's quite all right.' None of them moved to help him. Later, when Dad wasn't allowed to be there all the time any more, one of those psychiatrists told me that all of them had thought he got too involved in looking after me; he shouldn't have been moving me around without the proper training. It was all a bit Bruce Willis, he said, carrying people round. Perhaps that was why they hadn't helped: they disapproved; and maybe they didn't have the proper training either.

Once I was on the sofa I found I couldn't quite breathe without my oxygen mask on, so Dad disappeared for a moment, and went to get the oxygen cylinder, returning with it under one arm.

'Here we go.' He tried to smile, to make it seem like things were going to be all right, then put it on over my head, tucking the elastic of the mask behind my ears, and sat down next to me. He held my hand very tightly, and I turned my attention to the strangers sitting in front of us.

'So you're not eating at the moment, Kate, is that right?'

I hardly knew which of them was speaking. They all smiled at me with the same dispassionate face. It was only a day at work for them. No matter how kind they might have been, they were all thinking of their inboxes, their to-do lists.

'Yes.'

'Do you intend to eat again?'

'No.'

'Why not?'

'I don't need to.'

'Why do you think you don't need to eat any more? How will you live without food?'

'I'll have coffee.'

'But why do you think coffee will give you all the nutrition you need?'

With a triumphant gesture, I pointed to myself. 'Well, it's working all right so far, isn't it?'

There was silence in the room. I felt sure I had won the conversation with this convincing argument. I noticed that Dad had visibly relaxed next to me, and thought I must be doing well. Of course I was doing well, in a back-to-front way. He knew once I'd said that, once I'd insisted with a smile on my face that I would live on coffee for ever and that would be all right, then the judgement was made. I wasn't in charge any more. They wouldn't allow me to die; they would place me under a further section that allowed them to save my life. If I had persuaded them I was sane and deciding to starve myself on a rational basis, perhaps if I had explained my reasons, the trouble I had come through, things might have turned out otherwise.

In a quiet corridor aslant from the bustle of Grandad's house, waiting to use the loo and taking a break from greeting people, I'm stirred from the memory of what I've come through to stand here today by the smiling face of a cousin.

'Hiya, Kate!'

Fiona and her parents come to the party every year, even though they have to travel the farthest, getting up at God knows what hour to come all the way down here from their home on the Wirral. Perhaps being so far from the rest of the tribe means they're more committed to it, and that's why they always make the journey every May.

'Hi, Fiona, how are you?'

'I'm OK. It's been such a long time.'

'I know. I'm sorry. I've been a bit ill.'

'I know, love. I heard. I'm so sorry. Are you all right now?'

I shrug. I didn't want to have this conversation. I don't

want to lay myself open in front of this person I barely know. But I knew what would happen if I came to the party. And I know I have to start sometime. That's why I came here, after all: to start being brave again, carry on reminding myself how I'm supposed to live. 'I don't know really. It's like being an alcoholic. It's there, always, for ever. You just get control.' This is further than I meant to go, really. Fiona probably didn't bargain for this much truth. I could go even further now I've started, try to really show her the way I feel, wake her up to what I've been through, and tell her my favourite image of what anorexia is like, the final image of Primo Levi's book *The Truce*, which I read while I was still in the hospital, ghoulishly devouring tales of Auschwitz because they reminded me a little of myself and hoping none of the nurses would work out what I was reading. At the end of *The Truce*, Levi spoke of the morning call at Auschwitz that woke him every day, the cry of '*Wstawàch*', 'Get up.' And he finished by saying he didn't believe he'd heard it for the last time. He believed that a truce had been called, but it wouldn't last for ever. And a day would come when he would be lying in bed, and the sound would reach his ears again. The sound of a German voice outside his window calling 'Get up,' and the nightmare starting again. That's what anorexia is like sometimes. I can understand why Levi ended up throwing himself down a stair-well to his death. I can imagine he must have heard the call again. I know what that's like, to wait for the voice that will summon you home into suffering. I think, on reflection, I might not say this to Fiona. She probably hasn't heard of Primo Levi, anyway.

'A friend of mine had a sister who died from it.'

'Yeah? I'm sorry.'

Fiona becomes suddenly tearful. 'It's so good to see you. I'm so glad that didn't happen to you.'

'Yeah.'

'More people die from anorexia than anything else, you know.'

I try not to smile. 'I don't think that's quite true. I think you mean it has a higher death rate than any other mental illness. I don't think more people die of it than anything else.'

Fiona laughs. 'God, sorry, yeah, said the wrong thing. AIDS, obviously, loads of people die of AIDS.'

I'm glad I didn't tell Fiona about Primo Levi. 'I think even AIDS is still a bit of a minority pursuit compared to, like, heart attacks and cancer.'

'Of course. I didn't think of them. Of course.'

The loo door opens, and Fiona disappears through it. I wait on my own for my turn.

I began fainting regularly the afternoon after my sectioning meeting, my energy reserves completely exhausted. My body was eating my heart and all my bones were aching. A tube was inserted through my nose after my fourth faint, despite my screams, despite my protestations, and Dad was sent home so the doctors trying to save me could get on with their work.

I stayed in bed in the hospital for four weeks. Dad moved into my room in Bristol, so he could come and see me every day. I still can't bear to think of the tension there must have been between him and Mum in those weeks, when I was still adamant that I wouldn't see her. It must have been hell for him to mediate between the two islands of pain and isolation he lived between, his home and the hospital; to hold them together, and keep them apart. I was unfair on him, giving him all that to cope with, when perhaps what he wanted to be was weak and distraught, to collapse and give way to the grief of what had happened to his daughter. And it must have been hell as well, of course, for Mum. But I made myself ignore that. I told the nurses Mum's name for them to put on a list. They promised they wouldn't let her on to the ward, and because I was over eighteen that was the end of it, of course. I thought if I saw her the walls might cave in. She would sit by my bed and pretend we were close, pretend we were all in this together and she knew what was best for me, she could look after me, and the thought made me sick, I couldn't stand it.

I kept remembering Mum sitting me down on the closed lid of the toilet seat, and running the hot tap.

'What do we think of bad language?' she said in a shaky voice, taking the soap and rubbing it under the water with both her thumbs, so a lather started building. I watched it, burning in the brightness of my shame.

'It's bad.'

'And I won't have it in the house. You understand? I can't let you behave like that.' Mum turned to me, the soap in her right hand, her expression almost imploring. 'Open your mouth.'

'Please.'

'Come on, Kate.' She crossed the room and took my chin in her left hand, and I let my mouth fall open, because there was no point resisting Mum, no matter how hard I tried to make it stop: whatever Mum wanted would happen in the end. 'If you would just listen to me sometimes, I wouldn't have to do this. Why can't you ever listen?' I retched as my mum put the soap on my tongue and scrubbed, as if she was trying to bleach away darkness. The tears came springing onion-sharp into my eyes, and I let them.

'I'm sorry.'

'I should think so too. I should think so, Kate, I—' Then Mum stepped back, and I could see she was trembling. She seemed scared by what she'd done. 'You see what I have to do when you use language like that? What you make me do? Never do that again, all right?'

'I'm sorry.'

She turned away to the sink, and held her hand over her eyes for a moment. 'Stop crying. I don't want to see you till lunch.' Then I was alone in the room, and I let the guilt wash over me, and sobbed my wild heart out, because my mum hated me, my mum thought I was disgusting, and I hadn't even really done anything wrong but I knew I must be evil. I went to the mirror and looked at my eyes, and tried to clean up my face so it didn't look like I'd been crying. I knew that I mustn't show Dad all this, no matter how much I wanted to, or I'd only be in more trouble with Mum. I knew I had brought this sick soap taste on myself, and it mustn't be shared with anyone else.

I still can't quite tell what it was that she hated, unless it was the peaceful hours I took from her, unless it was the simple fact that I existed.

Time and again, my family said the wrong thing to me when they came to visit, all through my time in the hospital. That I was looking well, that I would soon be better, that the hospital was really very nice, wasn't it? All I saw around me was a prison. All I could feel was the bloating of my body. Whenever anyone tried to make me feel better, the thoughts would flare up, and I wanted to tear at my skin. It was damaging enough to hear from friends, but I dreaded Mum arriving, telling me I had brought this on myself, or that I had always liked to milk my illnesses a little, or that my vegetarianism might need setting aside now all this had happened, as if that had started everything, as if it was my own fault and a madness hadn't taken me.

Most of those were things I overheard Aunt Laura saying while she waited in the reception room to visit, over the subsequent months of my treatment. She used to come with Grandma and Grandad. Then after a while it was only her and Grandad who came, because Grandma was ill. That's another thing that hurts now, knowing that I wasn't there for her, that I missed so much of her sickness. And Laura and Grandad dealt with all that, the loss of a wife, a sister, and I've never asked them about it. We never talked about how they were, because I was too deep down in the well of my sadness. When Laura said things that upset me, I tried to tell myself it was just one person who thought like that, and Aunt Laura didn't know what she was saying, she didn't know how to react to what had happened. She expresses love like a woodpecker, battering away; she doesn't understand the subtler tones people sometimes needed to hear. But all the same, it made me panic when I heard her talk like that. I didn't know whether anyone would ever treat me normally again. What if everyone pursed their lips and shook their heads as they walked away from a visit with me, out of the hospital grounds, and thought I wasn't trying hard enough to get better? Or thought I had been selfish to cause so much pain? Or thought I was stupid to throw my life away like this? What if everyone still thinks like that now, and everyone at this party is whispering and shaking their heads to each other when I pass by?

While he sat with me through visiting hours, Dad arranged for me to be released from the contract I had signed for my room in the flat, excused a few months on medical grounds. Dad and everyone else knew ages before I had accepted it that I would be a long time recovering. He arranged with the call centre that I wouldn't come in for a while. I tried to shut out the humiliation of it all, of never being alone, of being watched all the time, even when I went to the toilet. And the shabbiness of using a commode, and having to be helped in the shower, and having to be helped to stand. I tried to smile at my visitors, and tried not to look too directly into the horror of the situation, the depth of my unhappiness, the depth of my fear.

'It hurts so much even to lie here.'

Dad was opening cards for me, showing me the wishes of people who'd heard about what was happening. There was a card from Grandad and Grandma in among them. I had just heard Grandma was ill, and that was like a nightmare to me, another person I was going to lose and me not there for them. The card was comically inappropriate to the situation – a high heel or handbag or something, I think, with glitter. I saw that Grandad had written it. He'd never written a card to me before. Every birthday, every Christmas ever had been marked in Grandma's handwriting; she had been the one who remembered all the dates and signed for both of them. Now I saw how ill she was in the neat and straitjacketed hand of my grandad. He must have stood mystified in front of the rack of cards and then seized on the one that seemed most feminine, pleased he was filling in for Grandma so well. He had tried to write her name differently, in curlier letters, so I wouldn't guess she couldn't sign it herself. I've never told him how easily I saw through it. I want him to think that it worked.

'Do you need more painkillers?'

'No. Yes. I don't know.'

'You can sleep soon.'

The best bit of the day for me and Dad was right at the end, when the other visitors had left, before the nurses had sent Dad away. Then we would share a bottle of fizzy water he brought every day from the hospital shop. It was the only thing other than still water I allowed myself to have; it was my treat, the most precious and exotic flavour in my world. I wasn't allowed very much, because the hospital had me on a strict water diet and I couldn't take on too much, but if Dad drank half the bottle with me then I was allowed my San Pellegrino. So we would sit together, watching the sun go down over Bristol, and say very little, or even nothing, and I would luxuriate in the tingle and thrill of sparkling water, the last luxury I allowed myself.

Fiona comes back out of the bathroom and smiles at me.

'So good to see you, Kate.'

'And you, Fiona. Lovely to chat. I'll see you outside in a minute, yeah?'

'All right.'

Fiona disappears back in the direction of the lawn. I duck

into the bathroom and lock the door behind me, and allow myself to bask for a moment in the happy seclusion of a locked door and a drawn blind, the hubbub of the party sounding distant through the window. I have to admit, it's going better than I expected, today. It seems I might be able to do it all. I can talk to people. And I've been looking around, but I haven't seen Dad or Mum, they can't have arrived yet. There's still time before I have to face that.

It is all about time, that's what I've learned, that's what heals everything, clichéd as it sounds. That's how I got out of the hospital. Slowly, agonisingly, things changed. For a long time the tube in my throat caused me a lot of pain and I avoided speaking at all, even to Dad, but after two weeks a doctor told me the tubes came in different sizes, and fitted a smaller one, and then I was able to talk again. As I left my starvation state behind the fog I'd been living in started to part; I was able to begin seeing more clearly that my life hadn't been worth living when I was very ill, that I didn't want to go back to how I had been then. Getting away from the hospital was more important than never eating again; if I had to eat my way out of there, then I would. The complete terror I'd started to feel about eating eased once my body had energy and my brain could work. After a while I was able to start taking in some of my calories without the tube. There was a coffee-flavoured drink that they gave me called Fortisip. It came in other flavours too, not just coffee, but that was the only one I accepted at first, because coffee had been the last thing I still allowed into my body before the sectioning; when I had got down to the very bottom and stripped all of life away, I'd still been drinking black coffee. The last taste in the world. When I was moved from the general hospital to the specialist unit I eased away from the tube completely, until I took all my energy from those coffee-flavoured drinks. The tube made it easier not to think about the treatment but it hurt, and there was something unhealthy about it too. To have your life piped into you, so you never really knew anything about it. It wasn't how things were supposed to happen to a person. Things were supposed to pass through the net of the senses.

There are photos of my family all over the walls of Grandad's downstairs bathroom: collages of snaps framed together to mark different years of all our lives. Looking around at them, I see once again the beaches of Salcombe where we all used to holiday together, the horses my grandparents kept that Mum and I would ride when we visited, the barbecues, the gin and tonics, the laughter of a family seeming united. I spot us in our raincoats, braving different winters, and down by the sea with buckets and spades. I recognise myself, stubby-legged and just beginning to learn to read, and Mum when she was young and uncertain and too long-limbed to be really beautiful. People caught in old photographs always look like early drafts of themselves to me, unfinished. I never think people look like they've fallen away from who they really are as they get older. All their lives, as they turn grey, as the lines grow deeper, people seem to me to be working their way towards their true faces, until the last face they present to the world is finally like the telling of the whole truth. We are always turning into ourselves, into the finished self people will remember us as having been when we have died, even though we were never really finished at all. Even though our stories might have had other chapters, if we'd just lived longer.

I come out of the bathroom and head back down to join the party. The bar, which I abandoned momentarily, is thronged with people waiting for the single bottle opener I've been using all morning, and I suppose I should go and rescue them all, but I've decided to take another five minutes to be peaceful, so I walk round the side of the stables, and look out at the field beyond the car park, enjoying the feeling of having escaped from my duties for a little while longer.

The specialist eating disorder ward was a calmer place than the general hospital. It was meant to be a community of people in recovery from the same kinds of trouble I had been in. I was in a medical bay at first, under constant supervision, but once I had passed three weeks without using the tube and my weight started to increase again – how I hated that feeling, dough swelling in an oven, the shame of a body distorted by fat again; or that was the image in my mind's eye anyway, no matter how often people told me it was healthy – I was given a room of my own. All the patients had a room, with a big window in the door so the nursing teams could always check on us, but with a view from a window, and a desk and a cupboard and a bed: the nucleus of a life available to us, the very basics. It looked a little like a boarding school. The days were filled with workshops and community activities, a hundred different ways of supposedly nurturing me back into the world.

Whatever it looked like, it wasn't like a school to those who were there. To me the place was like a gaol, and I hated every second. To be trapped; to be shut away from life; to be walled into that emptiness: it was the worst nightmare that had ever haunted me. All I did was eat, and wait for the next meal so I could eat again. It felt like a bitter irony, having avoided eating for so long. All I did was watch life running away from me, convinced the world had forgotten me, convinced that everything was passing me by. It was the same for everyone on the ward. I kept myself to myself most of the time, apart from other patients, determined to focus on getting out of that place, not making friends, but we did talk at mealtimes, and slowly I became closer to some of the young women I lived alongside. The ones who seemed determined, who could help me along. After visiting hours had ended I used to have a menthol with two other girls, Rachel and Ellie, on the balcony at the back of the ward. That was the only place we could smoke, because we were only allowed outside in the garden for thirty minutes each day. The rest of the time we were behind the locked door, in the prison. For the first month we didn't even go outside at all. Then we were given fifteen minutes to sit in the garden. After a few more weeks we were allowed a daily walk as well, and then at last we were given community leave, the chance to go into town for a few hours, the chance to go home for the weekends. Such was our agonising reintegration back into the world. The rest of the time we lay on our beds and waited for the next meal. All the patients fantasised together about the lives we had once had and the lives we might have been having if we hadn't been there. I used to talk about it with Ellie and Rachel. We dreamed of a hundred lives that wouldn't come true. We would plan huge menus of food we wished we could eat without feeling afraid. All of us struggled to pick out goals to cling to. Without a reason to get out of the hospital, with nothing but despair and the constant act of eating to fill our time, it was hard to get better, and sometimes we felt it was too deep and steep-sided a well to climb out of.

I tried to commit to my recovery. I wanted to get out of the hospital, and so I thought of Joe, and what he would want for me, and tried to draw strength from imagining that. I worked with a psychologist to analyse where my fear had sprung up from, how it could be reimagined into something safe. I was enchanted by this idea, that my whole life, the whole world even, could be reimagined. I could make it take a different shape and hold less threat for me, if only I managed to think things through.

A dietician worked with me to plot a route back into health through food. I started to work out the path I had taken to get away from eating, so I could retrace it in the opposite direction. The last things I had eaten were carrots, cucumbers, bananas. Single ingredients with very little in them at all. They were the first rung on the ladder back into life. The last food I had eaten with more than one ingredient had been a soup: pearl barley and tomato and root vegetables and lentils and onions. I made that my next step. After that, little by little, more seemed possible.

I didn't have that much choice in the way I was treated. Still under section, I had to do what the dietician said. I was supposed to eat six times a day, three proper meals and three snacks. It was exhausting, and constant, and frayed my nerves so I used to catch myself grinding my teeth again, digging my nails back into my palms. But they told me it was what I had to do to get out, so I committed to it, clinging to the diet plan they gave me, the yoghurts and biscuits and chocolate milk, because it was a way to not be in the hospital, a way to go home, wherever that might be. I spent six months as an in-patient at the unit on this relentless cycle before the doctors let me become an outpatient. I moved out and rented a new room in a different part of Bristol, closer to the hospital, and Dad paid the rent for half a year. He wanted me back home still, but I wouldn't go, insisted it wouldn't help me. So we set out on the plan I had made for myself, the plan of standing on my own two feet again. Little by little I started to kick the ladder of my treatment away.

That took a long time, and of course the process hasn't really ended, and perhaps it never really will. Once you have an eating disorder, you manage it for the rest of your life. It never goes away. The war is never quite over, even if it drifts right to the back of your mind over time, as it can with some people. I don't know what will happen for me, not yet. I will have to live my life in order to see what becomes of it, and how the song ends. I can't skip ahead and peek. Sometimes I feel like I'm winning, and sometimes I don't, and then I tell myself I'm a bad anorexic for doing so well, and sob out my heart while the dark of another hollow evening spreads around me like blood pouring out of a body. Sometimes I'll still pass a day without eating more than a few pieces of fruit, if I want to, or if I can't manage it, if Sam isn't around and I think I can get away with fasting without having to explain myself. I shouldn't, but I like to exert that control over myself. The idea it all started with, the feeling that I wanted to take hold of the reins of my life, is still there somewhere near the heart of me. Sometimes I still feel overwhelmed by the world around me, paralysed when I'm sitting in a café looking at a menu, or shopping for food, or thinking of getting on public transport and facing the grubby and degrading noise of the world I'm being squeezed through, like sausagemeat into skin. The fear is always waiting for me, ready to claim me, if a day takes a wrong turn. I'll always know that I could one day hear its voice again.

When I came to the end, when I had stripped myself away till only my skin and my bones were left to me, Lizzy had sat and held my hand and tried to bring me to my senses.

'I think you think you're doing this for Joe. But listen to me. The only thing any of us can do for him now is be alive, all right? And stick two fingers up to dying, and prove that life's better than death. You have to see this isn't showing loyalty to him. You have to live instead.'

It was a hard lesson, but I heard it; it reached through the fog of my illness and stuck like an arrow in the centre of me. And so I decided I was going to live, for Joe's sake, for Lizzy's sake, and try to stick two fingers up to death. I wouldn't turn away from the world I had been plunged into. I would find a way to live. And the fall would be hard, and I might break something when I landed. But I would fashion a parachute and live.

I find my way back to the bar to get another drink, fill my glass and look around me. Mum's walking towards me, smiling, determined. Panic floods through me. I'm so scared to see her face after we've spent so long apart from each other.

'Hello, darling.'

'Hello, Mum.' Mum gives me a hug, and I let her, lifting

my hands to rest them for a moment on her shoulders.

'I saw they had you out here running the bar again. Isn't that terrible? You'd think they could run to some proper caterers and let you actually see everyone.'

'I don't mind helping them – they do enough for us today, don't they?' I speak as bluntly as I dare, hating Mum for finding it so easy to criticise others when I know she's never in her life accepted any criticism of herself. I'm shocked at the hostility welling up in me.

'Well, yes, I suppose they do. Now, how are you, darling? How are you feeling?'

I shrug. 'I'm all right, I guess. It's nice being here.'

'Nice seeing everyone.'

'Not particularly. I just like this house.'

'Of course. Lots of happy memories for you here, aren't there? Of course, it's not so easy for me.' She looks back at the house as if it holds some secret, and I don't want to let her get away with that. She's nervous, I suppose, she doesn't know what to say and how to start talking to me. But that's no reason to be cruel to other people, to Grandad and Aunt Laura. There's no reason for Mum to play the victim today; she has no right, she shouldn't be standing here trying to make herself important.

'Why not?'

'Oh, I don't know. So many reasons. Much more than we could ever get into here. Wouldn't expect you to understand. You've always romanticised this place, I know. But I just think of this as a sad place, really.'

'It's a shame you think that.'

'There's nothing I can do about it, and I don't think I should have to apologise for feeling the way I do. It's just a sad, sad home, and I know you can't see it, but there are things you don't see, you know.'

'Well, I think Grandad would probably appreciate it if you kept that to yourself, as long as you're here. I know I would. I'm here to be happy for him, not sorry for you.'

Mum forces herself to laugh. She doesn't look at me. 'You've still got a temper on you, haven't you?'

Why is she sounding so aggressive? I suppose she's hurt like I am. I suppose that always makes people want to lash out.

'I'm just telling you what I think. I'm allowed to do that, particularly if I'm finding you offensive.' Mum turns to look at me now, and I fight down the old fear, the child's fear that I'll be in trouble for speaking out of turn, that I'll get told off.

'Why on earth would you be finding me offensive?'

'Because you're so ungrateful. You're so ungrateful for everything you have.' How have we made our way so quickly into these deep waters? I wish Dad was nearby to mediate between us. I can hardly imagine a way we can ease back into civility from here.

'Are you still working in that call centre then?' Mum asks.

'Yes.'

'How long has that been?'

'A while.' Mum sighs, and I feel angry again. 'What?'

'No, it's nothing, darling, sorry, I'm not trying to argue. I don't want to have an argument.'

'All right, but what are you sighing about?'

Mum's searching for words. 'It's such a waste of your potential. You're a talented girl, you shouldn't be sitting in a call centre, it's going to hold you back.'

'Don't call me a girl, Mum, I'm not a little girl. I don't want you to talk to me like I'm an idiot.'

'The best way of shaking yourself out of everything you've been feeling is to start taking life seriously again. Isn't it? Don't you have to decide that you're going to be well, isn't that how we do things? I know it all happens slower now for your generation, but really, it's not too soon to start building something for yourself, darling, that's the way you're going to start to feel better.' I feel nothing but contempt. I'm not saying anything to that. Mum fills the silence by reaching out and taking my hand. 'I'm sorry, darling. We're fighting, and I so don't want to fight. I'm just worried about you. I'm worried sick. When are you going to come and visit me, my love? When are we going to sit down and sort this out?'

I want to slap her, grab her by the ears, to scream. I want to turn and walk away. This is the woman who told me to move on from Joe, just weeks after the accident; this is the woman who told me I would waste my life if I kept on crying for him.

'You're not doing anything for him, being like this,' she told me, sitting next to me on my bed at home, the childhood bed I never wanted to see again. 'This is just you hurting yourself. There's no point to that. Do you understand? You have to find ways to move on with your life.' And then she wondered why I didn't let her near the hospital; she raged at Dad and asked why she couldn't be part of that illness. I didn't dare let her near me then, for fear she'd tell me I was only hurting myself; I ought to move on with my life. There was no room in her world for grief, no understanding that some things take time, need time, leave scarring that has to heal. And nothing's changed, has it? I can't believe she thinks it's OK to come here and tell me her complaints are important; that our falling-out matters, and needs to be dealt with. It's as if all she can see is her own life and her own needs, all she wants is her own happiness, and she can't imagine the needs or the life of anyone else. I want to scream at her. But that's the kind of thing she expects me to do. That's the way we used to communicate, and I don't want to go back to that place any more. I keep breathing, out and in. I take my hand away from where Mum's holding it.

'I don't know that there's very much to sort out, really, Mum.'

'No?'

'I just don't think we love each other very much.'

I don't look at her. I can't. It's too much, I shouldn't have said it, but I was hurting too much to hold my tongue. I can feel Mum's shock in the stillness that falls aching between us before she finds any words to offer in return. I feel like the party has gone silent around us. I've been too cruel. But then there's another part of me that thinks maybe something important has happened; maybe this was what I came here to say. This was the secret I wanted to get out, the suspicion that has been growing all my life. It isn't that Mum and I hate each other. There's just an emptiness between us instead.

'I . . . I'm sorry you think that. For me, it's not true. It's so not true.'

'OK. Maybe we can talk about it later. I'm busy now.'

'All right then,' Mum says quietly.

'I'll be able to leave all this in a bit. I'll come and find you and we'll have a proper talk,' I say.

'All right. I'll leave you to it then. Bye, darling.'

'Bye.'

Mum turns and walks away, and I know she's crying now. I hate myself for being so cold. I was cruel, really, I know I was. Dad asks me sometimes to try and imagine standing in her shoes, and I can see my coldness must be hard for her to bear. He likes to try and tell me that so much of the trouble between us could be scrubbed away if we just tried harder to understand each other. But I've never been very good at listening.

It was a lie to say that we'd talk properly later. I don't know why I said it. Those kinds of talks never happen; they never get anywhere. They fall apart because no one ever knows how to say what they're really feeling.

When have I ever managed to really say what I'm feeling? No one ever understands what it's like to inhabit this place I've found my way into. I've never managed to communicate that. To be grieving so fiercely, unable to eat, crushed all the time by fear. People tried to make out what was happening, but there was a shore they couldn't venture beyond. So they watched from the strandline and tried to imagine how cold the water must be. Then shouted out from time to time that I really should eat, I really should lift myself up out of the sorrow I was in, and hoped I could hear them over the waves, the storm raging.

I see Dad sidling towards me, trying to check I'm all right.

'Kate?'

'Hi.'

'Are you upset?'

'I'm OK.'

'Did I see you with your mum? Do you want to talk?'

I don't know what there is to say yet – I haven't had the time to think about the conversation. 'Maybe in a bit. I just need a minute, if that's OK?'

Dad nods. 'Of course. Sorry. Just wanted to check you were all right.'

'I'm OK.'

'I'll leave you alone then.' His face fills with love, and then he steps away from me. I step away from the bar myself, take a moment to stand at the edge of the flower bed and be on my own, and forget the people round me, and try to be calm again.

I'm probably standing in more or less the spot where Grandad fell.

He had the heart attack while he was gardening. He hadn't been doing anything particularly taxing, just weeding one of the beds, and Grandma looked out of the window, and saw him lying on the lawn, and rushed out to help him, and called the ambulance. He said later that he didn't remember any of what had happened for the whole of that day. Grandma hadn't seen him fall and wasn't quite sure how long he had been lying there. She only said he was very pale when she got to him. He lay there on the lawn like a fish plucked up out of the river and left on a bank.

I can't stop thinking about the conversation I just had with Mum. I feel breathless, dizzy, full of shocked elation, like a child who's just done something dangerous: defying a parent. A memory, I suppose, of other smaller defiances long ago, of what it felt like to answer Mum back when she was cross with me, or not to have come when I was called. I feel as though I've reverted to some previous age, having gone so long without seeing her, and fallen back into an older pattern. I can feel my heart pumping faster, the adrenaline coursing in me. My breathing's quick, now I pay attention to it. It almost makes me dizzy, this sudden rush. I focus on the walls of the house across the garden, let my eyes rest for a moment on the stables, the light of midday making the bricks sing, and imagine all the stories that must have played out inside that simple brick building. People who died long ago who loved and sinned there, and felt just as deeply as I did, struggled like I did, in their own different ways. If I could only make out all of them, glimpse every day that has flown through this garden, that might be perfect happiness.

As much as I want to ignore it, the truth is that Mum wasn't completely wrong about this place, this house; it isn't all beautiful. A sadness has fallen over it since Grandma died, and everything's very different now from how it used to be. Almost all of Grandma's things were cleared out when she died. And the toys in the barn, and the lost things in the attic, lying forgotten for so long, Grandad got rid of all of them. No one ever really said why that had happened, that striking of the camp. He simply ordered in removal men, gathered things together, and gave them to family, or to charity, and got it all out of the house as quickly as he possibly could. Perhaps he couldn't quite cope with the reminders of his wife all around him. He needed all of her to go if she was going, not just the body she had lived in. I've heard the same story elsewhere, from other mourners. People cope with loss in their own ways. Some cling to any reminder of the person they loved that they can hold on to; leave rooms untouched, that sort of thing. Some determine that they have to go on, they can't get lost in the remembering of what has been. So they strip away all the props and supports of their old life.

It's as if a great storm has swept through all these buildings, crumbling away whole generations of memory and belonging and home. Layers and layers of time have suddenly washed away. Now all that's left of the treasures that once filled those little treehouse rooms in the barn is memory. Now the only place I can still see my face in Grandma's dressing-table mirror is in my head. Only in my mind, and the minds of the others who saw it as it once was, is there any trace of the old glory of this place when it was happy, when it was the heart of a family, because no one ever thought to take a photograph of anything as ordinary as a stairwell or a storage space, to show the life in it and how it really was. I wish someone had thought to do that before it was too late. Instead a time will come when no one will have any reason to suspect that a child once doubled over laughing in those little attics, that sequins and rhinestones sparkled like jewels in the dim light of that barn. Someone will store hay or Land Rovers in there, or simply knock it down, and they will never think of its history, because the world never remembers anyone who passes through it, not really. The world is impervious and indifferent to all of us in the end, and it comes to feel like all the stories that ever rained down on us don't even add up to the names on a list of visitors, the names on a family tree.

Perhaps Grandad didn't know what else to do, or how to cope with the loss, because he never imagined it happening to him. Everyone had assumed he would go before her, after all.

I make my way back to the bar, feeling guilty that I've been standing in the corner of the garden not helping anyone. Chris, whom I also call an uncle but who is yet another older cousin, is helping himself to ale from the trestle table. He smiles when he sees me, and I smile back.

'Don't mind me,' he says.

'You're all right.'

'Your mum being a bit tricky, is she? I saw you were having a bit of a set-to.'

'I think it's probably me, really.'

'People always argue at parties, don't they?' Chris smiles again, and moves away.

I watch the crowd under the marquee. Fewer than eighty people have come, by the look of it. It's still a lot of mouths to feed, but there's undoubtedly an air of decline about the gathering. In my pocket I feel my phone vibrating – a text from Sam. *Sorry I missed your call. I know you're busy now, don't worry about replying. Hopefully speak to you later. Hope you're having fun. Xx*. I could just ignore him, but I decide I want to reply. *I wish you'd told me earlier that you didn't want to come. I woke up thinking you were going to be here.* Then I put my phone on airplane mode, because I've got enough to deal with already today.

I have to be careful, to manage my life, to try and make sure I don't give myself too much to deal with. I'm still in a fight, after all. I still have to will myself into staying well; it's just that these days I'm able to do it, whereas once I wasn't. And that's not nothing, that's a big change. So much has become possible. I'm able to live on my own, and have a job. Perhaps these aren't extraordinary achievements, but they feel extraordinary to me.

*

For a time after I moved back out of the hospital, I liked to go out and stand on the side of the flyover roads that ring round Bristol, and look up to the hills, and think about freedom. Then I'd look down into the river and the road, and up at last to rest my eyes on the stark silhouette of the Clifton Suspension Bridge, watching over everything. Bristol is a suicide's city, the image of that bridge always waiting at the edge of your vision, hanging there like a voice speaking into your head. But there's a story in the city of a woman who fell from the bridge a hundred years ago, and lived, because her petticoats made a parachute and saved her, and I have made that woman my patron saint. I like to think of her falling figure when I go and stand on the flyover. I like to imagine that she was me, because we have something in common – the fall didn't kill either of us.

The man whose arrival took Grandad away from the party comes out into the garden, blinking in the sun. He's looking around, like a boy on the first day of school. No one else seems to notice him where he stands, and he doesn't look like he recognises anyone. He spots the bar, and starts making his way towards me. Halfway across the lawn his eyes adjust to the day, and he realises I'm watching him, and smiles, and raises an open palm in greeting.

'I'm afraid I'm something of a gatecrasher,' he says in a gentle Irish accent.

'I know. I'm Robert's granddaughter. He said he had a bit of business to do with you. I'm supposed to help make sure you don't get interrupted.'

The stranger gives me a searching look. I wonder what he's thinking.

'I see. What's your name?'

'Kate.'

'I'm Frank.' He holds out his hand, and I shake it.

'You're a colleague of Grandad's then?'

Frank smiles ruefully. 'Something like that. I'm an academic myself, but we're consultants on the same project, sort of thing. You know how it is.'

'Sure.' I'm not sure I do know how it is, but there's no helping that. It's strange Grandad was so evasive, if this is all he was doing: talking with some retired academic.

'Grandad was sort of secretive about it,' I say and Frank nods absently, looking over the different drinks on offer on the table.

'I'm sure he was. It's a relatively secret project.'

'Intrigue and high drama?'

Frank smiles and shakes his head. 'Not quite. Just confidential, you know.' He picks up a glass and starts examining a box of wine.

'Do you want me to do that for you?' I gesture to his glass.

'No, don't worry.'

'It's what I'm here for.'

Frank considers this for a moment.

'Well, would you mind? I can't see how to do this, I've never poured from one before. That makes me sound very grand, doesn't it?'

'Perhaps you are.' I take his glass from him, and fill it, and hand it back. 'As you suspect, it's not very good. But it's drinkable.'

'I'm sure it's great.' Frank looks around the garden. 'These are your people then, are they?'

'Some of them, I suppose,' I reply.

'You don't feel much like you belong here though?'

'Not really, no.'

Frank appraises me more closely, his eyes narrowed as he takes me in, and seems to be searching for something.

'It's a very interesting area, isn't it? The way we used to build our lives around our families, and don't any more.'

'I've been thinking the same thing.'

'So what's your story?'

I wonder which story I should tell. 'Me? I'm the usual. A twenty-something looking for something to do.'

'What did you study?'

'English.'

Frank winces. 'That's the worst. You'd be more employable with a degree in surfing studies.'

'I know.'

'Where were you?'

'Royal Holloway.'

'Oh, yes. I like it there, it's all right.'

'It's all right, yeah.'

He carries on looking at me, taking me in, and his eyes seem clear and focused. 'What are you doing for work then, at present?'

'I work in a call centre in Bristol.'

Frank whistles. 'Jesus. Do you mind me asking how old you are? You don't seem so young to me that you still want to be working in a call centre.'

'I'm not,' I say, and leave it at that.

Frank empties his glass quickly, and puts it down on the table. 'Would you relocate for decent work?'

I look at him and he stares back, seeming serious and sincere.

'I might.'

'Well, I work at Oxford. My college library needs an assistant librarian, I think. Would you come for an interview if I could swing you one?'

'God, I'd love to, yeah.'

'There's a lot of specialist training you have to do to be any good at the job. But I wonder whether we could work something out. I'd be glad to see what I can manage?'

I wonder whether I hate that idea at some level. This is exactly how nepotism happens: it's all as well natured as this; it's just meeting people because you go to the right kind of parties. And it's still corrosive, even if people do it with the best intentions. But I shouldn't be turning down this kind of opportunity because of some principle. Everyone else takes their chances, after all. That is how to be alive.

'Well, if there was a chance to be interviewed, I'd love to be considered.'

Frank picks up his glass again, and refills it himself. 'All right then,' he says, thoughtfully. 'I'll see what I can do. It was good to meet you. I'll get your number off of Robert and let's speak again, if you want to.'

Frank smiles, then excuses himself, and leaves me on my own again. I wonder whether he meant any of what he said, whether I've genuinely just been offered an interview for a job at an Oxford library.

from Interview 66

After the bomb went off, I went back to the same café where I'd been given the go-ahead. Right by Southwark Cathedral. I was probably mad doing that, but I was shook up, I'll admit that, and things all felt different before CCTV. I almost expected the guy might still be there, sitting with his briefcase. So strange, a little nondescript gent like that causing so much chaos. That was how I felt about myself as well, little old me doing all that damage. Of course, we weren't really responsible. We just passed the message on, we carried out the will of the leadership. But I felt shook up. I watched this woman walking down the pavement outside while I had my cup of tea. She was looking shell-shocked herself, everyone was, and this young woman was in a daze, when a motorbike pulled up beside her. The guy on the bike took his helmet off, a young guy with a beard, and I could see they knew each other. Not that well, but he'd recognised her, so he'd stopped to see whether she was all right. They talked; I couldn't guess what they were saying. But while I was watching I thought this kind of poetry came into the moment, came out of nowhere and took them over, then took me over too. Because it was amazing, really, in a city of so many souls, on a day like that with the ash from the bomb in the air. He'd recognised her, so he stopped to say hello. And because of that, even the smallest talk was so intense, so beautiful.

Robert

GEOFFREY ARRIVES AN hour later. He must have got straight in the car and headed down as soon as our first call was finished, to have arrived so quickly. Someone in government clearly thinks this is important, too. His driver waits in the lane outside the house, engine running, ready to spring, and Geoffrey walks in through the gates on his own, scowling at the people he sees milling before him. I intercept him at the front door.

'This is a superb atmosphere in which to discuss state secrets, I must say,' Geoffrey mutters by way of greeting.

'I'm sorry. I didn't plan it this way, you know.'

'I suppose not. Where is he then?'

'In the garden with everyone else.'

Geoffrey arches back, recoiling in theatrical surprise. 'You've left him alone with that lot?'

'He's not going to go round telling people why he's here and what he thinks about it, Geoffrey. It wouldn't be in his interests, would it?'

Geoffrey appears to give this some thought before responding.

'No. You're right, of course. Is there anywhere private round here, or should I grab a drink and sit down under the apple trees with him?'

'I don't actually have any apple trees, more's the pity. I'll take you to my study.'

I lead Geoffrey through the house, running the gauntlet of the kitchen again, confident Frank won't have seen the arrival. In the study, Geoffrey sits down heavily in the chair Frank previously occupied, and eyes up the whiskey.

'Helping him feel at home, I see?'

I don't reply for a moment. My eye has been caught by a tiny rent in one of the pictures on my wall. I have seen it every day for years; I can't tell why my thoughts have snagged on it now. A sunset landscape, an empty field, a wood in the distance, a river running through it: a painting I was given long ago by my piano teacher, whose father, an RA, painted it a few years before I was born. There is another painting that Hattie liked which came to me the same way; it's hanging in a room upstairs, in a grander gilt frame: an image of two poachers stalking through a darkened wood. It is the first sketch of a better-known work that was eventually painted on to a larger canvas. Hattie always loved the speed with which our draft had been done, the urgency, the energy in the way the paint was layered on. She loved the life of it. I, myself, always preferred this unobtrusive sunset. I love the light in the sky, the feeling of dream about it.

I remember when the canvas was torn. When we moved here, Hattie put the corner of a hardback book through it in the middle of unpacking. We had been trying to carry too much in the rain, hurrying to keep things dry, and she tripped and fell. It is strange to think how every tiny mark in this room might hold some trace of her. I turn back to the whiskey.

'Would you like a drop yourself?'

'Not for me, thanks. That sort of gesture's going to become impossible very soon, you know.'

'Really? Why?'

'When you get down to it, it's rooted in something racial, isn't it? To offer an Irishman whiskey. Cultural, anyway. You wouldn't offer an African a banana, would you?'

'Good lord, Geoffrey.'

'I'm over-simplifying for effect, you understand. But they're phasing out this sort of thing in Whitehall. No more champagne for the French, either.'

'I imagine those kind of edicts have no effect on anyone's behaviour whatsoever, when champagne is involved.'

Geoffrey laughs. Of the two responses Geoffrey might have had to the ruining of his Sunday, he is taking by far the more productive line, it seems to me. He might have been in a bad mood because he's had to cancel golf or lunch or whatever he had been planning to go on and do with his afternoon, but instead he seems to be treating this as an adventure: a chance to see his old boss's house, and see me, for that matter, and to be whisked through the country in a chauffeured car, powerful and important, trailing secrets behind him.

'I think you're absolutely right,' Geoffrey says. 'People like champagne, don't they? If anything I think it makes it more exciting. Anything subversive is interesting, isn't it? Shall we call him in then?'

'You sound like a headmaster.'

'In another life perhaps I might have been, and I'd have been paid better.'

'I'll go hunting and bring him back.' I leave the room, Geoffrey sitting fat and pleased with himself and his joke in the middle of it. It is strange: there's something very new money about Geoffrey. Even though his family have been around practically since Domesday.

I find Frank in the shade of the lawn's far border, drinking wine and watching the marquee, standing alone as I guessed he would be. 'So sorry to have abandoned you like that,' I say.

'That's quite all right. I met your granddaughter while I was waiting.'

My eyes dart to the bar, where I last saw Kate standing. She isn't there any more. I look back to Frank, feeling hostile, protective, alarmed to think this man I was once so wary of is now circling my granddaughter, and see he has noticed me checking for her.

'I think she went into the house to find a bit of quiet.'

She probably went looking for somewhere to hide from her mother. I have an idea that Kate came to the party today to see her mum again as much as she came to see me, that the point of the day is some kind of reconciliation, at least some connection again. But that doesn't mean it will be easy.

'I see. Geoffrey's here; he's in the study. Shall we go back inside?'

'That's great,' Frank says.

I turn and lead the way back indoors, thinking of Kate, wondering what Frank said to her. Would he do that to me? Would he rope my family into our discussion as a way of making things harder for me? Perhaps. He has no idea, of course, how vulnerable she is. And even if he did, he might still have chosen to gain what advantage he could. I don't really know him.

I show Frank into the office, where Geoffrey is now on his feet.

'Professor Dunn,' Geoffrey says, 'may I call you Frank?'

'Of course.'

'We haven't met before. It's good to meet you.'

'And you, I'm sure.'

'You're here to talk about these Boston Tapes?'

'That's it.'

'I believe you have a perfect understanding of the situation, and you're only really here for reassurance.'

Frank raises his eyebrows, amused. 'I think it would be good news if that were so.'

Geoffrey nods. 'I'm sure it would. Robert has already offered you that reassurance, though, so was there something more you required from me that he was unable to give? Are you after some kind of commitment?'

I wonder at Geoffrey's brusqueness. Perhaps I'm not the only person to have called him out to press flesh and offer reassurances this weekend. Perhaps the car is still running in the road outside because Geoffrey has other meetings to get to, other negotiations to embark upon, other people to reassure. The fact I called him on his home number doesn't mean he was at home when he spoke to me, I realise now; the call might have been patched through to anywhere. Every covert contact the government had with the IRA may have been hammering on doors this weekend, clamouring for his time, trying to understand what was going on.

'I'm not looking for anything more than the reassurance

Robert has offered me, if that's all there is to it, if this isn't some kind of attempt to dig up a lot of old aggro and arrest a lot of old faces, you know. If you can assure me that's the case.'

Geoffrey thinks for a moment before speaking.

'No one will be brought in who doesn't need to be. Though I should add that no one will be spared questioning who is implicated in historical crimes by anything confessed in these tapes.'

Frank bows his head. 'All right.'

'You should know, though, that it's very much not the government position to start hunting people down. The dominant opinion these days is that there ought to be an amnesty, really. I don't see how the communities affected will move forwards until that happens. When the next election comes around perhaps we'll see if we can get that idea any oxygen.'

Frank is listening closely. 'I can tell that to my contacts, can I?'

'You're welcome to. I think everyone affected would agree there's value to the idea.'

'People might find it shocking, I think.'

'They might. But how do we move on, Frank? That's what we're trying to discover.'

Geoffrey turns to me then, and smiles. 'Thanks for letting us have the room, Robert. Much appreciated. I think we'll have no more need to trespass on your birthday.'

I am surprised by that; I almost feel cheated. There hasn't been a show at all. It's all over too quickly. 'Is that everything we need to discuss together?'

'It's a long drive for a short conversation, I agree. But I have a dinner appointment on the south coast this evening, and I don't think these things should be done via telephone. You've heard what you need, I hope?' Geoffrey looks to Frank, who smiles ruefully.

'I think perhaps we've said all there is to say for the time being, so I must be happy and take that home with me.'

'I think that's about right,' Geoffrey says.

'The only other thing I have to ask . . .' Frank adds. Geoffrey seems to be studying him intently.

'Go on?'

'I don't know everyone who's spoken to these interviewers, or what they've all spoken about. But one or two of them are men I've known a long time, men that I've known since my childhood. And I wanted to ask – I don't expect that my name would ever crop up in any of this, because I'm not anyone significant, I'm not some kingpin, am I? But if I were to crop up in relation to something or other, well . . . I knew men whose job was to execute those they believed had betrayed the Army. Those guys, they killed people, you know? That was all they really did, they killed people. And I was *persona non grata* with them, because I came and talked to you lot after Enniskillen. And there were other times when I spoke with you, and I don't know who knows what, and I don't know how all of it would look to guys who've already decided I'm some sort of collaborator with the Brits. Perhaps there'd be danger in it, you know?'

'You'd rather not see your name crop up, that's what you're saying?' Geoffrey asks.

'That's about it.'

Geoffrey nods thoughtfully. 'I don't think any of this ends up in open court really. That's my instinct. Though it's early days. But if some of it does, we can take that on board.'

Frank frowns, uncertain. 'Take it on board? How do you mean?'

'We can edit transcripts to focus only on what's relevant. And to protect people who are of ongoing use to our intelligence-gathering activities.'

'Am I of ongoing use?'

Geoffrey barks out another laugh. 'Well, who knows. But you're standing here now, someone's sent you, someone still knows your number. I won't ask who – I'm sure we know. It's probably in a file somewhere. But you don't have to worry. I'm sure we'd be able to draw a veil over anything that might compromise you, yes.'

Frank seems to visibly relax. 'That's great. I appreciate that, that's great.'

'Good.' Geoffrey claps his hands together, trying to conclude matters, trying to get away. 'Now, if you'll both excuse me, I must get away. Happy birthday, old man. I'll show myself out.' He offers me his hand, and I shake it. Then he makes his way out of the room and to his car, and is gone, and it seems to me in the wake of his departure that things have been left unchanged all around, as if he had never visited. I turn back to where Frank is standing.

'You feel you've heard all you need to hear, I hope?'

Frank seems unsure. 'I don't know what I've heard. I don't think I know any more than I did. If there was some game being played by someone somewhere, neither of you two would tell me about it. I don't suppose it matters. I don't think the people who sent me here are expecting much more than a straight bat from whoever I speak to. But I'll pass the news on and I suppose they'll compare it with whatever else they hear, and look for the cracks in the story.'

'It felt somehow anticlimactic, I think.'

Frank smiles. 'These meetings always are. The tide of the times isn't ever changed by just one conversation. If you or I were ever in the right rooms to make changes just like that, we're certainly not in them any more.'

'I fear those days are behind us, yes.'

Frank shakes his head ruefully. 'I don't mind, I don't suppose. I wouldn't want the responsibility now.' He turns and looks out of the window, and I know he didn't mean what he just said. He is as frightened of coming to the end as anyone else. 'I don't know. The politics of having me drive out here are impenetrable, really. It might have been just a way of reminding me they've a hold on how I spend my hours. You know? And it's a nice game to be able to get a man like him down from London at a moment's notice, and interrupt a day like this one you're supposed to be having. They might have just been enjoying themselves with that.'

'You sound rather bitter.'

Frank laughs. 'I think I am.' He looks at me, calculating. 'Can I tell you something? In confidence?'

'Will you regret it?'

'I don't think I will. I like you. I think I trust you, Robert. When I was a kid and growing up where I was, we all knew who was IRA on our estate. It was just part of our lives, like breathing. It was natural to know people in the IRA, like buying a pint of milk in the shop. And the thing is that I was IRA myself for a time.'

I say nothing, but I could feel my heart beating in my chest, heat on my skin, a restless sense of agitation. I was never told this. Who did the vetting on Frank? Did they just keep that detail from me, or did they miss this altogether, buried as it was under the respectability of who Frank had become?

Frank carried on speaking. 'I found ways to get away from it. I had to pay my way out, actually. I had a cousin who was shot dead by the Brits, and I got my place at university about the same time, and it felt very clear to me just then that there were two different roads ahead, and I couldn't twist them both into the one blade and keep walking along it. So I got out.'

'I see,' I say weakly.

'But before I did,' Frank presses on, speaking quickly, as if he needs to get everything out now he's begun, 'before I did, when I was a kid, I used to help with the transportation of parts for bombs, you see. And I used to help with the smuggling of guns, and play lookout on operations. Throw bricks at the Brits. And I used to participate a little in robberies that funded the Army. That's really what I don't want people to hear about, you see. I don't mind if they find out I used to talk to you, that's all right, I was trying to do good, even if everyone wouldn't see it that way. But I used to be another person, and I want that to stay buried. I used to live another life. I remember it sometimes, it feels like the flip side of me, this other side of my story that never got told. I don't want anyone to tell it and I worry a little that something could be on those tapes – just a name; sometimes all someone has to do is name a name and the world unravels, doesn't it? I like that old idea, if you know the name of a thing, you somehow own it. Rumpelstiltskin. There's a lot of truth in that.'

I watch Frank carefully. He isn't looking at me. 'I never knew all that,' I say.

'Does it change the way you see me?'

'Of course it does.'

'Well, then. I'm right not to want others to know then, aren't I?' Frank smiles, but he looks downcast. As if the thought of the past is dragging the life out of him.

'I think perhaps you are,' I say.

'I'm sorry I told you. I don't know why I wanted to share that with you.' He sighs, and turns to the window, where the late-afternoon sun comes filtering in, catching the crystal of the glasses on the desk. 'We get old, don't we? And we never get to talk about the old days any more, because no one remembers them. And sometimes it's nice to remember. I knew Enniskillen was coming, you know.'

I look at him sharply. 'What do you mean?'

'The guy I used to work with back when I helped moving bombs into place, he was still at it all those years later. None of them had blown up in his face, or whatever, and he hadn't been caught, so he kept on. And I knew there was something coming because he said as much to me. I always think I should have gone to you earlier. But I wanted to find a way to not be involved. I thought that would be sticking my oar in.'

'Bloody hell, Frank. You knew an attack was being prepared?'

'And I did nothing. And I live with it. I have to live with it. That's really what I don't want people finding out about, you see, that's what I'm worrying over. You can't go near something like that conflict and not end up with blood on your hands. There'll be blood on yours too; we both know it.'

I say nothing. He's right.

'Listen.' Frank seems to suddenly focus, to shake himself out of the sadness that had taken hold. 'I spoke to your granddaughter about a job. I hope you'll forgive me. I know a college that needs an assistant librarian; she seemed like she needed a break. It's not a political offer, it won't ever come back at you, I give you my word. I enjoyed talking to her and young people need breaks, that's all there is to it.'

It takes a moment for what he's saying to sink in. My mind is still on Enniskillen, on the man in front of me, who I thought I knew once, but has turned out to be someone quite different.

'That . . . that's very kind of you, Frank. Did she seem interested?'

'I thought so. She might have been being polite.'

'I must say, I would take a very dim view of my family being roped into any kind of—'

Frank holds up his hands in supplication. 'I promise you, Robert. I give you my word. No strings attached.' He picks up his bag. 'I'd better be going, I think.'

'You won't have another drink before you go?'

'I have to drive.'

We shake hands; the ritual is closing. 'Well then. Drive safely.'

'Enjoy the rest of your day,' Frank says. He turns and walks away through the house to get back in his car and drive away, and I look sadly at the whiskey on the table, the scene played out, another intrigue over. On the wall above my head, my piano teacher's painting watches impassively, and my eyes are drawn to it again. Incredible to think so many years have passed and I haven't taken the thing to a restorer to get that tear closed up. I am so glad now that I didn't; that there is an imperfection up there on the wall to remind me of her. I take a deep breath and head back out to the party.

I notice that Laura is no longer in the kitchen as I walk through. I find her in the doorway at the front of the house, looking out at the cars parked densely together, drink in hand. She must have seen Frank leave.

'Everything all right?' I ask.

She starts when she hears my voice. 'Oh, yes. Just having a breather.'

'I don't blame you. You've earned it.'

'Everyone's eating.'

'It's wonderful. It's extraordinary, really, when you think about it. What you do here every year. I'm so grateful to you. Everyone's having a lovely time.'

'You're not involving yourself in it though.' Laura looks up at me sadly, and I find I have to avoid her eyes. The guilt of having absconded, even for as short a while as it has proved to be, leaves me a little speechless.

'I'm afraid something rather unexpected came up.'

'That'll be why there was a chauffeur outside in the lane? I went out and offered him coffee but he said no.'

'That was kind of you.'

'I do all this for you, you know.' She faces me and fixes me with a look. 'There's no pleasure for me to be had from it if you don't want to take part. I do it all because she would have liked it; she would have wanted it for you. And I loved my sister very much, and I want to do right by her. In memory of her. You understand me?'

I shift uncomfortably. I feel wounded.

'She always used to work to make everyone happy,' Laura continues. 'That was what gave her pleasure. And she wanted you happy most of all. You were a lucky man. I don't know where she got it from. I was never as nice as her. And you remember Mother, of course. Mother was a terror.'

We both smile then, because it was true, she really was, though I'd never have said so when Hattie and Laura's mother was alive.

'I'm sorry I've been absent.' I think of saying more, but I don't know what I can say to Laura. Here I am, surrounded by family for an all-too-brief day, and still chasing after my work. When that has been over for long years, when it is only a phantom now.

'Don't apologise to me,' Laura says. 'Just get out there and mingle a little.'

'I will. I'll make more effort, I promise you. I'm sorry. I do appreciate it all, so much.' I think it would be unwise to say any more, but some impulse compels me to go on speaking. What is wrong with us all today? Why are the words flowing out? 'I know you and I haven't always been as close as we should have been, Laura. I know I've let her down in that.'

Laura turns away from me. 'I don't think she'd want you to feel like that.'

'No, you're right, she wouldn't. But you and I both know the reality, don't we?'

She looks at me again, and I am shocked by the sudden

discovery that she loves me. Laura loves me, and I love her in turn. We are the only route either of us has any more back into the memory of Hattie. I never saw till now quite how closely that binds us together. How much of our lives we have shared after all, though we've always felt far apart from each other.

'It's all right, Robert. We don't have to have big conversations on busy days, it's not the time for them. Why don't you go and finish your work, and I'll go out to the lawn and talk to people?'

'It's all right. It's all done.'

She looks hard at me, staring fiercely into my eyes to check I am telling the truth, then smiles. I suppose she believes me.

'Well, that's good news. You can get out there and do your speech now.'

I roll my eyes. Every year I have to give a speech, that has always been part of the day, and I always hate it, standing there, everyone looking at me.

Laura laughs. 'You go through. I'll refill this and follow in a second.'

I leave her, and come to the brink of the lawn, and look out at my family and my friends. Once, I would have looked for Hattie among them all. It's hard not to look for her now. It's hard not to listen for her laugh somewhere. I remember the sight of her moving among people on the days of other parties, a glass in her hand, seeming always so elegant, so happy with these people around her. I remember the feeling of pride when she turned and looked for me, when our eyes met, and in the midst of the gathered crowd the two of us shared, for a moment, the secret of having been in love with each other all our lives. I sometimes think very few people really know that feeling, but I feel sure I did. I feel sure in the way Hattie used to come over and take my hand, and kiss my cheek, and tell me I was late to give the speech, that we loved each other.

People see me and stop their conversations. Of course, I have been away from them; I have missed the lunch and half the afternoon. My absence must have cast a pall over things all day, and now everyone is waiting for me, more or less consciously.

And aren't they used to it by now? How have I been so fortunate to know people who will still travel to see me like this, when I have kept them waiting all my life? It has always been that way, really, though no one ever talks about it. I have always been away from them, doing other things, and everyone else is left behind. I wonder how many shadows I've cast through my life, which others have had to walk in. The party falls quiet, and I see Laura with her glass filled smiling at me, urging me on, so I raise my hand to ask for silence. Just beyond the people on the lawn around me, just beyond the limits of the day the eye can see, I can cast my gaze back across years, across all the time I have spent in this place, and I can see Hattie standing slim and filled with laughter on this lawn, lifting our baby up in the air as if to kiss the sunlight. I can see her turning to laugh with me, and the little cloth hat Hannah wore, and the yellow dress she had on, and Hattie's dress pale air-blue and bright and lasting for ever in the memory, in the sun. And I can see the spot where I had my heart attack, no more or less beautiful than anything else circling me now, no more or less human than everything else I have experienced. It has been part of life, and that is beautiful. I was weeding, the garden fork in my muddy hands, tired and unused to the exertion, of course. I had the soft weak hands of a pen-pusher, a presser of flesh. And I paused for a moment, stooped over a particular spot of the flower bed, and stared in bewilderment at the horseshoe I had unearthed from the ground beneath my feet. Twenty yards from the stable, and securely concealed underground, waiting for me like a secret. It must have been flung there once, long ago, kicked off by a horse, abandoned by someone who lived there before me – there was no way of knowing who. But the memory came to me of the time Hattie called to say Hannah had been kicked by her horse, and that she had been flown by helicopter to the hospital at Southampton. I remembered how clear and sharply defined every detail of my Belfast office seemed to me then, my senses sharpened, my heart rate accelerating at the discovery of danger to my family. And I remembered how another twelve hours passed before I got on a flight. How I had concluded the work on my desk, signed off a couple of purchases, and attended a briefing with the minister which I had felt unable or unwilling to delegate to anyone else, before I finally allowed myself to pack a bag and head home, to find my way to my daughter's bedside, and discover that she was in the operating theatre, and Hattie had sat alone for hours with no knowledge of what was happening to our child while I concluded my business abroad. How could I have done that to her? The guilt of that memory, the way I had failed time and again over all those lost years to do the right thing, and love the people closest to me as well as they deserved, washed over me, and that was when I felt the pain in my arm, and fell to the floor, and was taken in turn to the hospital. Was it the guilt of how I had lived my life that did that to me? Is that possible? Or was it only the exertion of an afternoon's gardening? Do we get all we deserve in the end, or are these things just chance?

I thought there would be time to make it up to her, and learn the lessons my life had to offer, and love her as I thought that she deserved, but things turned out differently. A few years later, she started complaining of always feeling tired. And so she went to the doctor. And that was the start of the end, and then it was too late for ever. At the end I tried to tell her I was sorry, tried to tell her it had always been for her, even when work took us far away from each other, but she wouldn't allow me to let it all out. It was too late by then, I suppose. The past had stopped being important for her, because she had so little present left to get any talking done. Better to talk about the reasons we had been happy. Better to talk about why we had loved our life together.

'I'm grateful, that's how I feel, I promise you.'

We both knew that wasn't the whole of the story. You can't only be grateful when you know you're going to die. You can't only say that you're ready, you've lost enough in the years that have gone, you're prepared to go on. You're always angry and afraid as well, as you lie there sweating your life out in the hospital bed. But she wanted to end our time together with a smile, and so she found one, and she wore it as gracefully as everything she'd ever done.

'I don't know why you'd ever feel grateful for having to put up with the likes of me,' I said.

She laughed, quietly, in the back of her throat. 'You brushed up all right. You were a rough enough diamond, but I brushed you up.'

It seems sometimes as though the beats of a life never end, but sing on for ever, echoing through the landscapes where they happened, waiting always for you to dive back in. I can see Hattie here, just beyond the corners of my vision, just out of sight of everyone else, the woman I loved, our baby in her arms and the light falling soft through the willow. I draw myself up to my full height and start to speak.

'Thank you so much, everyone, for coming today.' I look around for Kate, but can't see her. I feel close to her today. It isn't just that she arrived before everyone else. I feel our different losses make us closer kin, somehow. 'I'm sorry to have disappeared for a little while. I hope you will forgive me.' There's nothing else to say about that, is there? I abandoned them, really, and it is done, and what is the point of apologising further? 'It means such a very great deal to celebrate this milestone in the company of my family.' I wonder what I'm going to say about Hattie, how I can adequately remember her in the presence of all these people. I find now the thought is in my mind that I can't do it. Not this year, not again. I can't put myself through it. I stood in front of many of these same people in the church last year at the funeral, and spoke about her, and that is enough, that is all I can give. It is too raw, too awful still to be looking back in that way as we all journey ever further on without her. 'Of course, today is also a day filled with memory, as much as it's filled with you, and I appreciate very much this opportunity to think about the people who can't be with us today. We remember them, though they no longer remember us.' I stop. For a moment I stand in silence. 'So I'd like to raise a toast now to everyone who used to stand here with us, if you'd all like to join me. Let this day be about them, as much as it is about anything else, certainly as much as it's about my birthday. Because it's never been about me, not really. That's never been why I loved this day. It's always been about all of us.'

I get through the toast, drink back my drink and smile, then break the spell of silence that always circles around speeches with a nod of my head, and turn to the person standing nearest me, a cousin of mine named Matt. Matt is the son of my aunt's eldest daughter. For a long time he didn't come to these parties. He fell out with his brother and sisters so badly that when their mother died, he wasn't informed, and missed the funeral. He was left nothing in the will. He has struggled a little in his own life, losing his driving licence in his twenties because he was pulled over full of drink, and losing his job as a result of that. Of course, he has recovered after a fashion, but people never quite get over a thing like that. All the momentum goes out of them after such a setback, and some of the hope. It is frightening how the slightest snag can set you back for life. That is the fear I have for Kate, that she might take the same course Matt has, that she might never reach the mountaintop she once seemed to be bound for. Does it ever occur to Matt that his life is a poem just like hers is, that his dreams move me, his dreams are mountains? Of course not. Hardly anyone ever notices their lives are that kind of important. People are too worried about the washing-up, the holiday arrangements, the rent.

'That was lovely, Robert,' Matt says.

'Thank you.'

'A lovely thing to say.'

'Well.' We smile at each other, neither of us knowing what to say next. There is so much to talk about in anyone's life, we end up not talking about any of it. It's impossible to know how one might ever start crossing such mountains and meet.

'Did you get anything nice for your birthday?' Matt asks.

I despair, and put my hand on Matt's arm. 'That reminds me. Will you excuse me for a moment?'

'Of course.' Matt pats me on the shoulder with a meaty hand.

I turn and walk away, across the yard, into the dark of the barn that is still open from when Kate and I collected the trestle table in the morning. I stand as still as I can, and am silent. She is gone, my love, and I try, but I just can't bear it. I can't get used to it. Nothing gets easier. She was here, and that made everything all right, and now she is gone, and how am I supposed to live? How does anyone live without that prop to support them, the other half of their life? Who am I supposed to talk to when I become afraid?

I hear footsteps behind me at the door of the barn, and pinch the bridge of my nose, trying to compose myself, then turn to see who has followed me. I suspect before I see her – it is Kate.

'Are you all right?'

'I'm fine. It was all just a little overwhelming for a moment.'

'You're upset.'

'A little. It's all right. I'm all right.'

'Are you sure?'

'I think so.'

Neither of us speaks for a moment, and she knows I'm pretending as clearly as I do. My hands are shaking slightly; I can feel them. It feels strange to be speaking to each other in a new role. We have never played out this scene this way round before. It was always me picking Kate up after a fall, a graze on her knee, or finding her hiding under the stairs when she was sad. Or visiting her in Bristol while the dieticians coaxed her back into the world. But I suppose all the roles we ever play are temporary. Everything is recast in the end. It makes me feel so weak, to be leaning on her now, to be relying for strength on a girl who was a baby in my arms just a moment ago.

The truth is that I'm not all right at all. I have never been so old before, and I will never be so young again, and every minute of the day I grow slowly weaker. I start speaking again, and feel barely in control of the words as they roll away from me, hardly aware of what I am going to say before I say it. 'Sometimes I feel like I'm being punished. Or I'm going mad. It's been a year now, but really, all that stages-of-grief non-sense, it seems to me to be absolute rubbish. I don't think you ever get used to any of it. Because she's gone, hasn't she? And it's just, I don't know. It's just very sad. And it's infuriat-ing. I don't think it would even help me very much if I had the sort of faith that allowed for the possibility of a meaning-ful afterlife. Because I know I sound like a spoiled child, but I don't want her then, I don't want to wait, I want her now. I have been so bored and lonely and angry since she died, and of course you can have perfectly good conversations with other people, but it's not the same.' I glance at Kate, who looks as shocked as I am at how much I'm pouring out. 'No one else knows about all the other conversations I had with her, all the years and years, so there is no real stake in any conversation I ever have with anyone any more. No one else gets all the jokes.'

'I'm sorry, Grandad,' she says, and I know I must have embarrassed her.

What am I doing? This isn't fair. She doesn't want to hear all the troubles I carry. She has her own that she is coping with today. Everyone has their own, really, that is the secret to people. I wish I could find a way to bring my daughter and granddaughter closer together. I remember the way Hannah used to cry while she held Kate and tried to rock her to sleep, when she was just a baby.

'I can't do it, Dad,' Hannah said. 'It's too hard. I wasn't ready. I didn't know it would be this hard. I don't know how to do it.' Somehow, in the months after Kate was born, Hannah convinced herself she didn't deserve what she had been given. It set a pattern in the lives of both women that has never broken since. I wish I could have shown my daughter when she was young and things might still have been mended that she was good enough; she did deserve the luck that had come to her; everyone found life difficult, that was normal, that was all right. It didn't make her mad or strange. But I didn't know the words to say, and the moment passed, and by the time the vulnerability in her became clear, the die was cast for ever.

There ought to be truth and reconciliation in every stratum of the lives people live. All that laying out of things shouldn't be only reserved for the public sphere, the fractures in families are just as complex, just as terrible. I wish I could have sat them both down and talked things through. Perhaps I have got the balance wrong. Perhaps I ought to be trying harder to make a difference.

'What have you been discussing in your office all afternoon?' Kate asks. 'People are worried about you, you know. Has it upset you?'

'No, it's not that. I'm sorry I've been away from everyone.'

'It's all right. As long as you're OK.'

'You're very brave to try and get back to talking to your mother,' I tell her. 'I know that's part of why you're here today. I think it's very brave of you. I know it's hard, but we have to keep trying, don't we? Because family is what we have. Family is what will save us when we need saving. You and I both know that.'

'Yes,' she says, 'you're right.'

'Your mother wasn't well after you were born, you know. It was always a struggle for her.'

She puts her head on one side, puzzled. 'What do you mean?'

'It was postnatal depression. That was how they diagnosed it in the end.'

'I didn't know that.'

'She doesn't like to talk about it. I think it makes her feel ashamed.'

'Why?'

'She felt that she'd failed.'

'But if it was only just after I was born, that's a bit early to write the effort off, isn't it?'

'She found it very hard. It took her a long time to see how

she was going to cope. She always felt she'd let you down.'

Kate doesn't say anything for a moment. Have I done the wrong thing, telling her that? I wasn't sure whether she already knew it or not. If she could only see: they are both just frightened of each other; it's just that they can't break through to each other.

'She never told me that.'

'She holds her secrets close, your mum. You might understand that, I think.'

Kate smiles, in spite of herself. 'Maybe so. You're not so different yourself, you know.'

'I suppose I'm not.'

'We all keep too much to ourselves in this family.'

'Yes.' That was my job once; discretion used to be important to me. Perhaps I have prized that quality too highly, and taught my family to hold their stories in when they should have been sharing. Perhaps I should have had more regard for the value of simply opening up and talking.

'I thought it was wonderful, that you stood up like that, and said what you did,' Kate says. 'It must have been so hard. Grandma would have been very proud of you.'

'Perhaps. It doesn't help though.'

'No?'

'No, it doesn't help. All anyone wants is someone who likes them best. Someone who will put them first. I think that's all we need, really. That's what I find so hard, that I had someone. I had all that happiness. And now she's gone. I don't know whether we'll have any more of these parties after this year,' I say.

Kate looks surprised. 'Why not? Don't you enjoy it?'

'I enjoy it all very much. I think it's very important, to spend time with family – I think it's the greatest pleasure there is. But it could become very mournful if we plough on too long, couldn't it? Don't you think? And I'm eighty today, and that seems as good a milestone for bowing out of this sort of thing as any. I was forty when we came here – I've been throwing this party for half my life. Time for a break, I think. I've come to a good round number. If I don't wrap it all up now, I'll have to wait years for another good round number to tie things up.'

'Do things have to be tied up with a round number? Can't they just end when they want?'

'Oh, I don't know. People say it doesn't matter how many chapters a book has. I think it does, really. If you're paying any attention, a thing like that surely means something.' I glance out at the day through the barn doorway, at the house and the empty sky behind it, then back to Kate and the silence growing in between us. 'I'm sorry. All day, I've been talking too much.'

Kate steps forward and puts her arms around me. I feel the heat of her body, the sudden childlike silence linking us, and hug her back. It is closer than any words have brought me to anyone in so long, simply to share a hug. It says more than I know to explain, and I suddenly feel perhaps she understands me after all.

'It's all right,' Kate says. 'It's all right.'

I stand, a hand placed on my granddaughter's back. I hadn't recognised how lonely I felt today, not really. I can feel my shoulders shaking. I try to breathe, and the tension eases. I realise I am crying. I have started to cry, and Kate doesn't mind, she is happy to wait like this while I close my eyes and admit to myself how tired, how frail, how on my own I am feeling. I didn't realise anyone else could see it, the fear in me.

I have gone wrong so many times, taken so many turnings I regret, now I look back over them. And when Hattie died, I didn't learn the lessons of the years I had lost that might have been spent with her. I grieved on my own, I stayed here rattling round the house, when I could have been going to see Kate, and Hannah, and helping them both, and trying to bring them back together. Why didn't I think of that? Why didn't I try to be more like Hattie, and make people happy?

And the thought comes to me: It's not too late. You're still alive – just about, old goat; you can still do something about it. So why not act on this impulse, this sharp, clear moment, and earn the sympathy you're getting today?

I will change. I'm not too old to change. I will try and be someone Hattie would have been proud of, try and be someone who can help Kate. I will try and unlearn the circumspection of a lifetime, and be there for my family, my daughter and my granddaughter, the people I have been so proud of all my life.

from Interview 83

Back in the long ago, before Gaddafi got into supporting the IRA, every rifle that got into Ireland travelled the same way, behind a false panel in a locker on the QE2 *from America over to Southampton. From there it headed up to Liverpool or Holyhead by car or truck, only ever one gun at a time, mind, and then someone smuggled it into Ireland and into whatever arms cache was lined up. You couldn't dream up a system so inefficient, but that was the way that was open to us then. I was the guy used to run the scam on the cruise ship. I'd load the weapon on to the ship then load it off to someone at the other end. They used to rotate whoever picked them up, made it easier to track. One stranger after another, always the same kind of raincoats no one would remember, always the same kind of nondescript car no one would pull over. They'd take the gun off me and load it into the boot of their car, and then they were gone, and we never said much to each other.*

Kate

PERHAPS IF I were to tell the real story of my life, I would do it by writing a dream diary. That's where I see myself unfettered; there's no pretence in dreaming. In my mind's eye I appear as stupid or romantic or angry or afraid as I really am, and the pictures expressing my life don't have to conform as they do in life to what has physically happened to me, they only have to conform to what seems true from where I'm standing. A dream can't tell the whole story of a day, or a life, but it can be a way of telling the truth. It's the bubbling up and the clotting together of all a person's feelings, and perhaps that's a way of getting at the heart of them.

The strange thing about dreams, and the thing that makes them faithful, and the thing that makes them reliable as a way of understanding a person, is that they never stop happening, they never abandon anyone. We always dream. A person who achieves their ambitions simply finds the horizon has receded a little further, and goes on travelling towards it. A person right at the end of their life will still find when they fall asleep in their hospital bed in the evening that the brain needs to tell itself stories, to process experience, impose a shape on the images which have assailed it in order to make sense of them. Dreams, as far as I can see, are as natural and inescapable as the shadows people cast when they stand in the light.

I think if I could only keep hold of them all, and fashion the dreams of my life into one long chain, perhaps I might be able to make out the route I've been taking, and see where I'm aiming for. It will never be possible, of course. I will have to be like everyone else, and live in the space between reality and dreaming instead, and cling to what clues I can find to the code that would decipher me, if only I could ever make it out.

I emerge blinking into the sunlight outside the barn, and see my parents walking towards me, separating themselves from the crowd of people still milling around on the lawn. Dad speaks first, tentative and hopeful.

'Your mum said you wanted to talk to us.'

'That's not quite what I said, is it, Mum? I said I couldn't talk to you now and maybe I'd talk to you later.'

Dad flushes, distressed. 'I'm sorry. I didn't realise.'

'I just think we need to have a conversation, love,' Mum says. 'It's time we sorted this out.'

I suppose there's no point giving more of the day to evasion. If I wanted to hide, I shouldn't have come to the party, after all. 'All right. What do you want to sort out?'

'Why don't we all get a drink before we start?' Dad says. 'We're not in a hurry, are we? We just want to have a chat together.'

'Fair enough.' I shrug, moody like a teenager.

We walk to the bar and help ourselves, and I know both Mum and I are boiling inside, hurt and angry. In many ways we could be twins, really; we think the same things at the same time, and perhaps that's half the trouble.

'All right then,' Dad says, holding his glass of wine to his chest as though it might keep him safe from all that's about to happen. 'I suppose me and your mum wanted to talk to you because we want to know you're safe. That's all we care about. We just always want to know that you're all right. Of course, we both know it's best for you to keep yourself to yourself, while you're still getting better. And we know that's a long process and we want you to know we're here for you, as long as you're doing that, as long as it takes. We just want you to know that we love you very much. We're here for you, all the time, whatever you need from us.'

It's so difficult to know how to respond. I don't want to hurt Dad's feelings. I love him. I owe him everything. He saved my life by stepping in when he did. But there doesn't seem to be much honesty in simply biting my tongue, in staying silent.

'I think that's probably what you want to say, Dad, and thank you, but, Mum, I don't think that's what you want to talk about, is it?' I look Mum in the eye. I feel scared, but I won't look away. I will be strong today. We are going to actually talk to each other. Mum stares back at me, and it seems like defiance to hold her gaze. I wonder how dangerous a confrontation like this could be for me, how close I could come to sliding back into the black places I've been to if I have an argument with Mum now.

'I do wish I knew what I'd done to you,' Mum says. 'I do wish I knew what I could have done differently so that you didn't hate me.'

'Hannah,' Dad snaps at Mum. He is embarrassed and upset.

'It's all right,' I say. 'It's OK. People are allowed to feel what they want. It's all right you think that, Mum, it doesn't upset me. I don't know what I'm supposed to say back to you, though. Because we've said it all before, and it doesn't get better.' That's the trouble between us, really. I've tried explaining to her that she makes me feel unhappy. I've tried not speaking to her when that didn't work. But the problem is still there, tight like a knot, nothing moves it.

The first time I ever had a drink, I was standing here with my parents. For some people it's vodka at a friend's house, or lager at a bus stop, but I was trying to decide between Coke and Dr Pepper when Dad put his hand on my shoulder.

'Do you want to have a glass of wine, Kate?'

I was eleven years old, and the weather was hot that year. It was warmer than today; the sun seemed to beat down on us, golden. Perhaps that was only the colour of memories, but all the same that's how I remember it.

'I don't know whether I'll like it.'

Mum, who was standing next to Dad and watching us, leaned over then and gestured for a glass. 'You should try it and see, I think. For a treat. You might think it's nice.'

So I poured myself a half-glass of white wine, and took a sip, and didn't really understand why people were so keen on it, but finished the glass anyway. And my parents drank glasses of their own alongside me, and laughed with me at the faces I pulled because it tasted so tart and I wasn't used to drinking anything that wasn't fizzy and sweet. I remember walking with them over the lawn and sitting down on a bench that has fallen apart in the years that have passed since then. We watched the crowd: Aunt Laura drinking too much among them, and laughing too loudly, and Terry, one of the neighbours, laughing with her. Mum said she thought Terry and Aunt Laura were getting on very well together, and Dad laughed, as if she had said something much funnier than she actually had. Only now, thinking back, do I understand the joke. I can see the three of us, sitting together, all facing in the same direction. I wonder what I thought I wanted from life back then. Perhaps I didn't know. Perhaps I was still happy not thinking of the future, and going with my parents to visit my grandparents, and the world didn't yet seem big or frightening at all. I look at my parents now, and see how much taller than Mum I've grown, and can't help feeling like I've outgrown all those memories. I wish I could still be filled with that much hope, and feel that free of any worry, any care, and able to concentrate only on the taste of wine, the way the light passed through the glass when I held it up, the way Aunt Laura's laugh seemed sharp enough to crack glass.

'We're not here to upset you, Kate,' Dad says.

'I know.'

'It's so hard to have to watch from a distance, darling,' Mum presses on. 'We're left feeling so powerless.'

In a strange way, I know what she means. I came here today hoping it would help Grandad somehow. But it seems there's nothing I can do. When I followed him into the barn it was because I thought I recognised something in him during his speech – I could tell he wanted to curl up and turn into fire, into nothing, and not be speaking any more with all eyes on him. I know that feeling. I used to think it was only me that felt it. It frightens me now to see him so vulnerable. I tried to say something comforting to him just now, but I can tell it didn't help. So this must be what Mum means, what it was like for my family to visit me while I was ill, that fretting, powerless feeling when you see someone's hurting, and don't know what to change. All day, the humanity in Grandad has unnerved me. Have we ever spoken to each other before like we have today, as if we are equals, as if we might reach the different islands of one another's feelings? I wonder whether I have ever really thought about what it must be like for him now, properly set my mind to what it was to be him. Too often it's easy to think of someone like Grandad as being no more than the role he plays in my own life, not as a person who struggles with flesh-and-blood feelings. What he told me about Mum makes me wonder if I've been thinking of her that way too. An extraordinary thought – that under their different skins everyone I've ever met is feeling the same things I am, experiencing the same little dramas. All the problems of their lives seeming as vast to them, as all-consuming, as my own are to me. And does that mean all those problems must be important, and the world is completely beset around? Or might it mean that, actually, none of it matters at all?

People put up screens between themselves and their endings. I think that's how they cope. I suppose everyone needs a project to focus on, an image to hold their attention, so they don't have to think of what's next. When you're my age they can be very ambitious constructions, they can take in the span of a whole life. As time passes, the scale of what can be imagined changes, until the goal you set yourself has to happen sooner, if you want to be sure you can finish it. In the end, those projects all shrink down very small, to the seeing out of the year, the weeding of the garden, the making of a cup of tea, the taking of one breath after another. But people still call on their screens. Anything not to think about the ending until the time comes when you have to start puzzling out what that will mean.

On the day we're born, the future lies infinite before us, and all our lives can be spoken of as lying in the future. Then a change, a migration begins. Little by little you journey away from the place where you started, and start to grow a past for yourself, and trail that out behind you. In the end, a day comes when you have no future left at all, only the past tense to speak in.

What nothing in the world ever changes, though, is the present. The present is always only one day long. It's always now, and everywhere, and endless. And that's the most important screen we have to protect us – the world we're mired in, distractions and details and miracles of the everyday.

'I'm sorry you feel that, Mum. I really am.'

Dad can see that we're both becoming emotional. 'All that matters to your mum and me is that you know we're here for you. That's all you need to know. We're going to be here for you when you need us, when you're ready, we'll be there.'

I don't know what they want me to say to them. I wish I could tell them we could forget it all. I look up at the car park, and stop, surprised by a familiar figure. I only glanced across the roofs of the cars because my eyes were caught by the light. But someone is standing at the mouth of the drive, uncertain, silhouetted in the lengthening light, and when I look for a second time I realise it is Sam.

I thought the day had unspooled all it held for me already. I didn't see his arrival coming. I watch him over the roofs of the cars, looking around, taking everything in. All day I've wanted to be furious at him because he made me feel lonely, but now I see him there I find I can't feel angry. I want to feel happy that he's come, that he cared enough to give up a day. Even though I'm tired by everything around me. Even though he's arrived late, now all the heart is wrung out of me by talking to Mum, by remembering, by watching my grandad feeling so alone. For a moment I think of hiding, ducking out of sight, behind the wheels of a car, staying there till night falls and I can slip away, and then going home to Bristol, or maybe London on the run. Or I could turn now and flee from him, over the fields, stay in flight all through the hours of the dark till the morning, and see where my feet might lead me. I dreamed of that time and again when I was a girl, turning my back on it all and running away. I really wanted that. Does everyone young pass through that phase? But I'm old enough to see now that it wasn't a dream worth having. It wasn't anything to build on, the idea of getting away from everything. All your troubles come with you wherever you travel, and in the end they have to be faced down, and peace has to be made.

Grandad has just appeared in the doorway of the barn. He spots the young man standing in the driveway, looks back at me, and smiles. I guess he knows exactly what's happening.

'Hannah, will you help me with something in the marquee for a minute?' he asks, striding towards us. Mum looks at him, confused, her face still tense from our conversation, but follows him across the lawn anyway. Dad gives my arm a reassuring squeeze, and heads after them. I turn to face Sam where he stands, twenty feet from me, nervous like a first date, like a stranger.

He must have come in a cab from the station, which will have cost him far more than he had to spend, and he's looking for me. I walk towards him.

'Sam.'

He smiles in relief that I'm there, that I've found him before he had to go searching for me. He comes forward and we meet in the middle of the yard, and he kisses me, and I let him, but I don't kiss him back. I don't know yet what I'm feeling.

'Hi,' he says.

'You're here.'

'Yeah.'

'You weren't going to come.'

'No. I'm sorry about that. Stupid. Is there somewhere we could talk?'

I raise my arms and gesture round us. 'Not really. It's pretty busy everywhere here today.'

The party's breaking up, and people are starting for home. Already the young parents have left to start preparing the evening meals, and plates are being tidied away, and soon there will be glasses washed in the kitchen sink, bubbles climbing one above the other as the washing-up liquid lathers and dances round Laura's hands. All the work of the day will disappear as miraculously as it first came together; it will all be lost as if it never really happened. Men will arrive in a van to take down the marquee, and night will surely fall, and that will be the end of it for another year, the day of the party gone. We probably could find somewhere quiet to talk. But I don't want to make things easy for him. He hasn't earned that.

'OK.' Sam steels himself. 'Look. I came because I fucked up today. I realise that.'

'Right.'

'I should have come this morning. I don't know why I didn't. I got scared, I think. I was worried about meeting your family or something.'

'Why?'

'I don't know. The same reasons everyone is. And I think I have a bit of anger towards them as well.'

'What about?'

'Because they let everything happen to you. Because they didn't protect you enough from what happened. From getting ill.'

'What more could they have possibly done?'

'I don't know. I'm not saying it's rational anger. I'm just angry.'

'OK.'

'But as soon as I sent you that text I realised I'd fucked up. So I came to say I'm sorry.'

'OK.'

He risks a smile at me, and I smile back, because I like him. I can't help it; he makes me happy. I wish he'd arrived in the morning, but it still feels good to know he's made the journey now.

'And I've been thinking.' He becomes serious again. 'While I was on the train, I was thinking about us. I don't think I make it clear enough how important this is to me. And how much you mean to me. I don't know, I don't feel like I tell you enough. And I want you to know that you matter. And this isn't just a thing, you know? I care about us.' He takes both of my hands in his, and looks at me.

'All right,' I say.

'So I think I need to stop being such a loser, really. I need to stop not turning up for you, you know?' He pauses, uncertain for a moment whether to go on speaking. 'All I ever wanted was someone who liked me best. And put me first. I never had anyone like that. I always wanted that. And I feel like you've wanted it too, since I've known you. I don't know. I don't want to put words in your mouth. I've just been thinking a lot about this while I was on the train. But I suppose I feel like I want to tell you that I like you best. Of everyone. And I want to put you first. And I hope we might feel the same way about each other, even though I'm a dick and I bailed on you today.'

He looks young and frightened, no matter how sure he sounds, and I suppose it's because he's risking himself. I look in his eyes, and it feels like everything I need to be able to live might be there waiting for me. All the strength it will take to get through might be there, if I lean on him, if I take his hand, if I love him. All anyone needs is someone else who matters to them. Is that Sam, then? Can I find what I need in being with him?

'OK,' I say. 'It's cool of you to have come, after all, so OK.' He smiles at that. 'You know what this means though.'

'What?'

'You have to meet my family.'

Sam laughs. 'I thought that would probably have to happen if I came to their house, yeah.'

'You OK about that?'

'Yeah.'

'Just try not to be angry at them or anything.'

Sam shrugs. 'Fair enough. Where are they all?'

'That way.' I point to the marquee, and we start to walk. 'Was the train crowded? I always find it's really crowded from Bristol to Salisbury. They don't put enough carriages on.'

'I had to stand all the way, yeah.'

'And there's no 3G most of the way, so you can't really use your phone, so you get bored out of your mind standing around.'

'That was all right. I had a book.'

I watch Sam slyly from the corner of my eye as we walk together over the gravel. He's like a mystery to me, like a book that I want to read and haven't started.

I see that Grandad is standing with my parents, which makes things easier. I can get all the introductions out of the way in one go. Mum will find it harder to do anything stupid with the whole of her family around her. I approach them. Dad sees us first.

'Hello, love, are you all right?' he says.

'Fine. I just wanted to introduce you all to someone. This is my boyfriend, Sam. Sam, this is my dad and my mum and my grandad.'

'Pleased to meet you,' Sam says. He smiles and steps forward and shakes each of my family's hands in turn. I feel calm again now. The thing with anything frightening that ever has to be faced is that you only have to be brave for ten seconds. After that, it's done, and things can be easy again.

'Where have you come from, Sam? I don't think I've seen

you around today, did you just arrive?' Grandad asks warmly.

'I travelled over from Bristol.'

'Oh yes? Did you drive?'

'No, I can't drive. I failed my test, and now I can't afford lessons, not on a student loan.'

'You're at Bristol?'

'Yes.'

'That must be a lovely place to study.'

'It is, yeah.'

'So you caught the train, and got a cab from Andover?'

'That's it.'

'Very good. They never put on enough carriages from Bristol, do they?'

Sam grins. 'I had to stand all the way. But it wasn't too bad. I just stuck my head in a book.'

Around us, the paraphernalia of the celebration continues to be dismantled. And just beyond the limits of our vision, another day of our lives is falling away, unrecorded and unremarked, packed up with the tables and chairs, the plates and glasses. Whenever you see a person washing up a cup, if you look close enough you'll see them consigning something for ever to memory.

That's how the whole world goes. No tape will be made to stand for us after we're gone, and speak what we believed in. None of us matter like the people in history books, the people in movies.

from Interview 88

It was still dark, and the customs boat was bearing down. I knew we were fucked and they'd seize what we had on the boat. I remember the sky was very clear, stars out, and the light had just started lifting. Then the chop of the waves against the hull, and you see the light of the customs boat right on top of you, and hear the voice coming over the loudspeaker. I wondered who'd forgotten to pay the right guy off, how the hell it might have happened. I wondered whether the guns we were carrying would make it into the press, or whether the police would suppress the news. I thought of the old guy in the tweed suit who'd met me at Liverpool and supervised the pick-up, Fred or Frank or whatever his name was, but I wondered whether he'd been picked up and all, whether this was just a fuck-up at one end, or maybe customs had rolled up the whole operation.

Robert

WHEN THE DAY has ended I send Laura home, insisting I want to clear up by myself. She has done enough, I tell her, and I haven't pulled my weight, and she deserves a rest, an evening on the sofa. Most of the hard work has been done by the last of the guests already; they brought all the crockery and glasses into the kitchen, and helped put the bottles into black bags, and took the bags to the gate. What is left might well take the rest of the night and the next morning, putting on the next wash and running a dishcloth over the last one and storing it all back away again, but there's no way of hurrying it along, it just has to be done, so I might as well do it myself. Two people won't make the dishwasher get through its cycles any faster. And it isn't hard work to prepare the glasses for returning to Oddbins and potter round the house putting things back in order. Out on the lawn, the men from the marquee company work, and know their jobs, and need no help or supervision. I'm not going to let Laura stay and look after me, although I know she wants to see things through to the end, like the captain of a ship. But I tell her I don't deserve it today.

'Don't be silly, Robert, it's not a question of deserving or not deserving anything. I'm here to help.'

'But I can't do anything for you in return. I never do anything for you. So let me do this small thing, and save you the last of the lifting, seeing as you've already done everything else since first thing this morning.'

'You're looking at this all wrong.'

'Perhaps I am, but that's how I'm looking at it. Go home, Laura. Have a glass of wine and get a good night's sleep. I'm so grateful to you for everything. I feel so guilty you did so much. Please don't do anything more.'

She leaves, unhappy to be going, uncertain as to why exactly I am getting rid of her. After so many years of prickliness, she seems to view my insistence that I am thinking of her comfort with some suspicion. We're a work in progress, Laura and I. I suspect we always will be.

I am angry about the business with Frank and Geoffrey. I never saw so clearly how petty it all was before. The futility of it, the smallness of the discussion I arranged, and I surrendered the whole of a day. It feels like a bitter betrayal to learn that Frank knew about the planning of Enniskillen. Such a possibility never occurred to me for a moment, and I am bewildered by the reversal. It strips the relationship we shared of any vestige of trust, any sense of achievement. He could have said something, surely, if there was any bond between us. And he didn't. In all the years since, he never owned up to it, not until he thought he might get caught. So what did our collaboration ever amount to? I helped him take a place on the right side of the narrative, among those who had sought reconciliation, that was all. I helped him cross the floor on to the right side of history, when he was part of the conspiracy that killed those people all along.

My mind is so full of Frank that I can't quite concentrate on saying goodbye to Hannah. She and Michael are among the last to leave, and help pack up the things on the lawn, and put the chairs back into the house, and return the trestle table to the barn.

'Thank you for another lovely day, Dad,' she says.

'Do you think it was?'

Hannah shrugs. Of course, she knows what I mean. There's no one in the world who is closer to me any more, not really, so perhaps she always knows what I am thinking.

'Will you stop these now?' she asks. There it is again. She knows what's in my mind as well as I do.

'I think I will.'

'Probably for the best. It's sad though. Mum used to enjoy them so much. And so did we because they made her happy. We don't need to pretend we enjoy the business of seeing everyone like this any more, do we? You least of all. You've done your share.'

That is what I have always wanted, really – to have done my share. And perhaps in some ways I have, in some walks of life. And perhaps there is still time to do more, to be of some use to my family.

Hannah gives me my present, a map of the county she found somewhere and had framed, and wishes me happy birthday. 'It's terrible without Mum here, isn't it?' she says.

'Yes,' I say, 'it is.'

'I'm proud of you for getting through it.'

'Thank you.'

'I almost didn't come. When I got up this morning I thought I couldn't. I wasn't thinking.'

'Too painful?'

'I just thought I'd make it too hard for Kate. And I knew she was already here, and I knew she wanted to remember her grandma. I thought maybe I should stay away.'

'I'm glad you didn't,' I say. 'She came here for your mum, yes, and to support me, just like you've supported me by being here. But she came here to see you as well.'

'Do you think?' Hannah's voice wavers, and I see her shoulders drop a little, as if she'd been hunching them up without noticing until now.

'Of course. You have to be ready for it to take time. And it might not work just yet. But I think deep down you both want the same thing.'

'I hope we do.'

'You handled today well, you know. I was worried there'd be a scene.'

'Thanks, Dad. I tried, it's just – I don't know how to say it to her. I don't know how to say I'm sorry that I wasn't a good-enough mum.'

'None of us feel like we're good-enough parents, you know,' I tell her. 'I'm sure I wasn't. Half the time I wasn't even there.'

'You had your work.'

'I still felt guilty, all the time. It's part of being a parent. You work out with hindsight how you might have got things right, and it's hard not to regret the errors. When you think of the stakes.'

'Yes.' Hannah frowned, and seemed to be thinking deeply. 'That's it.'

'I know all this has hurt you. The way you haven't spoken.

But maybe you'll come out of it now. You never know, maybe you'll get there.'

'Maybe. Anyway. I ought to go.'

'All right. I love you, darling. Chin up.'

'Love you too. I'll go and find my things.'

Michael is waiting behind her at the edge of the room for his turn to say goodbye.

'Thank you for coming today,' I say. I can't help still seeing the man standing in front of me through the filter of the boy he once was. I've never quite got used to the idea that this man married my daughter. It's very hard to give people away.

'Thank you for having us.'

'Do you think things were all right between Hannah and Kate?'

Michael casts about, clearly wondering what to say. 'Perhaps they were as good as they could be. It's a slow process. There's a lot that wants working out.'

'Well, yes.'

'Time will tell, I suppose,' Michael says. 'People talk a lot about failure to launch. Have you heard that phrase? They use it about young people. The graduates who move back in with their parents, that sort of thing.'

'I think I've read that, yes.'

'As a rule it's an idea that I disagree with. I don't like the idea that everyone's career ought to be some great acceleration. There are people who are happier having life happen to them, and drinking it in, you know.'

'Of course.'

'But I think of that phrase a lot when I think about Hannah and Kate. Failure to launch. Sometimes, that's what it feels like. Something never started between them. Never sparked. I ignored it for a long time. Till Kate was ill, really. You can ignore so much, unless something comes along and really makes you look at it. Of course they love each other, but I don't know whether they ever really reach each other. I don't know what to do about it.'

'I don't know that any of us do.'

'But they do love each other.'

'Of course. '

We're both trying a little too hard to persuade one another, I think.

'Well, we ought to be going. Thank you, Robert. Thanks again.'

Once Hannah and Michael have driven away, I go back inside and stack the dishwasher in the way I like to load it, and run the hot tap till I can't hold my hand under it, then start to fill the sink with washing-up.

There are days my life snags on and I keep circling back to them. These are the roots of all I do, and if an observer were to lay those days lodged in my memory over the surface of my present, perhaps all my life would be explained, all problems solved, all wounds revealed. That has always been the beautiful thing about throwing this party – it's like hearing the refrain of my life return, the recapitulation of a theme that has shaped all the music, to gather the same people into the same place at the same time of year, and watch us all changing, and dance the same old dance. But this will be the last time. Without Hattie the heart has gone out of the ritual. I can't do it again. I'll retire from the entertaining business. I can only hope that in time to come, years after I have departed maybe, Hannah and Kate might look back on this as having been the start of something, the beginning of a thawing, of spring between them, and find today has turned into one of those curious, unexpected moments their lives snag on as well, the days that lend the rest of life their pattern and their meaning. Then perhaps this last party, with all the colour drained out of it, might prove to have been worthwhile.

The meaning of your life can creep up on you very suddenly. A day you didn't see coming; a person you didn't expect you were going to meet. Perhaps today will turn into part of the meaning of everything for them.

When the dishwasher finishes its first load I take out a stack of plates and carry them back to the dresser. I could have got Kate and her boyfriend to do the heavy lifting, because they are staying the night, but they have gone out for a walk together, and I didn't want to bring them back to earth from wherever they're wandering with dirty plates.

In Ireland, starving was always about honour. The old way among the peasants of that country, as I understand it, was that if someone had wronged you, you sat down at their doorway and went on hunger strike. And if you died there at the person's door, they were forever dishonoured, and reparations would have to be paid to the family of the deceased. To get the hunger striker up from where they sat, amends had to be made for whatever wrong you'd done them, and then they'd eat again. That was the history the IRA were drawing on, every time they used the hunger strike as a weapon. A history rendered sharper and more bitter, of course, by the horror of the famine in Ireland, which had seen so many poor people fall down at the feet of England, and fail to find salvation there. Perhaps that was a dishonour to England. And perhaps the turbulent memory of Bobby Sands and the nine other men who died on the hunger strikes in Long Kesh prison in 1981, which still echoed round the offices I had worked in when I arrived in Belfast, was spoken of so quietly because they brought a kind of shame on England. Certainly, I think the trouble that brought Kate so close to death is a shame on this country. On everyone who never helped her. On a society that put so much pressure on that poor girl. On myself, for not making any difference. I went in and saw her when she was in the hospital, travelled there with Laura and on my own, but I couldn't help her. The news of the disaster reached me like a rumour, passed beacon to beacon from miles away.

In my own youth, anorexics simply died, there was very little else for it. Or a few of them, if they seemed mad enough to whichever doctor examined them, were put away, and God knows what became of them then, but psychiatric hospitals at that time were not places one ever really emerged from again. Those people, I suppose, were consigned to a life's forced feeding. We should be glad those days are gone. I live through an age where gifted people have worked very hard to understand a problem, and as a result, an illness that would have killed my granddaughter when I was young has been turned into something she can live with, and recover from, and perhaps one day get clear of.

It seems like luck, the way it comes and claims you. Good luck and bad luck befalling you drop by drop, till the steady flow is a whole life, enough to fill a story. I don't like to believe in luck, not really. I tried never to allow for chance to play a part in any of my professional life: I was always a meticulous planner. But when you look at a person's life, that is sometimes what it seems like. Things just rise up and claim you, and mark you for greatness or mark you for tragedy, and the route of your life is mapped by forces entirely beyond you.

I look out of the window at the garden. Kate and Sam are returning to the house, holding hands, walking close together. It is beautiful to look at her, and see her surviving, and taking hold of what she can of the love in the world. She has come through. She can walk through an evening holding someone's hand again. She can smile in the light of evening as if nothing else matters.

In the storm of a life, there have to be arms that hold you, or the whole world can come to seem too terrible to face. I always wanted to protect Hattie from everything; I thought the job of a husband was to stop all harm ever coming to the one you loved, ever again. But Hattie died, and then all my ambitions were revealed to have been futile all along, to have been the ideals and dreams of a boy who didn't know the truth about anything. Sometimes people just die, and nothing can be done about it. I hope it still mattered to Hattie that I longed to protect her, and cared, and tried as the days ran down to keep doing what little I could. Perhaps it helped a little at the end of the long day to find at least the person you had ended up loving would have kept you safe, if there had only been a way for them to do so.

In the last days Hattie looked out at me from inside the prison of her body, and still her eyes were the same eyes I had always loved. I sat with her and held the hand of the love of my life, and we stayed silent, and looked at each other, remembering our yesterdays. They told you to try not to cry, because the dying need people to be strong around them. I cried every day. We had been so happy, and it seemed so unfair to know everything was ending. A heart attack was kinder. Something unexpected, something quick. Or if it were only possible to come and go like swallows, and never know that in a moment's time you would fly back out of the hall you had been momentarily passing through.

When she died it was her eyes that went. The eyes I had loved and kissed when we were young, when we were a boy and a girl in Oxford and courting, that went blank at last and told the end of her story. I closed them then, and kissed her for a last time, and she was released from the pain. I held my pain close to me, and guarded it, and never wanted to let it go, because no matter how much it hurt, it was all I had left of her now. It was all I had left that seemed worth keeping. Because what else could matter to me ever again, now she was gone? I am glad I had the time I did with Hattie; I am grateful for every kingfisher I ever saw; I am grateful for every evening I spent outdoors. The rest was noise.

Kate and Sam come into the kitchen, tired and smiling.

'Are you all right, Grandad?' Kate asks.

'Quite all right, thank you.'

'I wish you'd let us help.'

'I'm happiest getting on with things myself. Quite preoccupied today.'

'You know even if we don't have any more parties, you're not going to be able to get rid of us,' Kate says. 'We'll still turn up for your birthday, and take you to the pub maybe, and there'll be nothing you can do about it.'

Few are as lucky as I have been. I've been lucky all my life, because there have always been people who cared what happened to me.

'Oh yes,' I say, 'I hope we'll still have a gathering.'

They are beautiful, after all, the afternoons I spend with my family. It has been a great privilege to live them.

from Interview 93

In the eighties, I was part of a squad set up to go after high-profile targets. The assassination of a high-ranking Brit caused significant disruption, and also drew significant attention, of course. These kinds of wars are all about publicity. You're always telling the story of what you do, everything is an act, you're telling the story with every act. We used to get together drinking in this pub and identify potential targets. Usually we'd go after anyone. Sometimes people got ruled out because they were difficult to get to. Every now and then you'd get a veto for some other reason. They wouldn't let us go after Betjeman because he was a poet. Can you believe that? And there was a guy came to these meetings to run the rule over things on behalf of the leadership, and cross names off the list if he had to. If he thought they were diplomatically useful. Frank Dunn, his name was. Did a lot of messenger-boy work. He liked to say he kept his distance but he was the kind of guy had a hand in everything, I think, he just didn't leave much trace. Academic kind of guy, he had a job at Queen's, then ended up over at Oxford. He used to rule people out because they were more use above ground, kept out of their coffins. Like there was this civil servant we wanted to go for one time, say, there was a guy called Robert Shawcross. We thought we could get to him, but Dunn said he came in handy after Enniskillen, so we had to leave him alone.

Kate

SAM AND I stay at the house overnight, and it isn't like when I stayed here with Joe. We have a dinner of tomatoes and bread and cheese with Grandad, and then he suggests we might both sleep in the same room I slept in last night. I feel like a grown-up, to be allowed to take Sam to bed with me. And I feel sorry for Joe, because he was so young; he should have been right at the start of so many stories, but the world chose a different fate for him.

In our room, I sit Sam down on the bed and take his hands in mine. 'I want to tell you something,' I say.

'OK.' Sam eyes me warily.

'You said this afternoon you wanted to take me seriously. And I want that. I'd love that. I want to take you seriously too, and see what happens. So there's something you need to know that I haven't talked about before.' I look around me at the confines of the bedroom, the big dark wardrobe, the free-standing mirror. I wonder where to start. 'I spent the night with Joe here once.'

'Oh, right.'

'Grandad put us in different rooms, so we waited till we thought he'd gone to sleep and then Joe crept in here with me.'

'I bet your grandad knew,' Sam says with an involuntary smile. 'Bet he was testing you. Might have thought less of you if you stayed in your own rooms.'

It's a surprising thought. 'Why do you say that?'

'I don't know. I just like your grandad, I think he's cool. And old people were young people too once, weren't they, they know what happens. He was probably just testing you.'

I shrug. 'Maybe. Anyway, that's not what I wanted to tell you about.'

'What do you want to tell me?' Sam looks at me kindly, trying to put me at ease, and I realise I'm afraid he's going to judge me or hate me, or decide there's too much distance between us for him to cross after all. I try to breathe steadily, but I can feel my lip starting to shake, my eyes filling.

'I've told you about what happened to Joe,' I start, and allow myself to remember the night for a moment. I remember the call when it came, where I was sitting in the old flat in Kennington, the programme I was watching at the time. I remember the run to the Tube and the heat as I stood helpless, pressed against the doors, wishing I could somehow travel faster. I remember Lizzy's face at the hospital, the way she had to tell me what had happened to the boy we both loved.

'Yes.' Sam squeezes my hand, and waits, knowing not to speak while I search for words.

'The thing is that he isn't dead.'

Sam doesn't speak for a moment. 'He's not . . . ?'

'No. I just don't see him. He lived through the accident, but he was very disabled by it. He has no speech, no mobility. He has a respirator and he's in a bed, in a hospital in London for people who'll never get better. I used to go and see him at first. And I used to tell myself, no matter how much it cost me in here' – I beat against my chest to show him what I mean – 'I'd always keep going. I'd always sit with him for the rest of his life and not leave him alone. But I couldn't do it. I couldn't keep visiting him. It hurt me so much, and I started to get ill – you know what happened to me. I started to get ill and I just couldn't cope any more. So I stopped going to see him. That was when I left London. That was when I ran away.' I'm crying now, the tears running down both sides of my face. I do nothing about them. This is the story I never talk about with anyone, the shame that burns me from the inside out every minute of every day I am trapped in like amber, the cloying guilt that drowns me. 'I thought if I just got some distance from him, I could get back control of myself. I used to just go there and sit by him on those plastic chairs and cry, because I couldn't do anything for him, and that wasn't good for him. I think I upset him whenever I was there. So I thought if I went away for a month or two, I could go back and be strong for him. But nothing changed once I was away from there. I felt just the same. So I couldn't go back, because nothing was any better, everything hurt just as much. More and more time passed, and I didn't feel any stronger. I just stopped going. I abandoned him. I think that was why I started to punish myself, you see? I think that was how I got ill.'

And then after all that, when I was coming out of all that suffering, I had met someone. I had kissed another boy, and allowed the thought of life moving on to enter my mind. I look at Sam where he sits on the bed beside me, and know that part of the reason I need to tell him this now is that being with him feels like another betrayal, no matter how happy he might have made me. The worst feeling of all is being willing for life to go on. He'll need to understand that, if we're going to take each other seriously. He'll have to help me see the time I spend with him in a different light to the bleak cold light of the betrayal my whole life has been washed in since that night.

It was a long time before I let another person near me. Only my father, and Lizzy, and no one else. After the accident I spoke to no one except Lizzy for a little while, because no one else seemed real. The times we both visited Joe were the only times in my life when I believed that I was where I was supposed to be, no matter the pain the visits caused me. So I clung to her friendship, because Lizzy helped me get through the sorrow of those hospital hours, with her kindness, her patience. She found a way to be glad that Joe was alive, when sometimes I couldn't see one. She seemed to really believe it was better he'd lived like this than died, and that held me together for longer than I could have managed on my own. And no one else ever quite understood, and whenever I was anywhere else but there with Joe and Lizzy, I felt I was far from any sense of home, far away from the centre.

Sam still hasn't said anything. I can't tell whether he's giving me the space to keep talking, or just taking it all in. He nods again, then reaches out to dab with his cold fingers at the tears on my cheeks.

'I'm so sorry,' he says quietly. He looks stunned.

'I'm sorry I haven't told you. I didn't know how. It makes me ashamed that I can't get back to him.'

'So you don't go any more?'

'I can't. I think about it all the time, but I feel like I've failed him. I don't deserve to go and see him any more. I haven't gone there since my diagnosis.'

Sam swallows. 'It must make it very hard to be with me.'

I feel a rush of love for him then, hearing him understand. 'Yeah. Sometimes it . . . it feels like letting him down again,' I say.

'I can see that. So, are you trying to tell me . . . I mean – would you rather not be with me?' Sam looks at me, his face as innocent and kind as it always is, and I smile.

'No. I would really, really like to be with you, if you don't hate me for keeping that secret. I just have to learn how. And I have to ask you to be patient. Because it might take me a long time. To know how to be close to other people.'

'I get that,' Sam says.

'Do you?'

'I think I do, yeah. And you know what, that's all right. I can be patient.'

'Do you want to be though?' I'm waiting for him to tell me what he really thinks, to get up from the bed, to walk out and leave me.

'Yeah. I'd like to. I mean, if you'll let me try,' Sam says.

'All right then.'

'For what it's worth,' Sam says, 'I don't think you've let him down. I think you got ill. I don't think he'd think you let him down. I think he'd see it was pretty clear how much you loved him.'

He puts his arms around me, and for a moment I could swear I'm playing out two scenes with two different boys in this room at the same time. Sam could almost be Joe, those brief years ago, sneaking into the bedroom in the midnight's pitch-dark to hold me. I could swear that I'm living both feelings for an instant, as the days of my life weave into one another. And why not? Every gemlike, brilliant, different day meets with the past in the end, and becomes an irretrievable part of it, and perhaps in the mind's eye it's possible to leap and glide from one to the other.

It's only a passing illusion, and it's falling from me now like a dress from my shoulders. No one ever goes back. I thought of Joe because I would have liked to see him again as he was, just as I would have liked to try being young again, but that's another time now, another life really, and this is different. So I hold on tight to Sam and we lie down together, awake and silent, side by side and not saying a word till late into the night.

Sometimes I think I'm an island. Bound all round by sea, and all alone, with no hope of ever reaching out beyond myself, ever making land anywhere else and reaching some other person. Sometimes I think I'm adrift on a raft, and way beyond sight of the shore I set out from, and paddling in hope that there's an island out there somewhere waiting for me, caught in the tides as they turn me away from the direction I'm longing to travel. All I know is that I live held fast in the empty, vast embrace of the blue sky, the bright water, the loneliness I have learned to call being alive.

The following morning we have breakfast with Grandad and he gives us a lift back to Andover station, where they're putting up one of those second storeys to the car park made of scaffolding, like the ones you pass at Farnham or Fleet. The old flour mill looms half-derelict above it, and suburbia stretches out street after street on every side. We catch a packed train to Bristol, standing all the way.

By the next morning I've decided that I'll let things with Mum lie quiet for the time being – but not for ever. We didn't get very far when we talked at the party, but at least we tried. I still get angry and petulant like a child when I'm around her, and I hate myself for it, and don't want to bring out that side of myself. So it's going to take a little more time. I'll carry on meeting Dad in public places, and we'll have lunch, and I'll send my love to Mum through him, because that's all I can offer for now, but at least it's a start. Dad will forgive me for being so difficult. We're close, and nothing can interrupt that closeness now. He saved my life. I expect it makes him sad we're apart, because families are supposed to be all together, really, and he must want that as much as any other father. But it isn't really so strange for distances to grow up between people. Children always grow a little apart from their parents, just as the branches of any tree strain away from the roots and up to the light. I know that a time will come when I'll have to be strong, and speak to Mum again properly. I've realised, spending time with Grandad, that my parents are going to grow older. I don't want to run out of time to have the conversations we need to have. At some point, we have to decide what we want to be to each other in the final reckoning. Although that time is a way off yet, as far as any of us can know.

I get a call from Grandad the following week to say he's given Frank Dunn my number. The following day, I get a call from Frank himself, asking me whether I would still be interested in the assistant librarian position that he mentioned was coming up at his college. A week later, I go to an interview, imagining it'll most likely be a waste of time, just an excuse to spend a day seeing the sights in a nice city, a favour that won't quite come off because no amount of goodwill will compensate for my lack of experience. That isn't quite how things turn out. I'm offered the position the following week.

I talk to Sam about the offer. Really, there's never any question of my doing anything other than accepting. So we agree to try to make it work. If we are supposed to be together then a few miles between us for a little while won't matter all that much. Sometimes these long-distance relationships pay off, after all. I move to a village called Eynsham, a twenty-minute bus journey outside Oxford, and set about learning the lines of a new life, and Sam and I start to visit each other at weekends.

I love the library from the first time I set foot in it. The quiet and the beauty of it, the calm, and students bent over their books, and the invisible work of the library team holding it all together. A lot of my work is administrative, keeping the shelves in shape, that sort of thing. I get to help the archivist a bit with special collections as well, a big collection of medieval manuscripts and the books and papers of a theatre critic and the library of a poet. I like cataloguing all that. People's libraries are a window into who they were, a map of their thinking, their lives. That's a fascinating detective story to follow. I love spending my days in the service of thought, making new thinking possible, cataloguing ideas. It seems to me that I'm involved in making the most beautiful, dangerous, powerful, sensuous thing in the world available, and of course I have no idea where exactly my work leads the people who use the library, but I know everyone who comes through its doors is travelling somewhere I can't imagine, and that's an extraordinary thing to be in charge of.

Frank has lunch with me in the Senior Common Room about a week after I start. He tells me I won't ever see much of him round the college.

'I'm pretty much retired now. Only come in for the food really,' he says. 'And anyway, don't ever think you have to be nice to me or anything, if you do see me. I got you the interview, but you got yourself the job.'

Three months after I moved to Oxford I get a call from Dad to say Grandad has gone into hospital.

'No need to worry, love,' he tells me. 'It's just a chest infection – one of those things they have to be a bit careful over with people your grandad's age. He doesn't want visitors, thinks we'll be a bother I suppose, drown out *Test Match Special*.' I go to visit him that evening though. I remember what it feels like to be alone in a hospital. Once I'm there I find he has pneumonia.

'He's been ignoring a cough for weeks,' says the nurse who shows me in, shaking her head, 'so then of course he collapsed one morning and hit his head against a table on the way down. We had to give him stitches. These older gents are always hopeless about going to the doctor when something's wrong – mind you tell him to take better care of himself from now on, all right?'

Grandad starts when he sees me, tries to cover himself with a blanket. 'Kate. You don't want to be around places like this.'

I'm suddenly worried that I've done the wrong thing coming here, seeing his agitation, the way I've embarrassed him. His voice is hoarse when he speaks, as if he's been shouting.

'It's all right, Grandad,' I tell him. 'I wanted to check you were all right.'

'I'll be fine. Just a cold and a fall. I've been going too hard at things. I'll be all right in a few days' time.' He doubles over, convulsed by a cough, and I go to him, place a hand on his back, uncertain what to do.

'Do you want some water, Grandad?'

He nods. 'On the little table.'

I pick up a cup of water on the table by the bed, and hold it while he sips from it, clutching at his blanket with both hands.

'Thank you. So sorry.'

'Don't be sorry. You've got nothing to be sorry about.'

I can't stop looking at the bruise that's formed around the cannula, the great dark mark drowning most of his right hand, which seems so small and desiccated now, with the needle sticking out of it.

Before long Grandad has recovered enough to leave hospital, but when I visit him again at home, I find him quieter. Something has changed. I ask him how he feels, but he just smiles and tells me not to worry about it. Late in the autumn he has to go into hospital again.

I'm at work when I hear. Dad calls, and tells me he has bad news. I know before he says it.

'I'm so sorry, Kate, but I'm afraid your grandad's gone.'

It always feels the same when anything important happens

to me. It reminds me of the first time I ever told Joe I loved him. The same punch in the gut as the words were spoken, the same uncertainty drowning me as the world changed. I can't react at all for a few minutes after I hear, and then I cry, because I loved my grandad, and now the root of my family is torn out, and I don't know what in the world will hold us together any more, all those strangers who used to come together every May for the party. I hardly knew him, not as I would have liked to know him. I didn't give him enough of my time; it's almost as if I assumed that he'd be there for ever. And I loved him. Did he know that? Did he know I really meant it when I said it? I didn't say it enough. I don't know whether he was on his own at the end, or whether he knew he was dying. I wish I had been there with him. But I'm like so many grandchildren with their grandparents – I felt I loved him very much, but that didn't mean I saw him very often. That didn't mean I was the one by his side at the end. There was too much in between us, too much life, too many things to call me away.

I take the afternoon off work and go to see my parents. I haven't been to their house, the place I once called home, for a very long time, and it's strange to visit and find I've somehow become a visitor, and feel I need to ask whether I should take off my shoes when I come through the front door because it might all have changed, and besides I can't quite remember. Mum is inconsolable for the whole of that afternoon and evening that we're together, and I don't know what to do. I've seen Mum upset before, but I never quite believed it. It always seemed for show. I don't know how to reach her now, though I find that I wish I could help her. We sit on the sofa together, the three of us, a family, and hold hands. From time to time we break down and cry again, and then we hold and comfort each other. We say very little. It feels like the closest we've ever been.

'He used to make me breakfast every day he was home,' says Mum. We both look at her, waiting for more, but nothing comes. I lean tentatively into her shoulder, which is sharp and uncomfortable. 'Boiled egg and soldiers,' she continues after a moment, and then stops again.

'I remember your mum laughing about that,' says Dad, rubbing her back. 'He kept making it after you left home, gave it to her instead. Every morning, crusts cut off all neatly. Did she tell you about that?' Mum doesn't reply. Eventually Dad gets up to make yet another pot of tea that we won't drink.

'Do you remember that summer we went to Lyme Regis with him and Grandma, Mum?' I venture. She breathes out slowly.

'It rained,' she says, and I nod, feeling tearful again, but can't think of anything else to add. The threads of conversation keep fraying like that all day. It seems there's no way of touching the sides of grief, and slowing your fall as you plummet into it. I remember a story Mum told me once of a man who tunnelled all the way from England to Australia. I suppose that's what it's like to lose someone. You have to pass all the way through the centre of the earth before you come out into the light again, dizzy with the emptiness of losing something you need and can't have any more.

At the end of the evening, Dad gives me a lift to the station, and I catch a train back to Oxford. Mum and Dad tried to tell me that I was welcome to stay the night, but I refused their offer, smiling, saying I'd rather spend the night on my own.

And I meant it, but Sam's waiting at the flat when I get back there, so I have company. We don't talk, but only lie next to each other and listen to the traffic passing on the road outside, and watch the yellow car lights strafing the ceiling till we fall at last into grateful sleep. I reeled out all the words I had for loss after Joe's accident; I don't want to say it all again.

Grandad's funeral is held in the church at the heart of the village. The place is full, and I see it all for one last time: the world he built up around him, the people who used to fill the garden on the day of the parties. I sit between Sam and Dad during the service, Mum sitting on the other side of Dad, and we cry, and sing, and think of him. I can't find a picture for what has happened to him, how he can have just disappeared. How does anyone ever come to terms with the way that stories end? When the service is done and the coffin is being carried out, Aunt Laura has to stop in the aisle for a moment, and Dad holds her up while people watch, not knowing what to do.

'I can't,' she says, 'I can't.'

'Come on, Laura. It's all right. Come on.'

After the wake and the half-hearted speeches and the sandwiches cut into quarters and bad coffee in the middle of the day, and the love all around us, I take Sam's hand while the party starts breaking up.

'I don't want to go back to the house. I can't do it,' I say.

'OK.' He can see how serious I am: there's no point arguing about it. 'We'd better go then, I guess.'

'I'm sorry. I can't go back there. It would be too – I just can't go.'

'Will you say goodbye to your family?'

'Of course. Give me a minute. Why don't you go and wait outside?'

'I'd like to say goodbye too, if you'd let me.'

'Of course. Sorry. Come on then.' We cross the hall to where my parents stand. Dad hugs me, and Mum hugs me as well, and tells me I should do what I need to do, that's what's important.

We call a cab to the station. I wonder whether Sam understands, whether he thinks I'm mad now for leaving. But I have to close my mind to worries like that. Grandma and Grandad are buried side by side in the churchyard, and I can't bear it, that they've both gone on without me, that I'm left here. The taxi comes and we sit in silence in the back while it weaves through the lanes and finds its way into the life and ring roads of the town. At the station I pay the fare and jump out of the car and go in to stand on the platform.

'What are we going to do?' Sam asks. I don't know the answer. I can't go home now, back to Oxford and my flat and my bed. I can't go to Sam's in Bristol. Then I look at the boards in the cramped little ticket hall of the station announcing the train times, and I realise what I want, where I need to be, what has to happen.

We buy tickets and board a train, and pale winter light is on our faces as we head for London, the centre of everything, the blighted beating heart of the country in which we're living this afternoon of our lives. We change at Clapham Junction and catch a train for Putney, and still Sam doesn't ask where we're going, only sits with me and holds my hand, and I'm grateful because I couldn't have explained it, I don't know how to put it all into words.

What is needed is an amnesty, a forgetting. What might save us all is a way to put our lives behind us, and love facing into the future, not always turned back looking for the past. But the song of memory is forever calling. You can't just wash it away. It's everything people are made of.

What people want above all isn't just forgiveness. What people love is the dream of laying it all out into the open and letting the light play over the acts of their days, all crimes confessed, all sins revealed. The idea of amnesty is only the end of a process the whole world longs for: the comforting dark of the confessional, the ease of the psychiatrist's couch, the non-judgemental blank sheet of paper listening to them, and the giving up of sins into words. Only then, at the end of all that, do they long for some absolution to come from baring the soul. Above all what everyone wants to do is sing of their sorrows and sins.

We get off the train and walk, and reach our destination. Sam looks up at the building and still I don't think he understands, because he isn't in my head. He's never quite known how it all looks through my eyes. He hasn't seen everything I've seen. No one ever succeeds in learning the map of another person's life; they only glimpse the surface. We walk into another hospital, another corridor, another ward. Back into the centre of the world, the place where I want to be more than anywhere, the place I'm more afraid of than anywhere else.

Looking back, I know what happened to Joe became part of my own illness. I wanted to suffer as much as he did. I wanted to be trapped and half-drowned in a sickness like him, and make amends for having run away from him, and know what it felt like to be where he was. I wanted to be so ill he would believe I still loved him, even though I had let him down.

It didn't work out like that. He never heard anything about my illness. He never got any better as I grew worse. Nothing changed for him, and I didn't have control over the gesture I was trying to make, and it held me down under the water, and I couldn't take back what I had done. But that was part of why it started, all the same.

It was part of why I wrenched myself free of the hospital, too. Once I reached the bottom of the ravine of my sickness, I saw it had never been a way of getting close to anyone, only a way of getting close to death. So I used the thought of Joe to make me strong again, once I saw I was further away from him than ever. The patients on my ward used to say that the NHS provided a DIY recovery – lots on offer, but you had to put it all together by yourself. That was the hardest thing, that in the end nothing was healed by medicine or medical expertise – people recovered because they willed those recoveries into being; they fought until they could live in the world again. To ask so many people who were at their weakest to have to fight so hard seems very cruel, but that's the truth of the illness. Lots of people can't do it. There were people on my ward who had been there for years. People who were there to die, who never thought of leaving. They couldn't find a way to see a dream worth living for, so they carried on in the rut they were in, propped up by the endless sympathy and kindness and patience of the nurses, and the Fortisips fed to them by tubes, and the garden sits and escorted walks and unescorted walks and community leave that dripped like blood transfusions into the darkness of their days, the little heartbeats of freedom in the middle of the prison of it all. I chose to fight my way clear of that half-life. The light I aimed for then was the thought of Joe, the same light I had thought I was chasing in the first place, now leading me on in a different direction. He was the way I found to get strong enough to take on the role of a human being again, act out the part of a living person.

Joe sees us approaching before Lizzy does. She's sitting with her back to the entrance. Joe's eyes light up, and I laugh, because I know now that I am in the right place. Lizzy turns to see what Joe's smiling at, and stands and hugs me as we meet by the bedside. I know Lizzy always spends her Saturday afternoons here. I knew I would find them both here.

'Hello! We weren't expecting you,' Lizzy says.

'I know. I'm sorry. I just really wanted to come and be with you both. I hope you don't mind.'

'Of course we don't, it's brilliant. You're all dressed up.'

'Family do.'

'Your grandad's funeral.' Lizzy's face becomes suddenly serious.

'Yeah.'

'I'm sorry. Are you OK?'

'I'm fine. I just really wanted to be with you guys now it's done.'

'Of course. Well, we're so glad you came. You must be Sam?' Lizzy holds out her hand, and Sam shakes it.

'Yeah. Hi. Nice to meet you.'

'Do you want to help me get some extra chairs?' Lizzy says.

'Sure thing.' Sam follows her off through the ward.

I sit down beside Joe and hold his hand. I want to say something, but there's too much to say. So I stay silent, and we look at each other instead. Lizzy and Sam come back with chairs, and the four of us are together for the first time.

'I don't think you two have met before, have you?' Lizzy says, looking from Sam to Joe. I take my cue. This, I suppose, is what I came for.

'No, you haven't. Joe, I wanted to introduce you to my friend. This is Sam.'

Joe looks at Sam, and for a moment no one says anything. Then Sam speaks.

'Hi, Joe. It's nice to meet you. I've heard a lot about you.'

Joe looks away from Sam then, at me. All I wanted this whole time was to hear his voice once more. All I wanted was to speak with him again. He smiles, and for a moment I almost feel forgiven that I didn't die that night, that I wasn't there in the car beside him. And I think I can imagine what he might have said to me now, if only he could still speak.

Don't be stupid. That's not what I want. I want you to carry on living.

Acknowledgements

This book was written during my tenure as the playwright in residence at Keble College, Oxford, and was nourished and shaped by conversations I was able to have as a result of that position. I would like to thank Roger Boden, Yvonne Murphy, Sir Jonathan Phillips and everyone at Keble for affording me the opportunity to develop my work in such a supportive and enriching environment. Some of the thinking also got done while on attachment at the National Theatre Studio, and I am grateful to Emily McLaughlin, Tom Lyons and the rest of the team there for their support.

Thanks, from the bottom of my heart, to Laura Williams and Suzanne Bridson, Alice Youell, Kate Samano and everyone at PFD and Transworld; Lord Bew; Molly Waters; Checky Gardiner; Richard English and Angharad Vaughan; Gemma Oaten; my uncle and aunt, John and Sally Norris; Doug Rolfe and everyone at James's Place; Up In Arms, particularly the *Fear Of Music* company and the *Visitors* company, above all Alice Hamilton and Eleanor Wyld; and the staff and patients of St George's Hospital and Springfield University Hospital for their contributions to this story. Richard English's *Armed Struggle*, David Beresford's *Ten Men Dead* and Ed Moloney's

A Secret History of the IRA and *Voices from the Grave* were invaluable sources. Support and advice relating to eating disorders is available from the charities Beat and Seed, as well as from GPs and NHS Mental Health Services.

Thanks are due always to Bernard O'Donoghue, who started everything by arranging for me to visit the Yeats International Summer School in Sligo in 2009. I made my second visit to Sligo while finishing this book, and was reminded of how much I owe to that fortnight, that place.

When I started writing this story it was going to be about the Boston Tapes, because I believed two things about that project – that it was profoundly important, and that more people needed to know about what happened. Then life took hold, and the book became about other things as well, that are also of profound importance to the society in which we live, and also demand more concerted attention. I wish I had never gone through the year that led to the rest of this story; I would give anything to change the tape, so none of it had happened. But happen it did, and at the insistence of my wife, Charlie, I refused to let that stop my work; I fought to turn it into poetry instead. Perhaps it will offer some catharsis; if it helps one person feel a little less alone some day, that will be something. Charlie, I can only hope this tale has earned its telling, and this writer has deserved his dedicatee. To you, my love.

Barney Norris was born in Sussex in 1987, and grew up in Salisbury. Upon leaving university he founded the theatre company Up In Arms. He won the Critics' Circle Award for Most Promising Playwright for his debut full-length play *Visitors,* and his play *Nightfall* will appear in the inaugural Bridge Theatre season in April 2018. He is the Martin Esslin Playwright in Residence at Keble College, Oxford and has been named by the *Evening Standard* as one of the 1,000 Most Influential Londoners.

His first novel, the critically acclaimed *Five Rivers Met on a Wooded Plain,* was a *Times* bestseller and won a Betty Trask award. It was also shortlisted for the Ondaatje Prize and Debut of the Year at the British Book Awards. *Turning for Home* is his second novel.

By the same author

FICTION

Five Rivers Met On A Wooded Plain

THEATRE

Visitors

Eventide

Echo's End

While We're Here

What You Wish For In Youth: Three Short Plays

NON-FICTION

To Bodies Gone: The Theatre of Peter Gill